SOUTH OF THE HIGHWAY

A GABRIEL FORTUNA HAMPTONS MYSTERY

GLEN BERKOWITZ

IUNIVERSE, INC.
NEW YORK   BLOOMINGTON

South of the Highway
A Gabriel Fortuna Hamptons Mystery

*This is a work of fiction. All of the characters, names, incidents,
organizations, and dialogue in this novel are either the products
of the author's imagination or are used fictitiously.*

iUniverse books may be ordered through booksellers or by contacting:

iUniverse
1663 Liberty Drive
Bloomington, IN 47403
www.iuniverse.com
1-800-Authors (1-800-288-4677)

*Because of the dynamic nature of the Internet, any Web addresses or links
contained in this book may have changed since publication and may no longer be
valid. The views expressed in this work are solely those of the author and do not
necessarily reflect the views of the publisher, and the publisher hereby disclaims
any responsibility for them.*

ISBN: 978-1-4401-5158-3 (sc)
ISBN: 978-1-4401-5157-6 (dj)
ISBN: 978-1-4401-5159-0 (ebk)

Printed in the United States of America

iUniverse rev. date: 6/16/2009

1

It was the middle of May when Gasper Dupree, Captain of the Southampton Town Police, called to offer me what he termed a lucrative opportunity to serve as security for the opening night party of The Hamptons Designers' Showcase. The affair, the first big event of the ever-expanding Hampton's summer season, was scheduled for the weekend before Memorial Day at the Al Shareef Castle off Deerfield Road in Watermill. It was a hot ticket and getting one was considered quite a coup, especially if you gave a shit about fabrics, moldings, paint chips and bathroom accessories, which, of course, I didn't. Still, I hadn't heard my old friend's voice in a long time, and although I found it hard to believe he was calling simply to give me a chance at earning an extra buck, I kept my cynicism to myself and patiently listened to what he had to say.

I reminded Gasper that in spite of what I might look like I wasn't a bouncer and just like old times, as if six years hadn't slipped between us like a wedge, he responded with his old familiar laugh and said, "Fuck you, Gabe. You know what I mean." He went on to assure me that the attendees at this event, the rich and the rich wannabees, were not the types who go looking for any kind of trouble. They wanted only to rub shoulders with each other, to catch up on the latest divorces and gossip, and to see what new trinkets their brethren had picked up during the off-season. In other words, who was screwing whom? To find that out, they were willing to pay an admission price of one thousand dollars, with all proceeds supposedly going to The Southampton Hospital Fund.

Gasper said I could dress casually and would be free to mingle with the guests because for all anyone would know I was a guest. I could eat the food and drink the wine and if I got lucky with any of the attendees, well, that was okay, too. Should anything unruly occur, which Gasper again assured me would be about as possible as a meteorite from Krypton hitting me between the eyes, it would be my responsibility to step in and make sure things got settled without anyone getting hurt. For doing that, he said I'd be paid a cool thousand in cash. That sounded like a lot of easy money to take care of people who were generally so soft and pampered they drycleaned their underwear, but I knew that protecting that sort was what helped make the East End prosper. Gasper had only one request before hiring me.

"There's just one thing, Gabe," he said.

"What's that, G?"

"Don't bring your piece."

"You ought to know me better than that, G. I haven't taken the Smith & Wesson out of the locker since I retired from the force. Like I've always said, if I can't handle things with my hands, then I can't handle things. Nothing's changed with that."

Gasper went on to tell me how good it felt to speak with me, how sorry he was that he'd ever let a woman come between us and assured me that if I liked the job he could hook me up with a gig just like it every weekend, adding that with the connections he had with police forces from Montauk Point to Westhampton Beach, I could probably make a small fortune. I knew that a thousand bucks wasn't going to change my Hampton's status, even a hundred-thousand wouldn't do that, but it occurred to me that Gasper's way of thinking might have defined what an old-time local was; some poor sap who thought that a thousand a week might ever amount to a fortune.

It was Page Six knowledge that there were lots of extravagant for-the-rich-only parties every weekend in The Hamptons and it was common knowledge that the East End police forces didn't have the manpower to manage them. Things like traffic control, petty theft, drunken fighting and public urination were top priorities for the town and village cops, and there was no way they could also be responsible for public safety at parties held on private property behind locked gates. I figured that a thousand tax-free was a thousand tax-free and the possibility of rekindling an old friendship made Gasper's proposition even more interesting, but to be honest, winters can be lonely on the East End and it was the prospect of meeting some fine-looking women with unique designs of their own that made my decision a no-brainer.

I said dully, "Okay, Gasper. I'll take the job."

Gasper replied enthusiastically, "Great. It'll be good to have someone there I can trust. It'll be just like old times. You'll owe me for this one, Gabe. You'll see. It's a piece of cake."

I recalled that old times with Gasper had often brought nothing more than headaches and cake was not a staple of my perpetual low-carb, high-protein diet, but the job sounded sweet to me, too. I asked, "G, is there anything else about this thing you've left out that I should know?"

My old buddy cheerily answered, "Nah, it's a breeze. Meet me at The Paradise Bar in half an hour and I'll fill you in on the particulars."

I hung up the phone and slipped into a pair of old jeans and an even older oversized cotton pullover and drove into Sag Harbor to meet Gasper. We sealed the deal with a firm handshake and a couple of shots of Padrone and by the end of the night were in separate bedrooms out at my place with a couple of good-looking, blonde and leggy paralegals from New York City law firms. They'd come to The Hamptons to hook up with some bad-boy movie stars or a couple of rich investment bankers, but after a few drinks and some easy laughs forgot about their original plans and joined Gasper and me for a night of noncommittal sex under a shimmering full moon on Noyac Bay. After taking Mary-Ellen for the third time, I went outside, stood on my deck and marveled at the twinkling stars of a Hampton's night sky. It occurred to me that the summer season had not yet begun and already things were looking up. Just goes to show how wrong a person can be.

2

The party was scheduled to begin at eight, allowing everyone ample time to catch a tan, take a nap, partake in a little afternoon delight, and then get to the soirée with that glowing Hamptonian sunburned face that says, "I've got it all."

I didn't have any delight that afternoon and I certainly didn't have it all, but I did catch a little sun on my back deck and did some weightlifting in one of the small bedrooms I'd transformed into a well-equipped little gym. After showering, I gave myself a couple of strategic hits of Aramis just in case I got lucky and got dressed in what I considered to be sophisticated party wear of tan cotton chinos, a black polo shirt and black loafers. Knowing I wouldn't be one of the best dressed guys at the affair, I was confident I would be one of the fittest and left my home.

I'd been a rag-top man most of my adult life and that night was no different. With the top down on my classic '76 fire engine red Cadillac convertible, I left home and began my mellow drive through the cool twilight of a Southampton night. I cruised up Noyac Road inhaling the piney evening air and passed the modest downtown Noyac commercial strip of The Whalebone General Store, Noyac Realty, and Cromer's Market, acknowledged home of the best fried chicken and working man's lunches in The Hamptons. A half mile later, the Noyac Golf Club came up on my left, where I noticed a few hard core duffers clinging to the last of the day's light in their maddening attempts at breaking a hundred, and then on my right, the Noyac Marina flew by, its slips still half empty awaiting the boats of the Palm Beach crowd that would soon be arriving. Reaching the fork just past Bittersweet Lane, I bore to the left, and in the purple shade of tall oak and beech trees, began my sweet ride on undulating and serpentine Deerfield Road. Three miles ahead, on the right hand side, was The Castle.

I left my car with one of a hundred valet parkers in white shirts, black pants and bow ties and began my walk up the long graveled driveway. I recalled that the host of this party, Benjamin Al Shareef, had become pretty famous in the movie business and had recently won a couple of Oscars for his studio, producing a movie called *WEST BANK STORY*, the tale of a young Israeli boy and a Palestinian girl who suffer a star-crossed love in the Holy Land. The success of that film had made Al Shareef an international celebrity and the heavily populated Jewish communities of The Hamptons and New York City whole-heartedly welcomed the progressive, Muslim, celebrity film maker into their homes and temples. Walking along, I further recalled that a few weeks earlier The Times had done an interview with the guy, making it the featured article in its Arts and Leisure section, but there wasn't anything particular I could remember about the guy except that his hustle was the movie business, a good way, I figured, to meet beautiful women.

I came to a stand of tall white pines and turning it, found The Castle suddenly looming before me. It was dark and foreboding and I knew just from looking at it that no good could come from being in such a gloomy place, but I shrugged and told myself a thousand was a thousand and went on ahead. Crossing the drawbridge, I looked into the moat almost expecting to see alligators, but there was nothing below my feet but a thin stream of water that couldn't have protected The Castle from a class of angry kindergartners. The doors to the place were something else, though. Twenty feet high, six feet wide and four inches thick, they were fashioned from hard oak and were closed behind an iron portcullis that had to come from either a Hollywood soundstage or an actual medieval castle in Europe. Remembering that Al Shareef had taken his family's Middle Eastern money and had invested only a small portion of it into the fantasy world of American movies, I figured it had probably come from MGM's closeout sale.

There was a small lighted entry button beside the door on the left. I pressed it and a series of trumpets blared, announcing the arrival of

King Arthur or me. From the black mesh speaker located just below the button, a heavily accented Middle Eastern voice asked, "Yes?"

I answered in clear American, "It's Gabriel Fortuna."

A few seconds passed while I assumed the voice was checking his lists of names, and then the man with the accent said, "I cannot find your name. Are you with the caterers, coat check, or bar service?"

I smiled toothily into the small camera situated discreetly above the Herculean doors, stretched my frame to its full length and threw my shoulders back before replying, "I'm security."

"Oh, I see. Just a moment, please."

A few seconds later there was a buzz and the portcullis silently rose with none of the cranking and rattling you hear in the movies. The huge doors slid backwards on their hydraulics and little by little the inside of The Al Shareef Castle was exposed. Watching the place slowly open up, it occurred to me that the work of interior designers was often much like that of clothing designers; nobody in his right mind could wear many of the outfits created for runway shows, and if the grand entrance to The Castle was an example of what was inside, nobody in his right mind could have lived in many of the rooms recently designed in Al Shareef's place.

I walked into an arched entry foyer of irregularly shaped slabs of polished pink travertine marble surrounded by luminous magenta walls and all under a high-gloss kiwi colored ceiling that loomed twenty feet above my head. The impressive arched passageway was guarded by two rows of six armor clad Arab swordsmen from The Crusades Period, their backs against the wall and scimitars drawn. I thought I recognized the costumes from an old Tony Curtis movie I'd seen when I was a kid and assumed that Al Shareef, the guy who'd built and owned The Castle, had bought the outfits from the same movie lot he'd gotten the portcullis.

Entering the great room, a perfect square of sides of at least a hundred feet, I viewed walls of mosaic tile depicting scenes from Middle Eastern history, with an emphasis on history since not much of anything important to the rest of the world had come out of that place in about a thousand years. Except oil, of course. Plenty of that had been pumped out of that dry beach and there was a constant reminder of that on the wide expanse of floor, where a sand colored, wall-to-wall carpet lay displaying a map of the Middle East: geographical boundaries marked by dotted lines, large cities noted by stars, and oil fields marked by masses of small black crosses, which if you looked closely enough, were actually small oil wells.

The furnishings in the great room were composed of varying shades of camel leather and layer upon layer of thick Occidental silk, and I'd never seen so many ottomans in one place in my life. Potted palms were scattered throughout the place, sometimes in bunches of three or four, and lots of silk oriental area rugs were laying around, too, giving the place the feel of a great mullah's tent plopped down somewhere in the middle of the Arabian Desert. I remarked to myself that all that was missing was the camel dung, took a sniff to make sure I was right, and continued my tour.

Two wide staircases were carved into the walls of the great room, leading to the upstairs and downstairs levels of the twenty-four thousand square foot mansion, and two hallways, one at the eastern end of the house and the other at the western, led to the adjoining wings. Women in gauzy Muslim dresses and veils walked languidly around the room, their eyes cast down to the sandy carpet as they served drinks and pistachio halvah to the darker complexioned men who had arrived before me and who, I was sure, were part of Al Shareef's private security team. They caught me eyeing them and stared back at me as if I didn't belong in the place, and that was exactly the way I felt. I stared back at them and wanted to say, "Fuck you. This is my country," but checked myself, remembering that my job was to stop trouble, not to cause it. I was all prepared to bag the thousand and just leave the place and then something happened to change my night and my life.

"Mr. Fortuna, how nice of you to come."

I turned to my left and saw a stocky man of about fifty coming towards me. His hair was thin and black and shiny, like it had just been dipped into a bottle of Wildroot, and as he approached, his open smile grew broader, like he knew something I didn't know and was part of some private joke to which I wasn't privy. He got closer and I noticed a couple of thin old scars on his face that told me he wasn't always soft, and when I looked into his black eyes, because I knew what I was looking for, I could see that at one time he might have been a very dangerous man.

Stretching myself so that I was about a foot taller than the portly man in the off-white linen suit, I asked, "And you are?"

The man gave a small bow and replied, "Pardon me. I am Binyamin Al Shareef and this is my American home. At least it is when I am on the East Coast and not in New York City. You are Mr. Gabriel Fortuna, one of those recommended by Captain Dupree to guard my home against any mischief that might occur at tonight's event."

Neither of us extended a hand and I responded flatly, "There won't be any mischief." A few silent seconds passed between us before I added, "Nice place you have here, Mr. Shareef. Unusual, but nice."

My host's smile was gone but his sense of superiority apparently wasn't because he replied icily, "It's Mr. *Al* Shareef, Mr. Fortuna, and it is not so unusual." Smiling again at what he must have thought was putting me in my place, he added, "I have other homes very much like this in Southern France, Saudi Arabia, and Beverly Hills. This one is quite small compared to the others and does not contain all the comforts I would wish. You see, the people in Southampton are quite provincial and limit the size of home one may build. I was told it had something to do with protecting piping plovers and the underground water supply."

I didn't care much about piping plovers, but living on the East End, water was something I did care about and if this guy came from the sandy stretches of the Middle East it was something he should have been concerned with, too. Also, I didn't like his tone or that Mr. *Al* Shareef stuff. He sounded to me like he didn't think his shit stank and had graduated from one of those fine European colleges that limit their alumni to fops, scoundrels and other forms of Euro-bullshit.

I said flatly, "This place looks plenty big to me," and after taking another gander at the harem girls, the desert-sand rug and the private security goon squad, I added with appropriate 9/11 spirit, "unless you've got something to hide."

Al Shareef quietly laughed and said, "You Americans, always so serious when talking with people from my part of the world."

I responded coolly, "I can't imagine why."

Raising a bejeweled pinky finger, Al Shareef stopped one of the lovely harem girls carrying a tray of pink drinks in martini glasses. He turned to me and asked, "Would you care for something to drink, Mr. Fortuna? My religion does not allow me to partake of alcohol, but feel free to have something for yourself whenever you wish."

I had taken an almost instant dislike to the guy and wasn't about to take anything he was offering, except his money, of course, so I replied through tight lips, "My religion doesn't allow me to drink on the job ... and this is America; I always feel free."

Al Shareef made a tight little circle with his mouth but nothing came out of it except a tiny puff of air. My guess was he just didn't know what to make of me, and although he couldn't have liked any of his hirees giving him any bullshit, he wasn't completely sure that was what I'd done.

Satisfied that I'd shown Al Shareef I was not his typical employee but remembering that a thousand bucks was still a thousand bucks and who was paying me, I changed the subject and became a security professional, asking, "Who are the other people you have working here, Mr. Shareef?" Not wanting to let professionalism get too much in my way, I could not help but again leave out the Al part of his name, just to see if it bothered him as much as it made me feel good. By the way his right eyebrow lifted at my question, I could tell that it did.

To show he knew what I was up to, Al Shareef smiled pleasantly and answered, "But of course I have acquisitioned the assistance of others, Mr. Fortuna. By American standards, my home is quite large and is filled with many valuable objects. Captain Dupree assured me you were a very capable person, but I doubt that even one as intimidating as you could protect all my possessions."

A lewd smile slowly stretched across the Arab's lips that told me he was done talking with me and that he was now concentrating on someone behind me and over my left shoulder.

He graciously said, "Excuse me, Mr. Fortuna. A good friend has arrived with whom I must speak. Make yourself comfortable. I'm sure I will see you later."

I wanted to say, "Not unless you're the one handing me my pay envelope," but kept my mouth shut for that very reason.

On my own again, I passed through some of the smaller chambers of The Castle, each of which had been decorated by pricey interior design firms from New York, Rome, or Paris, and then proceeded downstairs to check out the indoor swimming pool, off limits during the party for insurance reasons, the bowling alley, the movie theater and the basement wine cellar. When I'd finally seen enough of what Mr. Al Shareef owned inside the walls, I decided to take a break and went upstairs to the stone terrace to check out what he'd done to the outside of his little palace.

I'd been coming out to the East End of Long Island for a lot of years before I moved out permanently, but there were still times its natural beauty could stun me, and standing on that terrace was one of those times. Looking west, beyond the marble Olympic pool and matching poolhouse, the formal and informal gardens, and the four acres of great lawn holding the large white canvas tent where cocktails and hors d'ooeuvres were to be served, was a hillside drop-off of at least two hundred feet allowing anyone standing on the terrace unimpeded views of the forests of Watermill, Hampton Park, North Sea, Shinnecock and beyond.

Much of that land was owned by the town and reserved for whatever good things the Southampton Town Council could come up with: medium and low income housing so that the locals' children might one day be able to afford a Hampton's place of their own, new schools to support the growing year round population, or assisted living and nursing facilities for the aging Southampton Boomers who would soon find themselves needing help because their ingrate children wanted the mansions and the beachfront properties for themselves and their parents out.

West of the reserve, hidden by the hills and the forest, lay some of the most prestigious golf clubs in the world, most notably Shinnecock Hills Golf Club, Atlantic Golf Club and The National Golf Links. Surrounding the forest were the brilliant blue waters of Little and Great Peconic Bays, already stocked with white canvassed sailboats gliding in peaceful packs or in lonesome grace to their evening moorings. Due North was Jessups Neck, jutting into the bay waters like a sandy warning finger, pointing at Shelter Island and separating Little Peconic from Noyac Bay. Beyond that lay the North Fork of Long Island with its new vineyards and old farms, and beyond that, the shadowy hills of Connecticut. To the South, about four miles from The Castle, was the Atlantic Ocean. From my terrace perch, I could see a dark ribbon of it floating between the verdant forest treetops and the deep and darkening blue sky.

I reminded myself that Al Shareef's property was, like my own, on the north side of Route 27, and did not compare in value to the land south of the highway, land that was nearer the ocean and the old

Southampton money, land that was home to the estates the robber barons built at the turn of the last century and the homes today's robber barons were building at the beginning of this new one. I wondered why, with all his money, Al Shareef had bought property here rather than on the ocean, and all I could think was that the locals living south of the highway might still have had enough clout to keep his kind out.

I shifted my gaze from some Canadian geese knifing through the sky in a perfect V-formation to one particularly large brown rabbit busily gnawing on the lowest branch of a perfect Golden Niobe willow stationed in the far corner of the great lawn. A gentle breeze blew in from the south, bringing with it the clean briny smell of the ocean. It mixed with the fragrance of the late May and early June flowers and I took a deep breath, fell into a trance and just like the brown hawk I saw sitting and staring down at me from the top of one of Al Shareef's chimneys, I was at peace with the world.

"Hello, Gabe. It's been a long time."

So much for peace, relaxation and serenity. With the sound of that voice, tiny beads of sweat popped on my forehead as if I was doing the last set of ten, three hundred pound reps on the flat bench. The ground under me suddenly became a field of eggshells, my knees went weak and I slowly turned.

There she was, five feet six inches of gorgeous in a turquoise miniskirt tight enough to show off a couple of full and dangerous curves without making her appear too cheap. Just as I remembered, she never really needed jewelry, her aquamarine eyes sparkling enough to outshine any polished stones, but she still wore a sapphire and gold choker around her long and lovely neck, just to show she had plenty of money to go with that dynamite body. Her hair was more golden than it used to be, a little less red, and hung down past her shoulders, partially covering what I knew was a perfect set, and it looked like she was still in the habit of traveling without a bra. Her cheeks glowed from a fresh tan and her mouth held an inviting liar's smile, her perfect teeth white and gleaming behind a pair of soft and succulent lips. I caught a flash of her wet, pink tongue and wondered if she'd exposed that on purpose, just to tease me, just for old times. Working my eyes down her fine, fine body, I saw she was wearing her trademark four-inch heels, one of dozens of pairs she owned and wore even to the beach because she thought they helped to make her legs appear longer and her ass sit higher, as if they ever needed any help. She was such a great piece; I wanted to be with her the moment I heard her voice. The problem was, I also wanted to run. I took a guarded step backwards and leaned against the railing.

"Oh, come on now, Gabe. Take that look off your face. I promise not to bite. Not unless you want me to."

I replied cautiously, "Hello, Teresa."

"Is that any way to greet your wife?"

"That's ex-wife."

"Only because that's the way you had to have it. I never wanted to get divorced."

"Sure," I responded tersely, "just so long as you could screw other guys when I wasn't around."

Teresa shook her head, laughed coyly and said, "When are you going to get over that? I explained everything to you. It was just business."

I responded icily, "Yeah, the oldest business in the world."

Teresa cocked her head a little to the left, took a step closer and through a naughty little girl's smile added, "Sometimes, in order to close a deal, I had to apply a little extra incentive. It's made me a good living, Gabe. I would have shared it with you and you know that."

I replied coldly, "No, thanks. Unlike you, I was never that hard up for money."

My ex-wife pouted insincerely for a moment and then said, "Oh, come on, Gabe, let's let bygones be bygones." Holding her arms widely, Teresa winked her right eye and issued her cheap siren's call, "Come over here and give me a hug. I saw how you looked at me when you first turned. Come on, baby, squeeze me tight and crush me into your chest. Honestly, Gabe, just looking at you makes my nipples hard."

I recalled instantly that honesty was something Teresa had never understood and all her trampy talk did was to remind me of how street she really was in spite of her expensive clothing and rich friends. Her nipples weren't the only things that had gotten hard, though, and not wanting to give her any satisfaction, I said, "No, thanks. It must be the cool night that's working your headlights. I think I'll keep my distance. Its safer."

Teresa sighed and bit her lip, actually making it look like she was troubled that we were not going to get together, but I knew that friendliness was never a strong part of her personality, either. She was all about power and money and had found that because she was drop-dead gorgeous, using sex was the easiest way for her to get what she wanted. Well, she'd fucked me in more ways than one and I was determined not to let it happen again no matter how much I wanted her.

Crossing my arms protectively over my chest, I asked, "What do you really want, Teresa?"

She answered demurely, "Do I have to want something to be nice to you?"

I snapped, "Yes, yes, you do. That's the way you're made. You have to want something and you have to get it or you aren't happy."

Teresa's sultry reply was, "I used to want you. I used to want you badly."

She followed that remark by sashaying up close to me and grazing the front of her skirt against my pants. From the widening of her smile and the twinkling in her eye, I could tell she felt my excitement.

In spite of my strong desire for her, I found the strength to say, "'Used to', are the magic words, Teresa. Remember my old saying, 'Fool me once, shame on you. Fool me twice, go fuck yourself'. Well, go fuck yourself a hundred times, Teresa. If you're speaking to me, it must be because you want something, and I'll tell you right now and upfront, I'm not interested."

Teresa was not at all flustered by what I'd said and kept her sultry smile, but I could tell that its earlier playfulness was gone and she was more about business. Taking a step back from me, she looked around to see if we were still alone, and when she was satisfied that we were, she whispered, "I need your help."

"Bullshit," I spat.

"Alright," she replied, still in a whisper, "I want your help."

I said, "That's better, but sorry, no can do. You're bad for my health. Get someone else to clean up after your mess."

A lean and hungry expression suddenly came over Teresa and she said, "Look, Gabe, I'm serious. There could be a lot of money in this for both of us but I can't do this thing alone. I'm onto something big, bigger than any deal I've ever done, but there are a few complications I can's handle, things a guy like you are good at. Can't we at least talk about it?"

I pretended to listen to Teresa's line about money and deals and how a guy like me was what she needed, but looking at her, all I could think about was how much I used to love holding her and kissing her and being in her, pumping away while she ground her soft furry wetness against me, her green eyes rolling around in their sockets and her voice screaming my name. And then, I thought about that incredible way she had of putting my dick in her mouth and using her tongue to …

"Gabe!!! Gabe, are you there?"

I shook out the cobwebs and found myself staring at the top of the deep valley that separated Teresa's beautiful pair. Weak from memories of bygone lust, I answered, "Sorry, Teresa, my mind was somewhere else."

Sensing an advantage, she replied huskily, "I've seen that expression on you before and I know where your mind was." Taking a step closer, she purred, "The offer is still there, Gabe, if you want it." Drawing a sharp fingernail down her throat to her cleavage, she finished her proposition by grinning salaciously.

I thought my head was going to explode, but I got a hold of myself and hollered, "Look, Teresa, for the last time, I don't want any part of your deals. You slept around and made a fortune selling yourself and real estate while spending me like I was nothing more than petty cash. I never wanted any part of your business when we were married, so why would I want any part of it now? And I don't know what you mean by, 'things a guy like me is good at'. I'm just an ex-New York City cop trying to live a good life in my own little piece of the world. I've got enough money to get by from my pension and savings and I don't need your money and I'm not interested in being with you tonight or any night. Now, get the fuck away from me and leave me the fuck alone."

Breathing deeply, I looked around and noticed that my ex-wife and I had become the center of attention for the guests that had arrived. It was eight-fifteen, and standing in front of Teresa with a hundred eyes staring at me made me realize that the only person who might cause trouble at the party wasn't a guest at all; it was me. Taking another deep breath, I blew past my ex-wife and got lost in the crowd that was beginning to flood The Castle.

After a short while of working my way through the growing crowd, I calmed down, and like Gasper had told me, not much of anything exciting happened unless you consider the arrival of the celebrity crowd thrilling. The place was the usual revolving door of magazine and television celebrities who sell good taste: Martha, Mario, Heidi, Emeril, Christie and more of the others who've become so famous they are referred to only by their first names. They came and went in a cavalcade of flashbulbs that promised to show their images in Dan's Papers or Hamptons' Life or Hamptons' Cottages and Gardens or in any number of the glossy trades that sell the ambience of this high rent locale. They had to leave quickly, though; there were other parties they'd promised to attend and other media opportunities that would help them sell their high-priced line of Hamptons Dreams.

Town officials were at The Castle, too, although it was common knowledge they didn't have to pay the thousand-dollar entrance fee. Dr. Eliot Sanders, President of Southampton Hospital, and Southampton Town Supervisor, Armand Conforti, were yukking it up amidst a glare of white light, seemingly unaware of the fact that most of the celebrity millionaires with whom they were clinking glasses thought they were nothing more than poor shnooks. They were drinking expensive wines and eating outrageous hors d'oeuvres of local crab, venison,and lobster, and although Dr. Sanders was well paid and Supervisor Conforti's landscaping business did very nicely, neither would have wanted to spend the money those eats and drinks would have cost them at any number of trendy Hamptons' restaurants.

The women that weren't the society grandmas or faghags that usually attend these kinds of parties were pretty damned good looking. Dressed in casual chic, they came in all sizes and colors and I'd have had to be blind to not know the place was jammed with models. I was eyeing one particularly tall and slim redhead of around thirty, making severe eye contact with her, thinking of what I was going to say when we were alone back at my place, and imagining what sound she would make the first time I placed my hand between her legs, parted them and petted her above what I imagined were a pair of cool and lacy silk panties. I'd gone so far as to fantasizing about how deep her breathing would become when I put myself inside her, and then, I heard the scream.

It seemed incredible to me that anyone could hear anything above the buzz, the drunken laughter and the generally well-monied uproar of the hundreds of people that crowded The Castle, but I remembered from my past life what a terrifying scream can do; it has its own way of rising above everything.

I raced to the staircase leading downstairs, pulled forward by the screams that came again and again until they finally stopped and turned into a long drawn out wail. Reaching the open doors to the off limits swimming pool, I saw Gasper standing at the far end, looking down at the water, his eyes focused on the white suited man bobbing face down in the deep end. Wrapped in my old friend's arms was a beautiful, olive skinned lady. She was wailing and every now and then I could make out what she howled.

"*Binyamin!!!! Binyamin!!!!*"

Again, I looked into the pool, recognized the large jeweled pinky ring of Binyamin Al Shareef, and raising my eyes, found Gasper staring at me with an expression that looked like he'd just stubbed his big toe into a sturdy table leg. I wondered what the hell had happened, where in the hell that redhead had gone to, and who the hell was going to pay me my thousand dollars.

3

Because I've got a cop's instincts, I stuck around The Castle for a while to make sure everybody got out safely. I wasn't getting paid any extra for it, and as far as I could tell I wasn't going to be paid at all, the man in charge of bill paying having recently departed the planet without taking the time to place me into his will. I tried to speak with Gasper, but being surrounded by town and county police, crime scene investigators and newspaper and magazine photographers, he seemed more nervous than I'd ever seen him, so I decided to just let him alone. Around midnight, Al Shareef's body was packed into a meat wagon and taken to Southampton Hospital. A few minutes later, I left The Castle and drove home.

Being around a dead man and rubbing body parts with my ex-wife had really gotten to me. Once home, I just fell into bed and every time I got a woody thinking about Teresa, I wound up losing it with the memory of Gasper pulling Al Shareef out of the pool to expose the deep gash in the dead man's forehead. Eventually, I got tired of tossing and turning and staring at my bedroom ceiling, so with the rising of the sun, I went out to my back deck to take in the tranquil morning sights and sounds of Noyac Bay. That worked to calm me for a while, but by nine o'clock, images of Al Shareef and Teresa began to attack again and I knew I needed some human contact to get off my bad ride. From the small double-hung window in my bathroom, I called across the narrow easement of trees to my next-door neighbors, Carla and Reggie, two thirty-something women who'd moved out to the East End a few years earlier to escape the hurly-burly life of New York City. They'd hoped to replace that craziness with the ease and quiet of a Noyac house on the bay, and then discovered that I was their next-door neighbor.

"Hey, Carla! Reggie! You guys home?"

A few seconds passed before Carla's soft and pretty face appeared at her bathroom window. She smiled at me and called through the trees, "Howdy, Stranger. Where've you been?"

I answered playfully, "Looking for girls for you guys. Problem is, I couldn't find any that might have been interested in you after meeting me."

"Screw you, Gabe," Carla laughed.

I replied through a rogue's smile, "In your dreams, Carla. In your dreams."

There must have been something different in the tone of my voice because Carla's face took on a concerned expression and she asked, "Are you okay, Gabe? You don't sound like yourself."

I answered unconvincingly, "I'm okay," and sounding more like my mother than my good looking, lesbian, next-door neighbor, Carla responded by saying, "Well, come on over anyway. We'd like to spend some time with you."

I was at their place in about three seconds flat. Flinging open their never-locked door without so much as a knock, I plastered a smile on my face and announced my entrance, singing, "Good morning, ladies. Gabriel Fortuna is here. Your problems are officially over."

Carla, dressed in faded blue Levi's, an old flannel shirt with a couple of strategic buttons missing and a pair of scrunchy old sweat sox, was seated on the tan paisley couch in front of the fireplace reading The Southampton Independent. She turned, saw me standing at the front door, and after a conspicuous roll of her large brown eyes, placed her newspaper neatly down on the the crushed velvet ottoman she used as a coffee table. Standing with her hands on her beautifully rounded hips, she gave me a very deliberate once over and finished her surveillance with a nod of faux approval. Through a put-on, sexy voice, she purred, "Oh my, Gabe. Don't we look handsome. Heavy date this morning?"

This morning? What's she talking about?

I looked down at myself and realized that I still hadn't changed out of my rumpled evening clothes, but before I could explain my sad condition, Reggie came barreling out of her studio carrying a large canvas. She settled it onto the tall easel standing in the middle of the room, placed her hands on her hips and studied her latest piece in the morning light shooting down through their skylight.

Reggie was tall and thin and not so pretty, compared to Carla's short and curvy and beautiful. She was wearing her ever present painter's smock, covered from collar to hem with years of dried paint, and a red beret of the kind you saw Rembrandt wearing in his self portraits. Despite the beret, Reggie was no Rembrandt. She had her own style, not at all dark and brooding like the old master's, and her paintings were considered quite good by many people who were supposed to know what they were talking about. She'd been offered a lot of money for some of her work, at least a lot of money to my way of thinking, and had decided not to sell, choosing instead to hold onto them for some future show she might have one day at one of the chic art galleries that were continually popping up on the East End.

"What do you think?" she asked, studying her work.

I walked up to the easel, looked closely at the painting and recognized Noyac Bay in winter with Shelter Island and The North Fork as background. Most of the bay was frozen, and a light trace of snow covered the ice, the ground, the trees and the distant shore of the island. Squirrel and deer tracks made small craters in the snow and the sky was a glaring white even though there were no clouds. A single bird flew through its blanched emptiness, and seeing it all alone as it was, I felt kind of sorry for it. Some branches rested on the shoreline and some stood stuck in the ice like gnarly black fingers, and a woman, who looked a lot like Carla in her red ski jacket, was bent over in the frozen distance, having just scaled a rock across the ice, watching it make a small splash where it reached the water.

I was moved by the painting and answered sincerely, "It's beautiful, Reggie, just like the rest of your Noyac scenes." Then, catching myself, I added sarcastically, "I'll give you ten bucks for it."

Reggie turned, looked me over and tossing me what over the years had become a familiar sour expression, responded to my offer, saying dryly, "Thanks, Gabe. You're a real patron." Then, softening for a reason unknown to me, she added, "You know, Gabe, we simply haven't got any space for this. Why don't you hold onto it until I have a show or until we get a bigger place."

I was a little surprised by this sudden talk of getting a bigger place, but I relaxed when I saw the quick and mischievous eye exchange between the girls. They knew I didn't have many friends and that their departure from next door would have left a hole in my heart as big as the stone quarry off Middle Line Highway. Also, if they left, who the hell knew who might move into their place? I didn't think I could live through two or three years of backhoes, demolition and reconstruction.

Confident that they were just pulling my chain, I defiantly replied, "You aren't selling anything and you aren't going anywhere. You're stuck with me."

Carla glided over to me, placed her arm through mine and with a warm and generous smile, replied, "We'd like you to have this, Gabe. Reggie painted it, I'm in it, and if you look closely, you'll see something of yourself there, too."

I looked at the painting, was again drawn to that lonely bird in flight and suddenly realized why I felt so sorry for it. After kissing Carla and then Reggie lightly on their cheeks, I said, "Thanks, girls, but it's too beautiful. I can't just accept it without giving you something in return."

The artist rolled her eyes, already anticipating the hard time I was going to give her, and responded, "Gabe, just take it. It's a gift. We want you to have it. Make believe Christmas comes early this year.

I reminded her that my mother was Jewish, that I'd grown up celebrating Chanukah and then, pretending to have come up with a great idea, cheered, "Let's make it Christmas for you guys, too. How about a menage? What do you say? Maybe I can turn you guys?"

Reggie rubbed at the cheek I'd recently brushed with my lips and gasped, "Please, Gabe, we don't need any turning. Just take the painting and go."

It occurred to me that it had been a long time since anyone had given me anything out of pure friendship and for the first time in a long time, I felt humbled. Cutting my bravado crap, I said sincerely, "Thank you, Reggie, and thank you, Carla. I promise I'll find a good spot for it."

"Yeah, sure," Reggie replied sarcastically, "but do us a favor and leave already. Your humility is killing me."

Not wanting to be alone, I stayed a while longer but never mentioned the murder at The Castle. My guess was that Al Shareef had to have a million enemies who wanted him dead and there was no reason to freak out the girls with my story of a celebrity killing in the Hamptons. They'd be reading about it in the papers soon enough anyway, that was if one of their friends didn't call to tell them about it first. At home, I leaned the painting against the wall over my fireplace mantel, centering it between pictures of my mother and father, my brother, David, and some photographic memories of me receiving citations for various acts I thought were just a part of my job but which others felt went beyond the pale. The painting looked great, adding something classy and soft to the otherwise masculine and sterile feel of my great room. I decided that I'd have to get the girls something in return, in spite of what they'd said, something that was personal and showed my way of looking at the world, as Reggie's painting showed hers. I got an inspiration, but I couldn't be sure if a Bowflex would fit nicely in their living room.

4

Under normal conditions, it doesn't take long for me to complete my workouts, but that day my routine lacked spirit. I didn't have the usual enthusiasm I felt in the weight room because not much was on my mind except Al Shareef's creased forehead and Teresa's big and beautiful breasts, but lifting weights was something I'd been doing since I was a teenager and the strength of my routine finally overcame my dark mood.

I started my workout with abdominals, knocking off three hundred stomach crunches and leg raises, and finished my midsection by working my obliques with two hundred, wide grip, broomstick abdominal twists. My bulk building, heavy lifting days were history, and with no one to spot me, I wouldn't take the chance of a heavy weight bar falling on my chest or head, crushing my heart or lungs or giving me that recently seen Al Shareef look. At six foot two and two hundred twenty solid pounds, I was happy with my appearance, my strength and my fitness level. Cables and plates worked just fine for maintenance, so I hit the universal.

After forty minutes of hard work, I was sweating pretty good and went to check my pump in the mirror. Throwing a couple of poses, I saw that I might need a little work on my left lat and was thinking that I must be favoring my right side when I heard the sound of tires kicking up gravel in my driveway. I checked the time and saw it was only eleven o'clock, still a little early for unannounced Sunday morning company, so considering my guests had not shown the courtesy of a phone call, I went to the door to greet them in my gym shorts and sweaty tank top.

I watched Gasper get out of his Trailblazer with some guy I'd never seen before. The stranger was wearing a crisp blue suit over a white shirt, a red tie, black shoes and aviator sunglasses and I took it for granted he wasn't dropping by to pick me up for church. They walked up to my front door and the guy in the suit stood pole-straight in front of me like he had a yardstick shoved up his ass. From his dress and his incredibly erect posture, any fool could tell he wasn't a relaxed local citizen. In fact, he might just have had the word FED tattooed across his forehead. Gasper, on the other hand, was dressed in jeans, a white t-shirt, and construction boots. His hair was a mess, he needed a shave, and the dark circles under his eyes told me he hadn't had any sleep. He stood slouching beside the Fed like he was either exhausted or in a state of constant surrender ... maybe both.

I flexed my wings a little bit for the benefit of Mr. Fed and said, "Good morning, G. You here with my thousand?"

Gasper's chin dropped a little more into his chest, but he recovered quickly and answered, "We'll talk about that later, Gabe." Pointing his thumb to the suit on his left, he added, "This is Agent Ralph Ledbetter. He works with Homeland Security and wants to ask you a few questions."

From the beginning of my career as a New York City cop, my instincts told me that when the federal government got involved with something it wasn't good for anyone. Working the beat, I never had much to do with any of the D.C. suits, but I heard about the way they worked from the detectives I knew and learned from them that what I intuitively felt was correct. Their advice was to always stay away from G-Men because they had a unique way of always fucking things up. I looked more closely at Mr. Ledbetter, his suit and his shades and his stick up the ass, and decided to behave appropriately. After all, there's no sense in making enemies.

"Mr. Bedwetter," I said and nodded in his direction.

Gasper rolled his baggy eyes and responded, "It's Ledbetter, Gabe. Listen, may we come in? There are a few questions we'd like to ask."

There was something I didn't like about having uninvited federal police in my house, so I blocked the door and asked, "What about?"

It was Ledbetter who curtly answered, "Look, we want to ask you a few questions, Fortuna. Any problems with that?"

It speaks!

I looked into Gasper's sad eyes and against my better judgement moved to the side and let them in. My place wasn't a palace but I kept it neat and clean. I had a couple of nice area rugs from Hildredths, a brown leather couch and two matching chairs form Chez Morgan, and a couple of nice oak side tables, two lamps and a forty-eight inch square glass and chrome cocktail table in the middle of everything that I got from Southampton Rumrunner. All of it sat in front of a fireplace that took up most of the western wall, Reggie's newly acquired painting sitting smartly on top of it. To the right of the fireplace was the hallway leading to the back bedrooms and the gym, and to the right of that, facing northeast, was the large picture window looking out over my deck and onto Noyac Bay. The kitchen was opposed to the fireplace, about twenty feet away, making most of my place what designers like to call a great room. I installed a butcher block topped island and some new appliances a couple of years ago, and I could probably have gotten a nice piece of change for the place if I ever wanted to sell, but this was my home, I loved it and I wasn't going anywhere.

Falling into one of the leather chairs and draping a leg over one of its arms, I asked, "Alright, what do you want to know?"

Gasper sat on the couch opposite from me, crossed his legs and said, "It's about last night. We want to ask you a few questions about your dealings with Mr. Al Shareef."

Ledbetter didn't sit. He walked around the room, checking out my lack of knickknacks and artwork, but stopped for a while at the fireplace to admire Reggie's painting. He turned and shot me a look that asked, 'where the hell did this come from?', and then continued his leisurely stroll around my place. I didn't like it when he reached the side of my chair, stopped and looked down upon me, so I stood and looked down at him. He didn't like that, shot me a stony stare and walked away.

Turning my attention to Gasper, I said, "What about last night, G? You were there. You got to the pool before I did."

Ledbetter had entered the kitchen area and was checking out the interior of my GE Profile refrigerator. He looked up after examining the fruit bin and said, "We were told that you and Mr. Al Shareef had a conversation early in the evening." Closing the refrigerator door, he stepped over to the matching Profile slide-in range and turned a knob. There were a few clicks before the electronic ignition lighted the gas, a blue flame erupting from one of the jets.

"Gas?" he asked in a surprised tone.

With an unmistakenly bad attitude, I answered, "It's the only way to cook."

Gasper was a regular cop, just as I'd been, and was as uncomfortable at being around a Fed as me. He wanted to get the questioning over with and to get the hell out of my house as much as I wanted him out, and broke off our culinary discussion by saying, "Now, about last night, Gabe. What were you and Mr. Al Shareef talking about?"

With no attempt at hiding my irritation, I demanded, "What's going on, G? I had nothing to do with the guy. I never met him before last night and was nowhere around him when he took his swim."

Ledbetter was examining my Fisher Paykel dishwasher drawers when he said, "I'm sure all that is true, but you were seen having a discussion with the man not one hour before he was found floating face down in his pool." Closing a drawer a bit too crisply for my liking, he added, "Being an ex-cop, you should know we have to talk to anyone who was seen around Mr. Al Shareef before his death. We need to come up with some kind of motive for his murder. You never know what might slip out, even from people who seemingly have nothing to do with the guy."

I wanted to say, "Fuck you, Bedwetter, and get the fuck out of my house," but I knew that would just be asking for more trouble, so I said, "I understand homicide routine, but what does Homeland Security have to do with a murder investigation?"

It was clear that Ledbetter had finally taken over my interrogation and that Gasper's job was to sit back and keep out of it. My old friend sunk into the soft couch and looked into his folded hands as Ledbetter answered, "Mr. Al Shareef was a prominent member of the Muslim community throughout the United States and the world. His work at bringing people together through film had made him famous. However, his somewhat progressive stance on the Jewish experience, and the USA in general, had made him very unpopular with many members of his religion."

I couldn't believe my ears and interrupted the Fed, belligerently asking, "Are you trying to tell me that killing Al Shareef was a terrorist act? You think he was killed because of his movies?"

My old buddies were right; G-Men always do fuck things up.

Ledbetter snapped, "We don't know why he was killed, Fortuna. That's what we're trying to find out. When we know why, we'll find out who, and hopefully we'll prevent any more anti-American feeling from circling the globe."

I shot Gasper a dubious expression, but he just shrugged and went back to studying his thumbs. Returning to Ledbetter, I said, "Alright, what do you want to know?"

He asked, "Why were you speaking with Mr. Al Shareef?"

"We spoke for only a minute or two. I didn't know who he was, but he approached me by name and introduced himself. He complained that he couldn't build a bigger house, that we were too provincial in Southampton and offered me a drink."

"That's all?"

"That's all."

Ledbetter's eyes twinkled and he asked, "Did he tell you he was banging your ex-wife?"

Again, I looked at Gasper, and again my friend shrugged, but this time he added a roll of his eyes before going back to his thumbs. I recalled my brief conversation with the victim, remembered the lewd expression in his eyes when he'd kissed me off and began putting things together.

I slowly answered, "No, he didn't tell me that."

"Well," Ledbetter replied through a thin smile, "he was. And from our preliminary investigation, we've discovered that he'd been nailing her for quite a while."

The Fed let this information sink into me for a few seconds and when he saw that it wasn't bothering me as much as he'd hoped, he crisply added, "We may have to talk with you again, Fortuna, but that will be all for now." Turning to Gasper, he said, "Ready, Captain Dupree?"

I wasn't about to let things end so easily and said, "Hold on a minute, G. I want to talk to you." Looking icily at the Fed, I added, "In private."

Ledbetter examined Gasper and let out a bored sigh just to show me how unimportant he thought I was. When he finished with that, he said, "Let's go, Captain. We've got a few more people to interview."

I screwed a disgusted look on my face and taunted my old friend, saying, "You taking orders from this guy, G?"

Gasper finally straighted his spine. He turned to Ledbetter and said, "I'll be right out. I'll meet you at the car."

The Fed stared at me from behind his sunglasses, threw a snort in my direction and left my house. Whether he'd said it or not, I knew he was considering me for the guy who finished Al Shareef. It would mean a lot for the government if it could quickly find the person who'd killed the world famous Muslim film producer, and it would probably get Mr. Ledbetter a raise in pay and big status within Homeland Security if he was the guy who broke the case. It was all bullshit to point a finger at me, though, and Gasper knew it. I was bristling from even being considered, but I was in it and I was going to stay in it until I was satisfied.

Gasper saw my slow burn percolate into a rapid boil, but before I got too hot to handle, he said, "Take it easy, Gabe. It's just the way this business works. You should know that. It's all a formality. You're not really a suspect. It's just something we've got to do."

I replied with a long, drawn out, "Fuuuuuuck you," and it occurred to me that unless the murderer actually was a towelhead on his way back to Qatar or Yemen or Dubai or any other one of those hot and sandy places in the Middle East, he was probably still in the Hamptons. I asked, "What's the next big event out here?"

Gasper answered, "You've got to be kidding me," and seeing from my surly expression I wasn't, added, "It's The Memorial Day Red, White and Blue Ball at Sylvester Hightower's place on Dune Road."

I responded forcefully and without hesitation, "I'm working it."

After a few moments of thought, Gasper replied weakly, "Alright. I'll have to get back to you, though."

I said, "Make sure you do," and noting my friend's sluggish body language, added, "And G, don't forget the thousand you owe me."

I didn't know if Al Shareef had been killed by a terrorist, a man or a woman, or if he'd slipped and smacked his head on the coping of his pool and the whole thing was an accident, but I knew I hadn't done anything to kill the guy and I didn't like being a suspect. To make matters worse, my ex-wife was somehow involved and that meant, if it was murder and the murderer was clever enough, he might find a way to point the arrow at me and then stick it straight into my back.

Gasper and the Fed left and I walked back into my gym, got my towel and was about to hit the shower when I caught my reflection in the floor to ceiling wall mirror. I was right; my left latissimus dorsi was definitely not in balance with the right. I went back to the bench and did three sets of one-armed rows with heavier weights than I'd used in a very long time.

5

The Whalebone General Store was the kind of place we used to call a five and dime and was where I presently picked up weekend editions of The Sunday Daily News, The New York Times and a weekly copy of the Southampton Press. I tried to read all three newspapers on Sunday because I felt New York was still my city, even though I rarely got back there, and the Press was pretty good reading for a small town paper.

Janet Maglie, the overweight, fortiesh daughter of Sal, the old guy who'd owned The Whalebone for as long as I could remember, stroked her long peroxide-blond hair, tilted her head coquettishly to the side and gave me the big smile she reserved for whenever I entered. Leaning over the counter while virtually spilling out of her sloppy, tie-dyed halter top, she said, "Hiya, Gabe. Didya hear about what happened at The Castle last night?"

I knew what Janet was asking for and it had nothing to do with the happenings at The Castle. I've learned that you don't shit where you eat, and The Whalebone was where I bought my papers, my lottery tickets, and occasional potted plants. Also, I liked Sal and didn't want to ruin my relationship with him, so I answered, "Yeah, outrageous, huh. Terrorists in Southampton. See ya," and rushed out the door.

I sped home, and after slamming the door to my place, threw the papers onto the cocktail table and fell into a chair with The Times. Al Shareef hadn't been dead for twelve hours and already his alleged murder was making headlines. On the front page, above the fold, were color pictures of The Castle, Binyamin Al Shareef, and his wailing wife being comforted by an obviously distraught Captain Gasper Dupree of the Southampton Town Police.

There wasn't much information to be had, but the banner said, *Binyamin Al Shareef, Prominent Muslim, Found Dead, Terrorist Connection Probed.* It occurred to me that that was the kind of headline that could increase circulation even for The Times. The article went on to say how local and federal police were investigating, working together to see if there were any international aspects to the death, but failed to mention that Gabriel Fortuna was a prime suspect because his ex-wife, Teresa Fortuna, had been playing harem with the recently deceased.

I went through the rest of the news quickly, barely looking to see how my Mets, those fucking pieces of shit, had managed to lose their latest ballgame, and was done with the paper by one. I fixed my power lunch of two tablespoons of hydrated kelp, two raw eggs, and fourteen ounces of soy milk in the blender, and while it was whirring, got dressed. After chugging my lunch, I hopped into the Caddy and headed straight for Easthampton.

If you know the roads, the drive to the trendiest of the Hampton villages is very beautiful. The trick is to avoid Route 27, sometimes called The Sunrise Highway, sometimes The Montauk Highway, but as I like to call it, The East End Distressway. It's a mostly commercial, sometimes two lane road that runs the entire length of The Hamptons, from Westhampton Beach all the way to the tip of Montauk Point, but after reaching Southampton Village, there's usually only one lane in either direction, with one or two traffic lights in every town and hamlet, and other lights where another main road bisects it so that vacationers north of the highway can cross and get to the ocean beaches. Most of the time, drivers crawl along the road bitching about the traffic and wondering why the towns can't add a lane or two to ease things, but I knew all the backroads and side roads even before Della Femina's kid published them and the only times you'd catch me on 27 was if I wanted to go to Saracen, or to Indian Cove, or to the Princess Diner.

Cruising along in the Caddy, I passed the Bacelona Neck Golf Course, Sag Harbor's State of New York Municipal Course, where for eighteen bucks locals can get pissed off playing nine holes on not-so-true greens and under-mowed fairways, and continued on to Swamp Road, where I made a left and drove for a mile through a pine forest filled with medium priced, million dollar homes. I reached Two-Holes-

Of Water Road, made a right and was flanked by larger homes of more acreage, places in the two million dollar range, and drove straight on for two miles until I came to the stop sign at Stephen Hands Path. The traffic wasn't too busy at this crossroad and only about thirty late model Infiniti, Mercedes, Lexus SUVs and Range Rovers drove past before I was able to bolt across and get onto Long Lane, the long and narrow street flanked by the village high school and its sports fields, a chicken farm and several vast tree nurseries. After a mile and a half of this and some amazing open skies, I reached the Village of Easthampton.

I parked the car on prosperous Newtown Lane and walked down the trendy street, passing a few art galleries, three European-style kitchen cabinetry shops and several gourmet delicatessans and cafes, each featuring either French or Pan-Asian delicacies, and although it was still only the Sunday before Memorial Day Weekend and the season had not yet officially begun, the weather was cooperating and the street was already teeming with people window shopping, sitting in outdoor cafes, or out hunting celebrities. I passed one of the Baldwin Brothers who was in dire need of a shave and a haircut and had let his gut get a little out of hand, an actor from The Sopranos without his toupee and whose name I didn't remember eating a doughnut outside Dreesen's, and turned right onto Main Street, where a befuddled and middle-aged Chevy Chase ran past me in a pair of snug white tennis shorts. In the middle of the block, flanked by Tiffany's and Cashmere Hampton, was the place I was looking for, Dreamland Properties, the principal owner of which was my ex-wife, Teresa Fortuna. I entered and approached the receptionist who had her face buried in some papers, busily doing whatever it is that receptionists do that makes them look busy whenever someone enters.

She looked up with appropriately bored eyes, and seeing me, emitted a slight gasp. Her eyes sparkled with possibilities and she straightened in her chair, jostled her ass a bit and threw her breasts out towards me, but after noticing my tightly set jaw, she knew my visit was all business and her little fantasy abruptly ended. Through a renewed expression of receptional boredom, she asked, "May I help you?"

I was pissed off and nervous about having to see Teresa, so I kept my lips tight and answered, "Teresa Fortuna, please."

"Ms. Fortuna is busy right now. Can you come back later?"

"She'll see me. Tell her Gabe is here."

"Ms. Fortuna gave specific instructions that …"

"I'm her ex-husband. Tell her it's important."

The receptionist sighed, pressed a button on her phone console and said, "I'm sorry to bother you, Ms. Fortuna, but a man who says he's your ex-husband insists on seeing you. Yes, ma'am. Right away." Replacing the phone, she said, "It's down the corridor and the last door on your right."

There were quite a few offices down the long corridor of Dreamland Properties, most of them filled with eager brokers seated behind their desks speaking with well-dressed New Yorkers wanting to buy their own Hampton's dream house. The flooring in the place was luxurious wall-to-wall carpeting, the air was filled with the sounds of soft flutes and violins, and there was a peculiar scent floating around that reminded me of money. I reached the door to Teresa's office, didn't bother to knock, and once again, when I'd opened a closed door on my ex-wife, it was I who was surprised. Unlike the last time, though, when I'd caught her in Room 110 of The Poseidon Motel pounding a hedge fund manager who was negotiating to buy a 20 acre lot off Further Lane, I wasn't going to let my consternation show.

I calmly said, "Good afternoon, G." Moving my eyes to the right, I added, "Teresa," and glancing and nodding to the other person in the room, I found myself unable to resist the temptation and said, "Agent Bedwetter."

Gasper rolled his eyes, Teresa smiled wickedly and the Fed grimaced. Like any normal guy, he already had a hard-on for Teresa and didn't like it one bit when I came in and took away his clout. He was shooting me nails through squinty eyes and from the way he was moving his fingers, looked like he was ready to yell, "Draw," and go for his gun.

Gasper reached out, placed his hand on Ledbetter's arm and turning to me asked, "What are you doing here, Gabe?"

"What's the matter, G?" I responded. "Can't a guy visit his ex-wife? Maybe I want us to get back together?"

I checked out Teresa, forced a smile and watched her eyes sparkle. She didn't care about me, I knew that, but I remembered how she always liked to see men fighting over her.

Ledbetter barked, "Not when she's part of a murder investigation. You used to be a cop. You should know better."

I snapped back, "I don't know anything. As far as I'm concerned, I came by to talk with Teresa about some old pictures she had of my family that I'd like returned. If there's a problem with that, I'd like to know what it is so I can call a lawyer and find out just how full of shit you are."

Gasper broke in, saying, "Take it easy, Gabe. Like I told you before, it's all formality. There are things we've got to do." Turning to Ledbetter, he asked, "Are we done here?"

The Fed glared at me and then turned to Teresa, at whom he glared even more intensely. She nudged her shoulders back barely an inch and pushed her braless breasts toward him ever so slightly, causing the Fed to quickly lose his angry expression. Being a Federal agent and a consummate professional, Ledbetter recovered from Teresa's come-on faster than most guys did and said, "We may have further questions for you, Ms. Fortuna." Turning back to me, he warned, "This isn't over yet." Without another word, he stormed out of the office with Gasper trailing in his wake.

Teresa closed the door behind them and twisted the little knob on the handle to lock it. Turning to me, she said demurely, "He doesn't like you."

I responded, "That goes both ways."

Teresa circled me like a vulture waiting for its prey to completely cash in. When she realized I wasn't intending to be her afternoon snack, she finally asked, "Why *are* you here, Gabe?"

I wanted to ask her what the story was between her and Al Shareef but I knew if I came right out and asked, the best I would get would be a lie, so I said, "I could use some money. I'm thinking about taking you up on your offer."

Leaning back against her desk and spreading her legs provocatively, she asked, "Which offer is that?"

She was wearing beige cotton slacks, tight fitting, the way she liked to wear everything, and I could make out her soft mound calling to me. I pretended to be deaf and answered, "You remember, the one that needed a guy like me."

Teresa raised an eyebrow and replied, "That takes in a lot of territory."

I responded, "I don't know. I'm a pretty simple guy. There are only a few things in which I specialize."

Smiling seductively, Teresa left her desk and sidled across the room. Stopping right in front of where I stood and placing her right hand exactly where she wanted, she cupped my strong erection over my pants and said, "Mmmmm, this is something I could use you for."

Teresa closed her eyes, brought her lips to mine and kissed me. I thought she was going to suck the tongue clear out of my mouth and for a couple of seconds I actually swooned. There was a rushing between my ears, I felt like I was losing my balance and without thinking I placed my hand on Teresa's magnificent ass and pressed her hard into me. She moaned a moan I remembered well and it was like an alarm bell sounded. A shock of fear passed through me and I pushed her away. We were both breathing hard.

With half closed eyes, she panted, "What's wrong, Gabe?"

I pressed my hand against the wall to catch my balance and standing on jelly-legs answered, "You're wrong, Teresa. You're all wrong for me." Gulping down some air, I decided it was time to get to the point and demanded, "Now, what the hell were you doing fucking around with Al Shareef?"

Teresa regained her composure a lot faster than I did. She combed her fingers through her hair, licked her luscious red lips and went back to sitting on top of her desk. Crossing her perfect legs, she whispered, "You really had me going there, Gabe. For a moment, it was just like old times. I still like the feel of your hand on my ass. I don't have to tell you how much I liked placing my hand on you."

I'd finally come down to earth and shot back, "Fuck you, Teresa. Somebody you were screwing is dead and the police are pointing at me because they think I might still have something for my ex-wife."

Teresa sighed with boredom and responded, "It was business, Gabe, just business. He had a piece of property I wanted and I was trying to get on his good side. No big deal."

I barked, "No big deal! The guy is dead. That's a big fucking deal."

Uncrossing her legs and opening them widely, she asked, "Jealous, Gabe?"

I looked at her contemptuously but knew she might have been right. Being around her had mixed me up so much I didn't know if I was jealous or not, and kissing her while her hand was on me had sent my head reeling, making me want to tear her clothes off right there in the office, but I did know one thing for sure, as great a piece of ass as Teresa was, she wasn't worth the trouble doing her would eventually put me through. Pulling myself together, I asked coldly, "Why did you want to hire me? You said there was a way I could make some real money."

"That offer is rescinded, Gabe. You should have taken me up on it while it was on the table." Undoing a couple of buttons on her blouse, she licked her lips and added, "The other offer is still open."

I don't think I ever wanted anything so bad in my life, but I found the wisdom to resist and warned, "Teresa, if you've done anything to fuck me up, it won't go well for you."

Unbuttoning two more buttons and spreading her shirt so that her beautiful breasts and their round pink nipples were pointed straight at me, she said, "Gabe, honey, the door is locked and the rug is thick and soft. Why don't we do something for old time's sake. After we're done, I'm sure we'll both feel a lot better. What do you say, Gabe? I don't mind a little rug burn. As I recall, neither did you. It's been a long time, Honey. Why don't you come over here and let nature take its course."

There was nothing more to say. I knew that if I stayed a minute longer I would have been in her and that would have opened up a whole new world of trouble for me. I unlocked the door and left the office with Teresa's throaty laughter following behind me, but I'd gotten what I'd come for. Teresa had wanted something from Al Shareef, and it was always what she wanted, land and money.

I passed the bored receptionist, opened the door to Dreamland Properties and hit the street. Across the way, at the Easthampton Movie Theater, the marquee showed that an old Arnold movie, *Pumping Iron*, was playing. It was the one where Arnold psyches out Lou Ferigno to win The Mr. Universe Contest and the one that got me into lifting weights when I was a kid. Needing time to cool off from Teresa and even more time to figure out my next move, I crossed the street and entered the movie house.

6

I watched the movie twice and left the theater a little after five o'clock, pissed off that I was never fully able to concentrate on Arnold's magnificent glutes because I'd spent the entire three and a half hours thinking about Al Shareef and Teresa and still found it hard to believe she could have had anything to do with his murder. Teresa had always used sex to get what she wanted, not a fucking crowbar, and although she had no scruples and was capable of doing just about anything, an act of murder was something I just could not believe she could commit. Still, I'd been wrong about her before, plenty wrong, and as I walked out of the darkened movie theater, blinded by the late afternoon light, I hoped the memory of my hand on Teresa's perfect ass wasn't blinding me as well.

I was in no rush to get home and decided to take Route 27 to make sure the going was slow. It was a Sunday afternoon and being near six o'clock, the going was even slower than I'd anticipated because most of the pre-summer crowd was heading back to New York City for the beginning of their workweek. I crawled along, thinking about Al Shareef's broken forehead and Teresa's superb tits, but once past the burdensome traffic light in the middle of Watermill's downtown, traffic suddenly opened up and I made an uncontested left past the pumpkin patch and pulled into The Princess Diner's parking lot.

The Princess was set up much like any other good diner. Owned by married Greeks, Nick and Katerina Constantinopoulos, it seemed like every type of food was on the menu. Prices were higher than you would have liked them to be, but were still reasonable when compared to most of the other restaurants out here, and your plate was always filled to its rim, everything coming with a mountain of fries. There were booths along the window and tables on the floor, the colors were beige and turquoise and nearly all the walls were mirrored. The clean and tidy tiled restrooms were immaculate and located behind a door at the end of the counter, along with the payphone.

When I was a young man, The Princess was the place I'd go at four in the morning on a Friday or Saturday night if I hadn't gotten lucky in one of the clubs. It should have been called The Last Chance Diner because that was what it really was. Looking back, I guess it could have been called The Hand Job Diner, too. There weren't any waiters in The Princess, only waitresses, and of those, more and more were South American or Mexican. My favorite server was Esmeralda Santiago, a twenty-eight year old Costa Rican sex-kitten with jet black eyes, café au lait colored skin, round curves on a short, strong body, and a pair of hands that held some of the most beautifully sculpted fingers I'd ever seen. I'd often admired those digits as they wrapped waxed paper around the breakfast burrito I sometimes ordered to go, and had also wondered if she'd like to give the same wrap job to Senor Fortuna.

"What *ees* the matter, Gabriel?"

I was seated at the booth across from the register, thinking about things I had lined up for tomorrow when I heard the voice. I looked up and there was Esmeralda smiling down at me, her ballpoint pen in her left hand, her pad in her right, and the top two buttons of her blouse open to reveal just the right amount of Latina cleavage.

I smiled and said, "Hi, Esmie. Nothing's wrong. I was just thinking."

Leaning over a bit more than most waitresses do so that I could get a really good look down her blouse, Esmeralda replied, "Well, do not theenks too much. I do not likes eet when ju gets that loco looks een jour eyes."

I slowly looked her up and down, playing around like I did whenever I stopped in the diner, and although I'd never been really serious about making it with Esmie, after the show she was putting on, I'd never been more truthful than when I said, "You're looking good tonight, Esmie."

She smiled like a little girl, blushed a bit and said, "Well, I am nots on the menu, Gabriel." Placing the top of her pen in her mouth and gently pressing the tip with her tongue so that it clicked and the point flew out its end, she teased, "At leese, nots now."

Sighing, Esmie closed her eyes and her pad, built up some resolve and said, "I cannot waits any longer for ju to wakes up to me, Gabriel. Ju have not beens here for weeks and I meest ju. I spends too much time lookings at the door for ju. Oy, mio. Gabriel, I works until eight. What do ju say ju waits for me to ends my sheeft and we goes to your place. We can cooks our deener there. No?"

I reminded myself of my cardinal rule, don't shit where you eat, but hell, I was really stressed out and as far as I was concerned Esmeralda had become takeout. I was about to say, "Andalay," when Gasper appeared.

He gave Esmeralda a sour look and said, "Get me a coffee and get lost."

Sliding onto the bench seat opposite me, Gasper picked up the metal container of milk, lifted its lid and took a sniff. Puckering his face, he placed it back under the music box and brought the covered little Half and Half containers sitting against the mirrored wall closer to him.

He said, "I've got to talk with you, Gabe," and I replied, "I think we've spoken more in the last day than we have in the past six years." A dark shadow crossed over his eyes and Gasper added, "Don't make jokes; this is serious."

Esmeralda came with Gasper's coffee and another for me. She frowned at the cop when she placed his cup on the table, but smiled at me, telling me our date was still on, if I wanted it.

Esmie left us and I asked, "Well, what do you want, G?"

"What were you doing at Teresa's this afternoon?"

"Like I told you, she's got some things of mine I'd like back."

"Bullshit. The only things she's ever taken from you were your balls, and judging from the little senorita's smile, I'd guess you've already gotten those back."

I wasn't about to take any of Gasper's shit, police captain or not. Sitting across from me and staring at me as if his eyes would be enough to stop me from doing whatever it was he didn't want me to do, it was my guess that our years apart had caused him to forget who I was. I needed to remind him of that and said, "Go fuck yourself, G. If you've got a problem with me seeing Teresa I'd like to know why, but don't go thinking you can tell me what to do."

Not taking well to my suggestion of what he could do with his dick, Gasper responded with unusual vigor, shouting in the crowded restaurant, "This is a murder investigation, Gabe! Al Shareef was a prominent man! He may have been killed by Arab terrorists, or Muslim haters, or business people who wanted some of what he had, or ex-husbands of women he was giving it to!"

I saw red with Gasper's last suggestion and blew up, blasting Gasper with, "You've got to be shitting me! You can't believe that I'm the one who killed Al Shareef!"

Noticing the questioning looks from the surrounding diner's patrons, Gasper turned it down several notches and replied through tight lips, "It doesn't matter what I believe. Al Shareef was rich and prominent. The Feds want to get someone quickly and get this shit behind them. They don't need front-page headlines about rich Middle Easterners getting whacked in the United States. And I've already heard from the goddamned Town Council. They want this shit wrapped up quickly, too, and believe me, you'd be the perfect fall guy. You never show anyone any respect, and if you hadn't noticed, you're not exactly the most well liked guy in Southampton. Even if not convicted, arresting you would quiet a lot of people until this thing blew over."

I was stunned. The sudden involvement of the council bothered me because it could prove troublesome. That group had real power out here and if the people on it wanted to, they could try and stop me from building an add-on to my deck. I barked, "What the fuck does the Town Council care about Al Shareef?"

Gasper stoically answered, "They don't like it when a celebrity gets killed out here. Its not good for property values."

I wasn't in any mood for Gasper's bullshit warnings, so I looked hard into my old friend's eyes and said, "Get the fuck out of here, G, and keep the fuck away from me. I'll do whatever and see whomever I want." Pointing my thumb over my shoulder to where Esmeralda stood watching, I added, "Now it's your turn to get lost."

Gasper slid out of the bench, stood over me and took a wrinkled white envelope from his pocket. He slapped it onto the table and said, "Here's five hundred. You didn't do a very good job and you're lucky to get anything so don't complain that I still owe you. I just hope you don't need this as part of a hefty retainer for your lawyer." Through a remarkably sour puss, he added, "Stay away from Hightower's place this weekend. Your services are not required." And just like an old-time, local cop, he left the table without putting anything down for his coffee or for Esmeralda.

Esmeralda returned just a few moments later, dressed in her street clothes of white sneakers, tight blue jeans, and a tighter white t-shirt under a Wrangler blue denim jacket. She said, "I hates that man," and slid in opposite me, her round little breasts pressing against the flimsy cotton of her shirt. Pouting cutely, she added, "He always geeves the girls a hard time, acteeng likes we don'ts belongs."

I explained, "He's an old-time local, Esmie. Changes come hard for some of those people."

We left the diner together, took the Caddy to my place and were making out in the great room before the front door closed behind us. Our lips were glued together in a passionate kiss as I carried her into my bedroom and the only time I took them from her mouth was to give her soft, sweet kisses on her shoulders and neck. After laying Esmie gently on my bed, I removed her clothes slowly. All the while she panted like a Latin kitten in heat, mewing sounds and words in Spanish that had me longing to have her. I kissed one of her nipples and she groaned and arched her back, forcing her entire lovely breast into my mouth. I lingered there for a while and made loud slurping sounds that combined harmoniously with her little Latin moans, creating a beautiful bedroom symphony. Working my lips slowly down her body to that soft place where I intended to really work some magic, I got hung up on her bellybutton ring, momentarily getting the tip of my tongue caught in its little golden hoop.

Esmeralda swiveled her hips a bit as I was unloosing my tongue and was able to slip her hand down my body to where my erection was lurking inside my pants. She felt it, squeezed it and then unzipped my pants, taking my incredibly swollen penis into her sculpted hand. A few seconds later, she moved her grip a little further down my root and took a delicate but firm hold of my bundled cajones.

Her skin was beautiful and soft and smelled like pot roast and her long fingers were just as wonderful as I'd hoped they'd be. I moaned with every pleasurable stroke she gave me and when it came time for some really serious business, I turned her over and took her from the rear.

She groaned, "Oy, Poppi," with my first stroke and then began to mumble and holler things I'd never heard before and knew I might never hear again. With all the pressure backed up in me from a day's worth of false alarms, I had to fight to save myself from cutting loose immediately, and somehow, I was able to hold off long enough for Esmeralda to come several times before I pulled out of her and shot my load all over her backside.

We made love three times that night and she fell asleep with her head on my shoulder and her arm draped across my chest. I didn't sleep much, though. I kept falling in and out of it, awakened by dreams I could not remember and spending most of the night looking at the ceiling, thinking about Teresa, Gasper, Ledbetter and Mrs. Al Shareef, to whom I was determined to pay a visit the next day.

7

At seven o'clock, I was already out of bed and in the kitchen, mixing up a powershake and getting ready to take the five-mile jog along Long Beach Road that I always took on days I didn't lift. I guess the whirring of the mixer woke Esmeralda because she came out of my bedroom wearing nothing but a thong, a smile and two of the most beautiful brown nippled little titties a man could ever wish to see. Wiping the sleep from her eyes, she took quick and playful little steps towards me, but even though I'd had a great time with Esmie the night before and truly appreciated how she'd taken my mind off things for at least a little while, the night was over and I had things to do.

"Good mornings, Gabriel," she cooed, coming around the island and wrapping her arms around me in a playful little hug. "Ju are too much mans for a leetle girl likes me. I am so sores between my legs. I weel theenks of ju with every steps."

I didn't respond to Esmie except under my running shorts, where her loving hug had brought about an unanticipated morning stretch. Her eyes were gleaming with bedroom possibilities when they looked up into mine, but when they saw my sudden lack of interest, in spite of what nature might have suggested, a wave of disappointment swept over her face and she released me.

Crossing her arms over her pretty little chest and changing that pouty little disappointed expression into one that was totally pissed off, she asked stiffly, and with not a small amount of belligerance, "Ees sometheengs wrong, Gabriel?"

"No, Esmie," I answered, shutting off the blender.

I was measuring out some whey and didn't need to look at her to know she was getting angrier because heat was radiating from her body like a car's fender left too long in the sun. Now, it was true that Esmeralda was a lot hotter than any bowl of chili she had ever served me, but I was already beginning to feel crowded. Last night was over, we'd both had our fun, and it was time to move on. I frowned and wondered what it was about some women that they thought they owned you just because you'd given them something for which they'd asked. Coming over here was Esmeralda's idea, not mine, and although I'd heartily agreed with it and enjoyed our little tryst, I'd see her again when I had the time and now just wasn't the time.

I said, "Esmie, I've got some things to do today and I need an early start. As much as I'd like to put in a little more time with you this morning, I just can't. I've already called Harry over at Town Cab. He'll pick you up at nine and take you wherever you'd like to go."

Esmeralda dropped her jaw and looked at me like I'd just killed her puppy and she was president of the Animal Rescue Fund. She moved her head sideways and back and forth like a surreal Egyptian dancer, bugged her eyes, built up steam, dropped her jaw a little more and screamed, "So, ju theenks ju can jus' haves your fun and tros me out?"

It suddenly occurred to me that Esmie might have been the most dramatic woman I had ever met and I quickly looked around to make sure there weren't any loose knives lying on the counter. When I was sure there weren't, I answered as calmly as I could, saying, "Take it easy, Esmeralda. No one is throwing you out. Last night was great but I've got things to do. I'll call you and we'll do it again some time."

"Calls me? Ju don'ts even haves my fuckeeeng numbers. Do eet again somes time? What are ju going to do? Comes to the diner and after eatings your fucking burrito, asks me eef I weesh to goes homes weet ju so ju can plays with my chocha. I am no fuckeeng puta, Gabriel. Ju cannot jus' fucks me and forgets me."

I'd been in this scene a thousand times and it never gets easier. You can't be understanding with women when they get this way because they take it as weakness and come at you even harder. With the supreme confidence of knowing I was right and the cajones to do what had to be done, I said, "Look, Esmeralda, you came on to me. We both got what we wanted, and now I've got some shit I need to take care of and

I can't be with you. There's food in the fridge. Make yourself some breakfast, get dressed and leave. The cab will be here at nine and take you wherever you need to go. Thanks for last night; it was great. Leave your number on the counter and I'll call you when I get the chance. I'm going for a run. Don't be here when I get back."

I chugged my shake and didn't wait for it to settle in my stomach because I didn't want to hear any more of Esmie's bullshit. As it was, she was busy cursing in Spanish, running around the great room like a pollo with its cabessa cut off, and although I didn't understand most of what she was saying, I caught the gist of it from words I'd learned on the beat in the South Bronx, words like maricon, becho, chocha, and the universal, muthafuck. I left my house to the sound of Esmie screaming in a Latin crescendo, "Ju weel not gets away weet this, muthafuck," and began my jog. Hoping she'd be gone when I got back, I knew there was nothing more unpredictable than a Latina who knows she's been screwed and thinks she's been scorned, but I had places to go and people to see and I needed to be alone.

Wearing my new white Nike running shoes, a pair of blue Adidas running shorts and a matching blue Champion t-shirt whose sleeves I had cut off so that my arms and deltoids could catch some sun, I set out into the cool spring morning. I rounded the turn past where the Salty Dog used to be, now some god-awful, low-rise condos, and padded onto Long Beach Road, heading towards the traffic circle two and a half miles away, where I would make my turn and head back home. I was working a nice pace and my mind began wandering, as it did any time I did anything aerobic. I thought about Esmie and Teresa and Gasper and Ledbetter, but at the traffic circle, where I made my turn, I began imagining my upcoming interview with Mrs. Al Shareef.

I remembered how she'd wailed the night her husband was killed and realized she might not want to meet the man some suspected of his murder. I went through the questions I intended to ask and hoped that she'd be forthcoming, and then I thought about the way Gasper had left me at the diner. He'd made it pretty clear that I was in trouble and that he wasn't going to be much help to me, old friends or not.

Coming to the end of my jog, I was only about a half-mile from home when I checked my stopwatch and saw that I'd made great time. It was only eight-thirty and Esmeralda was certain to be at my place for at least a while longer and I didn't want to argue with her, so I pulled over and went to my bench to rest. As I neared it, I read the bronze plaque nailed to its back, *In Memory of David Fortuna, Loving Son and Brother, 1968-1979.*

"Hi, Dave," I said, nearing the memorial. "I've got some big problems. I sure wish you were here to help me."

Dave had been my older brother by two years. Its funny how when most kids are young, the older brother takes things out on his younger sibling, but that wasn't the way it was between Dave and me. He was always good to me, and all I remember is laughing with him when we played and crying with him when either of us felt sad. It seemed like we shared everything; at least that's the way I choose to remember things. The worst day in my life was that Saturday I was in our bedroom, when I was watching television and heard the phone ring. There was a short, choppy conversation in the hallway and then Dad came in and sat on the edge of my bed. From the look in his eyes, I could tell something terrible had happened.

I was only nine, a year too young to play on the Noyac kids' hockey team, but David, being two years older than me, could play and was already considered a little star. The Peewees met every Saturday at Trout Pond Park and practiced during the morning hours from nine to eleven. My dad told me that David had chased a puck that had gone out of bounds, had skated past the red flags that had been placed as warning markers and had fallen through the ice. By the time they were able to get him out from under, he was gone.

I've never really gotten over his death and I never really had a chance to say good-by to him, not unless you consider touching a cold stone and walking away holding hands with each of your parents a fitting farewell. It was at his funeral that I learned that nothing stays the same, that all things do come to an end, and that if you want to live your life the way you want to live it you've got to be ready for anything because anything can happen. Those were tough lessons for a nine year old but I learned them. I got this bench through the town a few years ago. My parents cried the first time they saw it and said it was the finest thing I'd ever done. I don't know about that, but I'm glad I did it.

I sat there for an hour, just to make sure Esmeralda would be long gone before I got home. Most of the time, I stared blankly out at the bay, checking out the early morning windsurfers and watching the gray, morning mist lift and then disappear into the light blue sky. I admired the elderly joggers and walkers lapping the parking lot for their morning constitutionals, and regarded the sunlight reflecting off the sandy bluffs of North Haven Point. I felt my brother's presence, and when I rose to finish my jog, I was able to go at a leisurely pace, no longer nervous about the police, the murder, or Esmeralda.

I got home and was happy to see Esmeralda hadn't ransacked the place and destroyed whatever things I might want to hold onto. That was nice of her, I thought, and spoke highly of her character, too. Maybe I would give her a call after all. That was how I felt before I entered the bedroom, the scene of our lovemaking, and found the shredded sheets and red-lipstick message on my wall, "*Thees is not over, Muthafuck!*" I recalled that Ledbetter had said the same thing to me just yesterday without the mother-loving ending and again considered how things were certainly not going my way, at least not yet.

I threw the ruined sheets into a green, town garbage bag, showered and got dressed in a pair of brown linen pants, a white linen shirt, a tan linen sports jacket and a pair of cordovan lace up shoes that looked more official than loafers. I didn't have a tie and hoped that I still looked like a cop without one and dropped my old NYPD badge into my breast pocket. It wasn't a detective's shield and it was from New York City and not from out here, but I hoped that Mrs. Al Shareef might be too distraught or unknowledgeable to know the difference.

Before leaving, I went to my sock drawer and pulled out a large gold ring with a high dome bearing my initials, GF. My folks had given it to me a long time ago, as a present for passing my detective's test before I became the first and only detective in New York City history to demand a demotion and got placed back onto the beat because sitting behind a desk was just too damned boring. Since I hadn't gained weight for over twenty years, the ring still fit the middle of my right hand perfectly. I hoped I wouldn't need it, but I didn't know what to expect at The Castle.

Just as I was about to hop into the Caddy, I saw the dent and small sneaker print in the left rear fender. *Fucking Esmeralda!* I had violated my cardinal rule and had shat where I ate, even if it was takeout, and realized I had no one to blame but myself for what had happened to my car. I knew I'd get the dent fixed the first chance I got, but first I had to see Mrs. Al Shareef and ask her some questions about her husband, his property, and if she knew of any threats that had been made against him. I hoped that during the interrogation the name of my ex-wife did not turn up because that could prove very embarrassing and end my questioning very quickly.

I drove up Deerfield Road, reached The Castle and parked my car in a side lot of gray gravel. The portcullis was already raised and I pressed the welcome button at the door, but this time there were no trumpets signifying a royal visit. Instead, there was nothing except the almost immediate return of a heavily accented Middle Eastern voice asking, "What is it you want?"

Looking up at the camera, I took out my shield, showed it to the lens and said, "Police. I'd like to speak with Mrs. Al Shareef."

The voice responded, "Mrs. Al Shareef has already spoken with the authorities. She wants to be left alone."

I placed the shield back into my pocket, relieved that whomever I was speaking with had not asked me to place it directly in front of the camera and said, "This won't take long. There are just a few more questions we'd like answered and we'll be on our way. We're sorry if there's been any inconvenience. We do want to let the family alone and understand your grief. We promise to keep this short. If you please, let *us* in."

I didn't want to overplay my hand and say, "*We* could always get a warrant," because I'd learned that you always caught more flies with honey that you do with vinegar. I was anxiously wondering if the person behind the voice was trying to figure out who the hell *we* or *us* was and sighed with relief as the doors began to glide back, admitting me into The Castle.

To my eye, the place looked worse in the daylight than it had during the evening hours of the party. Maybe it was because all the joy and anticipation had been taken out of it, but I'd been to murder scenes before and it was always the same; no matter how expensive the layout, it was always decorated in 'SAD'. Entering the great room, I found three men waiting for me, two of them in their thirties, thick, olive skinned and brutish, and the third, a young man is his early twenties, thin and scowling. The young guy was in the center and stood a step in front of the thugs who were positioned protectively on either side of his narrow shoulders.

I walked up to the three, looked at the kid and using the first name that came to me, said, "I'm Detective Costanza. I'd like to speak with Mrs. Al Shareef , please."

The kid answered in perfect English, with no trace of an accent unless you consider Yale and Connecticut foreign countries, "I am Yousef Al Shareef. My mother is unavailable. She is too upset to talk. Anything you want to ask, you can ask me."

Trying to look as sympathetic as I could, I replied, "I understand, but it is important that I speak with her."

The kid was glowering, trying to figure out what to say next, when one of the bodyguards leaned over and whispered into his ear. Suddenly stiffening, young Al Shareef's eyes sparked angrily and he said, "Mustafa recognizes you from the party. He says you are not a policeman, but a hired security guard. Is this true?"

I looked at Mustafa and saw his wide grin show off a solid gold front tooth. The other guard stood as stiff as a statue, his hands at his sides, but I noticed his fists were balled tightly.

I answered, "Mustafa must be mistaken. Look, Yousef, all I want is five minutes with your mother and I'm out of here. You can be there when I speak with her. I assure you, I'll make this as quick and as easy as possible."

The kid snorted and said, "Let me see your badge, Detective Costanza. I must be sure you aren't someone who has come to kill the rest of my family. We can trust no one."

I guess I took too long to go to my pocket because Mustafa took a step towards me with nothing but vengeance in his eyes. He grabbed at my throat with both hands but I got my arms between them, forced them apart and a moment later smashed the bodyguard in the mouth with my right fist. I heard the click of my ring against his teeth and he went sailing head over heels, collapsing against one of the ottomans. The other guard was fast, but not fast enough, and as his fist came at my left temple I was able to duck below it. I felt it graze the top of my head as I brought my fist into his groin with everything I had and felt his eggs flatten under my knuckles. He screamed and bent at the waist, and with no reason to hit him again, I lightly pushed him over. He fell and immediately assumed the fetal position, moaning and groaning in the universal language of pain. The whole thing took maybe five seconds.

Turning my attention to the young man, I said, "That didn't have to happen. Please, Yousef, all I want to do is talk," but I could see the kid was building up steam and was about to charge. I was going to grab him and hold him and try to talk some sense into him, but I didn't have to do any of that because the moment he took his first step towards me, a strong woman's voice echoed in the greatroom, "Yousef!! Stop!!" I looked to the staircase on the left and saw Mrs. Al Shareef.

She was standing with her left hand against the wall and her right over her heart, dressed in American style in what looked like clothes from the latest Ralph Lauren window off Jobs Lane in Southampton. Her hair was long and black and shiny and it hung down past her shoulders, framing her heart-shaped face perfectly. Her skin was olive toned, as I'd noticed the other night, but in grief she was far more beautiful than she was when she was in shock and wailing. She looked to be about forty and had probably been not much more than a kid when the deceased Al Shareef had married her. I couldn't help but think about what she must have looked like when she was younger and what it must have been like to have been with her in a tent somewhere in the desert, making love on a silken rug, when I heard the guard on the floor moan a little louder and saw him slowly rising to his knees.

I called, "Mrs. Al Shareef, I'm sorry for what's happened here and I'm sorry about your husband. All I want is five minutes of your time and you'll never have to see me again."

I knew what I was saying was only half true. I was sorry about what had happened, but I also knew that there was every possibility that I would be seeing her again.

She didn't speak a word but motioned me forward with a wave of her hand. Four more guards suddenly appeared beside her and I was startled into thinking I might have to go to work again, but they passed me without even a sideways glance and went to help their fallen comrades. I leaned over, picked up a golden tooth from the floor that had a 'G' imprinted on it and handed it to one of the guards helping Mustafa to his feet, saying, "Tell Mustafa, I'm sorry."

I walked over to where Mrs. Al Shareef had taken a seat at a table beside a mosaic of the Emperor Saladin defeating a Crusader in battle. Her eyes were deep black pools floating in crystal white irises and surrounded by even deeper black eye liner. They were nearly hypnotic, and when she looked at me I had to blink several times to keep my mind on murder.

I managed to say, "Mrs. Al Shareef, I have some questions of you."

She stared deeply into my eyes and asked, "What is your true name?"

I thought there was no longer any reason to lie and answered, "Gabriel Fortuna."

That was a mistake. I had every reason to lie and I knew it the moment I gave my name and saw Mrs. Al Shareef's eyes widen.

"You are the husband of the woman with whom my husband was having an affair?"

"Ex-husband," I replied.

I wanted to ask, "Why would your husband have an affair with Teresa when he's got something like you at home to warm his bed?" but then I remembered what a great piece of ass Teresa was and the things she would do in bed to make a man happy, so I kept that question to myself.

Mrs. Al Shareef said, "No matter, my husband has had many women during our marriage. It was his weakness. He prayed often for deliverance from it. I hope Allah has forgiven him."

It occurred to me that Mrs. Al Shareef was more than a bit understanding about her husband's affairs and that if more women had her sensibilities the divorce lawyers out here in The Hamptons would be going broke. Returning to business, I asked her about the people her husband kept in contact with in The Hamptons and she told me she generally stayed out of her husband's affairs but knew that he often spoke with Teresa and Gasper, and various members of the Southampton Town Council, especially the president himself, Armand Conforti, who had visited The Castle several times in the weeks prior to the murder. I asked her what she intended to do with the twenty-plus acres The Castle sat on, and she told me it was not up to her. Her eldest son, Yousef, was to inherit all of his father's worldly belongings and what he did with it, she added, was of no consequence to her. She went on to say that she was returning home the next day, as soon as her husband's body was released from the Medical Examiner's office in Southampton Hospital, where the required-by-state-law autopsy was to be performed to discover the exact clinical reason for death where homicide was suspected. Mrs. Al Shareef told me she was distressed because according to their religion her husband should have been buried the day after his death, without the expressly forbidden performance of an autopsy. New York State Law superseded her religion so long as she was in the United States, and she prayed that Allah would be forgiving and allow Binyamin entrance to Paradise despite the scars.

I knew that Mrs. Al Shareef, her dead husband and her son weren't going anywhere for a while. There was going to be an investigation and I knew that anyone who might be involved in the victim's death, including Yousef Al Shareef, the son who stood to inherit many millions of dollars, and Mrs. Al Shareef, the wife whose husband was busy screwing the local talent, had better get used to living on the East End.

When we were done talking, I thanked Mrs. Al Shareef for her time and stood at the table watching her slowly ascend the steps leading to her bedroom or wherever she was going. Her slacks fit perfectly and I loved how the little bit of extra she had on her round full ass fell just outside the panty line that framed it. I turned to leave and found Yousef Al Shareef standing behind me, flanked by his four body guards, including an awfully ugly and grimacing Mustafa whose golden tooth had been awkwardly replaced into his jagged and swollen mouth.

I said, "Nice meeting you, Yousef," gave a quick bow and followed that with a jaunty, "Take it easy, Mustafa." Hustling around the wall of body guards, I made for the front door as quickly as I could.

My next stop was Southampton Hospital, where I planned to spend some quality time with the recently deceased, Binyamin Al Shareef. I recalled that Stacy Nichols was the head nurse over there and that over the years she and I had shared a few interesting times together. I was hoping she'd be able to get me into the morgue where I could check out Al Shareef and maybe even get me a couple of minutes where I could speak with the doctor who'd performed the autopsy. Jumping into the Caddy, I tried my best to avert my eyes from the dent in its fender, *Fucking Esmeralda!,* and started thinking about Stacy Nichols, her starched white nurse's uniform and those white stockings she held up with those sexy white garter belts. As I recalled, she was a *head* nurse alright, a real *head* nurse.

8

I drove south on Deerfield Road until I hit Edge of Woods Road, another serpentine, tree-shrouded, two lane black top, where I hung a right into deeper forest. Passing the Krzywski Farm, whose furrowed fields in a forest clearing were just beginning to show the green sprigs of its late spring crops, I continued past open fields of wildflowers, a few small corrals, and a new planned subdivision, Grand Estates of the Woods, where the only woods left were those that surrounded the one hundred and twenty-eight acre parcel of land that had been cleared of every living thing and was presently nothing more than a large pit of dirt, sand and rock. Reaching David Whites Lane I made a left where there was acres of open farmland to my left, but spoiling the bucolic scenery, a recently developed subdivision on my right. I knew that it would take the farmer on the left a lifetime to earn what his neighbor had earned in a moment by simply signing on the dotted line and surrendering his property to the highest bidder, so, if Mr. Farmer wanted to sell, how could anyone blame him? At Route 27, I had to wait only a few minutes for the light to change before I raced across the highway and reached the south side of Southampton, the ocean side, the really, really rich side. The sign, Southampton, Established 1640, Oldest English Settlement in New York State and a cooler ocean breeze greeted me. I continued over the Long Island Railroad tracks, made a right onto Old Town Lane and parked.

Southampton Hospital is a mostly red brick building surrounded by large trees and manned by scores of volunteers. It's a good place to go for emergency surgery or a full body cast if you've fallen out of a tree or off your roof. Locals use the hospital all the time, but weekenders and summer people always go back to the city for any real medical attention, thinking that the doctors in the city are more qualified than the doctors out here. They're wrong, but don't try and tell that to a millionaire who always has to have the best, even when the best is just another guy trying to make as much dough as he can so that he can buy an estate out here, too.

I entered the hospital through the emergency room entrance and walked up to the elderly white haired lady in the navy blue cardigan seated behind the admitting desk. Slowly taking her eyes from the screen, the old lady looked up, smiled sweetly and asked, "May I help you?"

I answered through a pleasant smile of my own, "Is Nurse Nichols available?"

The old lady put her right hand to her hair and primped it a bit, adjusted her ass more comfortably in her orthopedic chair and said, "I think so. Whom shall I say wishes to see her?"

"Tell her Gabriel Fortuna is here."

"Gabriel Fortuna," she echoed in a lovely singsong voice, "what a lovely name."

"Thank you," I replied.

I smelled Stacy coming before I saw her. She always put on too much Fire and Passion perfume and I'd told her that, but she said it was her trademark fragrance and that she liked her men to be aroused by the time she reached them. Sashaying down the hall from x-ray, she saw me standing in the emergency room and a big smile spread across her face.

"Hi, Gabe," she called in the smoky voice she proudly attributed to a great many afterglow cigarettes.

I said, "Hi, Stacy. I need to ask a favor of you."

Placing her hands on her provocative hips, she took a step back and announced, "That's what I like about you, Gabe. We spend a weekend in bed where we do everything one human can sexually do with another, and then I don't hear from you for six months, until you come by my place of work to ask a favor of me. Some girls would think you've got some pair of balls ... but I won't." Smiling lasciviously, she added, "I *know* you do.

I took a deep breath, raised my hands defensively between us and said, "Please, Stacy, I'm not fooling around. I really do need your help."

Stacy sighed and asked, "Alright, I've never known you to shoot me down before. Something big must be up. What can I do for you, Sugar?"

"I need to see the body of a stiff you've got laid up in here."

"That's no big deal. None of them are going to complain."

"The stiff's name is Binyamin Al Shareef."

Stacy pursed her lips to emit a low whistle and then said, "Now that's going to be a problem. He's the victim of a murder and has just undergone an autopsy. The police don't allow anyone to view a murder victim until the report has been officially forwarded to them. The hospital doesn't ever allow it."

Pressing close to Stacy, I said, "Please, Stacy. Do this for me and I promise you a really good time on your next weekend off."

Stacy moaned with my suggestion, leaned into my ear and murmured, "You won't be sorry." Taking my hand, she added, "Let's go."

The morgue in Southampton Hospital is located in the basement and is all cool white subway tiles: floor, ceiling and walls, except for the body drawers against the far wall opposite the door. They are rectangular gray metal with thick aluminum handles. Stacy pulled the handle on drawer number 8 and a sheet-covered body rolled out on a cold metal slab. I pulled the sheet down and there was the blue-white face of Binyamin Al Shareef. The groove that ran along the dead man's forehead was narrow and deep and had a slight taper as it crossed his head, a little thicker over the right eye and narrowing ever so slightly over the left. There were no other marks on the man's face except for the old scars I'd noticed when we'd spoken, and I was just about to pull the sheet further down to see if there were any other telltale signs of struggle or murder when the door to the morgue opened to reveal a man dressed in surgical green and tortoise shell eyeglasses.

He appeared to be in shock, seeing me and Stacy alone in the morgue with one of its guests laid out before us, and through a reddening face, demanded, "Nurse Nichols, what is the meaning of this?"

Stacy answered through a put-on little girl's voice I'd never heard from her, "Oh, hello, Doctor Greenberg. This is my friend, Gabe. He asked if he could see Mr. Al Shareef's body."

I was where I wasn't supposed to be, doing what I wasn't supposed to be doing and here was a doctor wondering what the hell I was all about. My ally, Nurse Nichols, had gone into a lousy Shirley Temple routine and things were definitely not looking up, but I wasn't going anywhere. I still needed some answers and the medical man was probably the only person who could help me.

The doctor, standing rigid and tall in the doorway, declared sternly, "This is unacceptable, Nurse Nichols. You'd better have a good reason for this, or else."

Looking back into the hallway and then shutting the door behind him, the doctor pulled its handle to check that it was closed tightly and then pushed in the little button to lock it from the inside. Crossing his arms over his chest and then assuming the well-known pissed-off boss position, he waited for an answer.

Stacy didn't appear to be too disturbed by Doc Greenberg's blustery attitude and responded coquettishly, "My friend has some questions for you, Doctor." She seemed to forget all about me as she sashayed towards the doctor, whose mouth had dropped open to allow for some very deep breathing and the escape of a trickle of saliva that had begun to meander down his chin. Swiveling her hips recklessly, Stacy approached the drooler and slapped her right palm hard against her right buttock, the smack simultaneously echoing crisply in the sterile white tiled room while producing a tiny leap and flinch from the doctor's vibrating body. Suddenly changing character and becoming something more akin to Xena, the warrior princess, than a little girl on the good ship Lollipop, Stacy threw a hard command at the trembling physician, "I want you to answer every one of my friend's questions, Doctor ... and I want you to answer them now."

Dr. Greenberg turned to me, moaned and asked, "Yes, how may I help you?"

Not knowing how long the doctor would stay under Stacy's authoritative spell, I quickly asked, "What killed Al Shareef?"

"A ... pole ... of ... some ... sort ... was ... smacked ... across ... his ... forehead," Greenberg moaned.

"What kind of pole?"

"Some … thing … shaped … like … rebar."

By now, Stacy was breathing huskily into the doctor's ear and her hand was making small circles at the crotch of his pants. Taking short, throaty gasps, he sounded more like a locomotive struggling up a very steep hill than a doctor of forensics.

Knowing the telltale signs of an imminent orgasm, I quickly asked, "What else can you tell me?"

"There … were … traces … of … graphite … IN THE WOOOOOOUND!!!!"

The doctor's body slid down the slick tile wall and I knew I wasn't going to get any more out of him. It didn't matter, though. I'd heard enough. After opening the door and checking the hallway, I turned back to Stacy and said, "I owe you one, Stace."

She laughed and said, "I expect more than one. See you soon, Gabe."

Checking the doctor's ecstatic expression as he sat on the floor, I knew she was right.

9

Located on Hampton Road, about a quarter of a mile from Southampton's six square blocks of downtown shopping, is Town Hall, a large and solid three- story brick building that at one time was the schoolhouse for all the village's children. The original town hall, another austere and solid red brick building, was much smaller and held only two stories, but four ionic columns decorate its front entrance as a reminder to its former prominence. It sits on the northeast corner of Hampton Road and Main Street and is now the home of the local Saks Fifth Avenue Department Store's women's annex. Is that perfect, or what?

The present Town Hall in Southampton is where all the important tax records, land deeds, maps and surveys are stored and where all village and town meetings are held. It's also where the major administrative offices are located. They include: Land Management, Community Development, Public Works, Highway Services, Parks-Recreation and Human Services. Enforcement agency headquarters are there also, including the Town Police, Fire Prevention, and The Code Enforcement Office of the Building and Zoning Division. I'd been coming to The Hamptons for over thirty years and I'd driven by the place a million times but I'd never stepped a foot inside. My dad and I dutifully paid our tax bills and we weren't ever looking for permission to renovate. It was just Town Hall, a place I could go if I ever had a problem. Well, I had one now and I was going to see if my tax dollars were at work.

After parking The Caddy in the Town Hall parking lot, I took the side entrance into the grand building. The place had a strong feeling of age about it, with high ceilings, marble columns and hardwood floors that creaked and echoed off the granite walls with every step I took. At the information desk, I was told where to find The Land Management Office. The people working there were very nice and competent, treating me as if they hadn't met someone who'd said, "Please," or "Thank you," in years. They knew where to find every piece of paper showing ownership, land boundaries, covenants and restrictions and in no time at all presented me with the town map of The Castle and its surrounding area.

As I already knew, the twenty-two point seven acres that belonged to the Al Shareef Family was located on Deerfield Road, with road frontage of point six miles. The nearly rectangular piece of property went back into the woods for more than half a mile and was surrounded by other properties, most of which were five acre lots. The Town of Southampton owned the land-locked reserve of over five hundred acres directly behind and abutting The Castle property, and the nearest road access to that undeveloped parcel of land would have to be cut off Deerfield Road. The last thing I discovered before leaving the office was an application placed by the town, releasing the five hundred acre reserve for unspecified building permits.

Teresa was fucking Al Shareef, so there had to be something special about The Castle property. What was it? Did Al Shareef want to sell? Was he looking to buy more? What was it about this piece that made it so valuable he had to be killed? Did Muslim terrorists suddenly want to move to The Hamptons? Did they need special permits to house their camels?

I knew the answers to my questions were right in front of me, but I couldn't see the forest for the trees. What I did know for a fact was that it was after noon and I was getting hungry. I couldn't go to the diner for a burrito; Esmeralda might be there to bust my ass. So, I decided to head into the village and hit The Driver's Seat for a nice quiet lunch and to see if I could figure out what the fuck was going on.

Southampton Village is not as trendy as its cousin, Easthampton. Neither is it as quaint as its northern kin, Sag Harbor. It fits nicely in the middle, with expensive and inexpensive, local and national chain stores comfortably fitted together so that year-rounders and summer people can buy whatever they want whenever they want. It was a beautiful morning and driving around with the top down always had a way of calming me, so I decided that lunch could wait a while. I made a left on Main Street and a right on Job's Lane, oldest street in The Hamptons, and drove past beautiful Agawam Lake and its perimeter of white-clapboard and cedar-shingled mansions until I reached Gin Lane, home base for some of the oldest money on the East End.

At the end of this rich man's avenue was Saint Andrew's Church of the Dunes. Tucked serenely behind the ocean dunes and sea grass, Saint Andrews is a red, shingle-clad building with green-trimmed windows that has long been a part of the coastal landscape. It started out in 1851 as a lifesaving station, but in 1879, Dr. Gaillard Thomas bought the property and turned it into a church. Time moves slowly there. Hymnals are from nineteen-forty and the American flag that flies from its rooftop was brought back from Europe after World War I. People in the village like to say that the church started as a lifesaving station and still is one today, saving souls as well as lives.

The church is built on the ocean dunes across from Lake Agawam, along whose shores early residents of Southampton built their homes. Many of those worshippers rowed or sailed across the picturesque lake to attend services and the legend of the nameless woman who rode a gondola to weekly services has entered into the realm of Agawam myth. Two towers are perched at the top of the small building, the first a lantern cupola that allows sunlight and moonlight into the church interior, the second holding the bells that ring on Sunday mornings, summoning parishoners to church. The pews are original, dating from 1879, and the walls are decorated with tablets that recount Southampton history from its beginning in sixteen-forty. Ten of the stained glass windows that line the walls are from Louis Comfort Tiffany and are considered to be among his early masterworks. Saint Andrews is rich and quiet, old and beautiful, and as good a metaphor for the village as any windmill could ever be. It was also a place where Gasper and I would sometimes go late at night with our weekend dates and if Reverend Smith ever found out what had happened in the third pew one night between me and the Shapiro Twins I'm sure I would have been banned from the East End forever.

I circled back to the village and parked on Job's Lane in front of Colette's Consignment Shop, where I waved to Dagmar, the pretty blond Swedish salesgirl who worked the shop when its ex-model owner wasn't around. She was dressing the windows in vintage Chanel, Gucci, and Givenchy gowns in preparation for the influx of summer vacationers, and watching her working in the window, I noticed that she'd put on a little weight during the off season. That wasn't a bad thing because her Nordic ass was filling out her vintage Sasson jeans better than ever and I told myself that I would definitely have to give her a call when the crap I was involved in was over.

Crossing the street, I went into The Driver's Seat, a local restaurant that served up pretty good and not too expensive food. There were indoor and outdoor tables available, but I needed to think and didn't want to talk to anyone, so I chose to sit at the bar, away from the lunchtime crowd that had already filled much of the side room.

"Hi, Gabe, what can I do you for?"

It was John Stuckart, the bartender in the place for as long as I could remember. John was like the bartenders you saw on television or in the movies; he was always drying a glass with a white towel and was always ready to talk about your problems. He had a very sympathetic ear, so long as the conversation was about your life, and as usual, he came out of the bar's shadows drying a glass and smiling.

"Whattaya say, John," I answered. "What's good today?"

"Nothing," he replied amusingly. Placing down the glass, he rested his hands on the bar and added, "But I hear the shrimp salad is almost fresh."

My mind wasn't on food, but I was hungry, so I half-heartedly responded, "Good enough. Give me a sandwich of that on whole wheat and double up on the shrimp salad. I'll take a bottle of Peconic Water, too."

John threw his chin at the door to tell me someone was coming and left me alone. I wondered what the problem was because John usually liked to speak with whoever entered the place, even if it was always bullshit, but I didn't have to wait long to find out why he'd gone.

"Gabe, what do you say we take a booth?"

It was Gasper. I turned around to see if he'd calmed down since our diner discussion, but knew I'd have to find that out later because Ledbetter and some other guy with an even longer stick up his ass were flanking him on either shoulder.

I asked, "What's up, G? What's with you and Fed Number One and Fed Number Two?"

The new guy spoke quickly, not giving Gasper the chance to properly introduce him, and said, "My name is Frank Stern. I'm with the FBI and we have to talk. Some bad shit went down the other day and we've got to bring it to a conclusion before things get out of control."

I looked at Stern and said, "What's the magic word?"

Stern looked at Ledbetter with a sneer and asked, "Is this guy fucking with me?"

Ledbetter smiled and appeared ready to say something foolish to his buddy, something like, "Let's take this guy outside and teach him a lesson." That would have been their mistake, gut Gasper interrupted and said, "Please, Gabe. It's important."

I acquiesced for my old friend's sake and the four of us went to a quiet table in the front of the restaurant. I sat first, followed by Gasper and Ledbetter, but the new suit stood behind his chair and stared at me. I figured this was Intimidation 101, a required course in Fed School, and calmly said, "Sorry, Stern, but I date women. If you're going to keep looking at me like that people might get the wrong impression."

"Wise guy," the Fed responded through a new and more intense sneer. Then, he pulled out a chair and sat.

Ledbetter began his spiel without any niceties, saying, "Listen, Fortuna, we want you to keep out of this investigation. You're corrupting evidence and speaking with people who may have something to hide. We don't want you alerting them. You have no authority and are just getting in the way." Pointing a finger in my face, he finished his harangue through a threatening and exceedingly annoying tone, adding, "I'm not going to tell you again; keep out of this."

With my best I-don't-give-a fuck-attitude, I responded, "I never wanted to be involved with this shit until you mentioned I was a suspect. I think that information allows me to do some snooping on my own. What do you think, G?"

Gasper had been sitting directly across from me, staring into his wet palms and trying to stay out of it. When I drew him in, he looked at me and answered, "They're right, Gabe. Stay out of it. Whether you're a suspect or not doesn't matter; you're no longer a policeman."

I barked, "So, I'm still a suspect! Holy fucking shit! Just because my ex-wife of six years screws a guy doesn't mean I'm going to kill him. I hadn't even seen Teresa for five years before the other night. I couldn't give a fuck who she was balling!"

Ledbetter leaned across the table and through a tight grimace said, "Listen asshole, stay the fuck away from Teresa, the Al Shareefs, the medical examiners and any other persons or places you've been to or are thinking of going to where it concerns this case. If you didn't kill Al Shareef, then it could have been any number of people, including terrorists, Muslim or American. This morning we received a message from a Muslim terrorist group taking responsibility for the murder of, 'the traitorous dog whose films preach love for the Jews and the Americans who worship them'. It came over the internet so we're having trouble tracing it. Yesterday, we got one from Patriots For A Clean America, claiming responsibility and saying, 'Death To All Towelheads'.

I said, "You don't believe any of that shit, do you?"

Stern's face brightened and he broke in, asking sarcastically, "Are you confessing, Fortuna? Bringing in a confessed murderer would put an end to a lot of the confusion and save taxpayers a hell of a lot of money. We could forget all about these hate organizations and just bring you in. What do you say, Mr. Fortuna? Are you confessing to the murder of Binyamin Al Shareef?"

There was nothing at the table but silence for a few seconds and I guess the Feds thought they'd gotten their point across because the new one, Stern, the one with the bigger stick up his ass, said, "I think Mr. Fortuna gets the picture. Let's go. I've got some faxes waiting for me at The American Hotel."

The two Feds stood to leave and Gasper, staring at me as if he was Dr. Phil about to impart some down-home wisdom, said to his new buddies, "I'll catch up with you in a second." Without any further acknowledgement to me, the two Feds left the restaurant and then, when he was sure they couldn't hear, Gasper asked, "Well, Gabe, what are you going to do?"

I answered succinctly, "I'm going to eat lunch."

"You know what I mean. These guys aren't fucking around. They will take you down."

John came over and placed a thick sandwich in front of me, the sides of it covered with cascading shrimp salad from where the kitchen help had cut it on its diagonal. I picked up a wad of the spillage between my thumb and forefinger and popped it into my mouth. It wasn't even as fresh as John had said, but he wasn't a liar and I couldn't complain; he'd told me honestly when I'd sat that nothing was good.

I looked at Gasper coldly and answered, "You know I didn't kill Al Shareef."

He responded, "I know it, but those guys don't. They don't know you and they don't like you. All they see is a great looking woman, a jealous big mouth of an ex-husband, and a stiff who could bring about international problems."

I moved the shrimp salad around with my fork and said, "You know as well as I do that if Teresa was screwing that guy it was all about land and money. Stop thinking about movies and terrorists, G. The answer is here in Southampton and it has to do with The Castle."

Gasper sat quietly for a while, staring emptily at me, chewing at the inside of his cheek and looking like there was something private on his mind that he was never going to share. Finally, he stood and said, "All I can tell you, Gabe, is to leave it alone. It'll pass. They'll figure out you didn't kill Al Shareef and move on. Now, you're just giving them reason to keep after you. Just let it go."

I figured that Gasper was trying to help me out, but both of us knew he wasn't getting far. I decided to change the subject and asked, "Will I be seeing you at Hightower's Red, White and Blue Ball?"

Gasper's lip curled and he said, "I told you not to go there."

I replied, "You said I wasn't working it, G. I'm going there to have some fun."

Gasper responded a little more harshly than I liked, saying with more than a little bit of warning in his voice, "That's a private party, Gabe. Where'd you get an invitation?"

I answered him with a mischievous grin. He knew I didn't need an invitation. Who the fuck was going to stop me if I wanted in?

Gasper pointed a finger at me, much like the Fed had done, and repeated, "Stay out of this, Gabe. For your own good, stay out of this." Then without a good-by, he left.

I took a bite out of my sandwich and through the restaurant window watched the trio of lawmen cross the street get into Gasper's

Trailblazer and drive away. I also saw Dagmar in Colette's window bending to pick a small item from the floor and again found her new ass quite remarkable. In spite of my unfriendly conversations with police at every level, the sight of Dagmar stretching her denim covered backside brought a wistful smile to my lips. My mouth was full, but I called out anyway, "Hey, John, where's my water?"

10

I left The Driver's Seat and drove home along North Sea Road, stopping at The Hampton's busiest traffic light at the intersection with Route 27. On the corner to my right was the Seven-Eleven Store, the biggest money maker in town. It was open twenty-four hours a day, seven days a week and it was always packed with workers buying donuts, coffee, cigarettes, soda, milk, corndogs, newspapers and anything else they might want or need. During the daytime hours, the place was ringed by Hispanic laborers waiting for a local contractor to stop his four-wheel-drive and say, "I'll take you and you and you," before packing them into his vehicle and taking them over to Mr. and Mrs. Rich's estate, where he would have them do spring and winter cleanups and dig ditches for thirty-five dollars per man hour from which he paid them eight dollars. The contractor kept the rest. The more clients he had, the more day laborers he needed and the richer he became, making landscaping a very good business on the East End.

As I drove, I reviewed my circumstances and the people who could have been involved in Al Shareef's murder. There was Teresa, my fucking nympho ex-wife, Al Shareef's wife (as forgiving as she seemed to be about his conduct, I still had never met a woman who liked it when her husband was giving it to someone else), Yousef, the son (the kid was going to come into a bundle with dear old dad's departure), terrorists, which I quickly discounted no matter what the Feds thought, and that was about it. I knew I didn't do it and I didn't think any of the other suspects had either, although I wasn't so sure about Yousef. Sons do funny things when hundreds of millions of dollars and a mother's happiness are concerned. I knew I was missing something and I just couldn't get it out of my head that it all involved real estate, knowing that if Teresa was in it in any way it just had to do with land and money. I resigned myself to meeting with my ex-wife again to find out more about what she was doing with Al Shareef and I just hoped I would be able to keep it in my pants, because if I didn't, Teresa would definitely have the upper hand.

I reached my house, made a left and pulled into the driveway. Getting out of the Caddy, my eyes were drawn to the fender, and once again I was reminded by the dent made by Esmeralda's kick. Leaning over to examine the crease more thoroughly, I sighed with exasperation and decided I'd have it to bring it into Stump McNamara's collision place the next morning to have it repaired before I went crazy looking at it. I had my fingers inside the fold and was wondering just how badly Stump was going to rip me off, when I heard the gravel scratch behind me and turned just in time to see a booted foot coming my way.

I blocked the kick with my left forearm, and immediately punched the guy who had delivered it square in his cajones. He yelped like he'd just had a lighted torch shoved up his ass, jumped back and fell to the ground with his hands between his legs, writhing in pain and yelling like a coyote. I quickly rose from the fender and saw three young Hispanic men racing at me from out of the forest with malice on their faces and thick, leafless birch branches in their hands. Each guy had a small skull tattooed above his left eyebrow, signifying their membership in a local gang I'd read about in The Southampton Press called The Latin Zombies.

The three were crowded too close to each other to take full swings at me with their lumber, so when they were in range I stepped forward and threw my first punch at the Zombie on the right, catching him squarely on his jaw. His eyes rolled back in his head and he folded to the gravel like a set of cheap Venetian blinds, but I didn't have the time to admire my handiwork because I had to give my undivided attention to the other two Zombies who were cursing in Spanish and trying to separate from each other so that they could get a good whack at me.

The Zombie on my left got some elbowroom and swung his thick stick, catching me on the left bicep with a loud, *whoosh and thwack*. A searing pain went through my entire arm before it went numb, but ten million concentration curls had done their job. The bicep was harder than the branch and the lumber shattered into a thousand pieces, throwing splinters of wood into the air and into my assailants face, allowing me the moment I needed to deliver a hard, closed fist to his skull, just above his left ear, where I felt my ring penetrate thick bone and lodge itself. He went down, but I had to pull to get my fist out of his head and prepare for the third guy, the one in the middle, the one who looked a lot like Esmeralda.

"Muthafuck!" he screamed through a thick Spanish accent. "Ju theenks ju can jus fucks my seester! She was a fuckeengs virgin, man! She was savings herself! I weel keels ju!"

Esmeralda had been as much of a virgin as I was, but you can't talk sense with a Latin Zombie when he wants to kill you. My left arm was useless, but I still had my right arm and two good legs and still felt dangerous. The Zombie came at me quickly and swung his three-inch thick branch at my head. I ducked below it, kept my eyes open and up to see where he would be going with his next move and had to duck lower when he reversed course and whipped the branch back the other way. He then took a step backwards, pointed the stick threateningly at me and glanced around at his three compadres on the ground. Two of them were out cold and the other was still writhing, probably praying that his balls would work again or just fall off so that they would stop killing him.

"Listen, Pancho," I hollered, holding my right hand out, palm up like a cop trying to stop traffic in a busy intersection, "I didn't mean to dishonor your sister. All we had was a little fun. Honest. I like her. I'm going to call her again."

"Calls her? Muthafuck! I am goings to keels ju! Ju rapes my seester and then tells me ju weel calls her and do eet again! My name ees Enrique, Muthafuck, nots Pancho! Ju shoulds knows the names of the man who weel keels ju. Now, Muthafuck, ju dies!!!"

Enrique was far too excited to fight well and made the mistake of coming at me with the stick held high above his head, the obvious intent of which was to bring it down on top of my skull where it would certainly, to his great pleasure, break open my rather thick Anglo skull. I discouraged this possibility with a swift kick to his groin, causing him to stop dead in his tracks and bulge his eyes like a couple of swollen Emperor grapes. He gasped and doubled over and I lifted his face with a knee to the chin, finishing our little disagreement with a right to his eye, just above his tattooed skull, stamping a GF above it so that he'd remember with whom he'd fucked.

Three Zombies lay out cold in my driveway and the fourth was still on the ground, curling and uncurling like a medium sized snake praying to Jesus Cristo that the fire between his legs would extinguish. I was wondering what I was going to do with them when I felt the bottle smack against the back of my head, producing that awful, *thunk,* thick green glass makes when it hits skull.

I went down to a knee and looked up to see an enraged Esmeralda holding an old Coke bottle. She was breathing hard, poised to deliver another blow and I could see the fire in her eyes, but I remembered the intimacy of the night we'd just shared and knew that I might still have a chance with her.

"Esmie, baby. Don't do it," I begged.

Esmeralda replied with a misquote of a famous line from an old Mae West movie, "Ju do me wrongs, Gabriel. Ju cannots jus fucks me and forgets me. Look at me," she bragged, simultaneously throwing her curly black locks back and her gorgeous little breasts forward, "I can haves any mans I wants, But I chooses ju. And ju dees me likes dees? No ways, Gabriel. No fuckeeng ways."

I tried to put things into proper perspective and said, "You've got me all wrong, Esmeralda. I'm not dissing you. I really do like you. I want to see you again. I want to spend a lot of time with you. Really, I do."

Esmeralda's face took on a skeptical expression and she responded, "Ju means that, Gabriel, or ju jus fuckeeng weets me? I no likes eet if ju jus fuckeeng weets me." Turning her eyes to the Zombies scattered on the ground, she added, "Ju knows, der are more Latin Zombies where dees fuckeeng *patos* comes from."

I placed my hand over my heart and said, "I mean it, Esmie. I'm looking forward to being with you. All I need is some time. That's all, a little time."

Opening her eyes widely and raising the bottle again, warnings that I'd better come up with a suitably short period, she asked, "How much times do ju needs?"

I answered, "A few days, a week or two at most. I'm busy with some important work now, but I'll get back to you and we'll have some fun. I promise."

"Ju better nots be fuckeeng weets me, Gabriel. I do nots wants ju to fucks weets me. I weels comes back and ju weels nots likes eet."

I rose from my knees and put my hand on the glass bottle she held. I was relieved at feeling the flow of blood in my left arm and confident I wasn't going to have to clock a woman, a woman who just the day before had banged me like a pinata filled with her favorite candies. Kissing Esmeralda's forehead and then reaching around to give her ass a nice little squeeze, I said, "I'll call you next week." She smiled and I knew I was safe from her, at least for a while.

Esmeralda turned and walked into the woods, stopping in a little clearing where the Zombies van was hidden. Moments later, she returned with it, and I helped her load her brother and his friends into the back. Laying in the rear of the van, Enrique was able to raise his head and stare at me through the one eye that wasn't swollen shut. He said, "Dees eesn't over, Muthafuck," just before I slammed the door into his face. It occurred to me that he was the third guy to tell me that within the last two days, and three strikes usually meant you were out. Esmeralda threw me a bright smile from the side view mirror, looking as if nothing bad had gone down, and jammed the gearshift into Drive. She peeled out of my driveway spewing gray gravel backwards, stinging my legs and my face.

I was exhausted and could have used a couple of hours of sack time, but I didn't want to return to the house where I'd be all alone with only my thoughts for company. I needed to be outside, in the free and open air, so I took a walk down to Long Beach Road and strolled the beach until I reached David's bench. I took a load off and checked out the sailboats floating on the bay and the gulls and terns hovering above it. The wind whistled over the waves and the laughter of children playing in the cold bay water echoed in the distance. It wasn't enough to make me feel good, but it was enough to take away a lot of the craziness I was feeling. Taking a deep breath, I released a long and slow sigh, and then closing my eyes, breathed the salt air and listened to my bayside world.

11

By ten-thirty the next morning, after about four hours of sleep and lots of pacing, I'd finished my bicep/chest routine and was on the road to McNamara Collision off Mariner's Drive in Southampton. It was a body and chasis outfit that was nothing more than three closed bays in a medium sized industrial park off the Long Island Railroad tracks and David White's Lane. Hidden by tall evergreen and deciduous trees, the unattractive park of warehouses, storage facilities and small business headquarters did not interfere with the sightlines of Hamptonites who wanted to live in a constant state of Nirvana, and provided a good hiding place for the necessary but not so attractive business ventures of a prosperous and growing town.

I pulled into a short driveway and stopped The Caddy in the asphalt courtyard that was McNamara Collision. A hard drinking guy of about fifty-five, Stump McNamara had been in the dent-fixing business most of his adult life, and like many Southampton locals, had taken over the business from his father. He used to do all the bodywork himself, until that boating accident of thirty years ago that cost him his left arm. The story goes that Stump was water-skiing in Peconic Bay with his latest summer girlfriend and a couple of her buddies. He'd already polished off a case of Bud, and never having been famous for his balance, even when sober, was trying anything to improve his performance on the skis and his chances with the girl. He wrapped the towrope around his left wrist to make sure he wouldn't lose contact with the boat, drunkenly figuring he could pop back up on his skis if he fell, just like the guys on

Wide World of Sports always did after they went into the drink. The boat took off and was doing forty miles an hour in a matter of seconds, but when the drunken driver and the rest of the crew looked back, Stump was gone and the only thing the boat was pulling was half an arm. Hence, the name Stump. His given name is Michael, but nobody calls him that, not even his fellow members on The Board of Trustees of the Freeholders and Commonalty of the Town of Southampton, an elected body of five persons, chosen by the voting public every two years and deriving its authority through the Dongan Patent, a three hundred and fifty year old doctrine that controls land in public trust.

When most people think of Southampton, they think of yachts and mansions and movie stars, but that's the transient crowd, the non-voting summer people who come here for parties and networking and to avoid the sweltering heat of a New York summer. The vast majority of people who make up the East End voting public are townies of modest and often less-than-modest means whose families go back generations, much like Stump's. In fact, there's been a member of Stump's family on the Board of Trustees for a couple of hundred years. Stump, himself, has been on it for ten; he's very popular with the locals.

I called, "Hey, Stump," and entered his cramped office.

It was a little before eleven, but already Stump looked as though he'd put a fifth under his belt. His eyes were swollen, his lips were chapped and his complexion had that unhealthy and uneven red look that heavy drinkers get, giving his face the weathered appearance of a catcher's mitt at the end of a long season. I thought it was a little early for even Stump to be so far into the bag but I didn't know what was going on in his life and anyway, it wasn't my business. Besides, I had my own problems and wasn't in the mood to hear any of his. As always, plastering the wall behind his desk was the best collection of pinup calendars I'd ever seen. Whenever I was in his office I barely looked at him, the fantasy girls giving me a convenient excuse to avoid his blotchy mug.

"How ya doing, man?" I asked, ogling Miss May. She was hanging naked on the back wall, her legs spread wide and her eyes twinkling as she provocatively dangled a stick of straw between her teeth.

Stump looked up at me with bloodshot eyes and said, "Whattaya say, Gabe?" Splashing down a shot-glass of rye onto his paper filled desk, he stood and held out his huge right hand, adding, "Haven't seen you for a while, kid. How's it going?"

It's an amazing thing how guys with one arm compensate for their loss. Stump had made himself the best one armed golfer in The Hamptons and had become the pride of the blue collar set during town tournaments, beating almost every wealthy club member who had the use of two good arms. Once Stump got his fingers around a golf club's leather grip, there was never any slippage or turn in the shaft, and because he hit all his shots with a squared clubface, every ball he hit flew straight and true. Stump's reputation as a truly great handicapped golfer became so widespread that he took to carrying a golf club with him wherever he went. Usually, he took along oiled, wooden-shafted, vintage clubs from a collection he'd painstakingly amassed over the years, and it was town knowledge that Stump possessed golf clubs that once belonged to Bobby Jones, Walter Hagen and Gene Saracen.

I went to give Stump's right hand a shake, made sure I had a good grip and immediately began squeezing. He applied the same kind of pressure to my hand as he placed on his golf grips and as we shook he grinned insanely, leaning his puffy face into mine and snorting bad breath. Beads of sweat sprouted on his forehead and after thirty seconds of what looked like might be a standoff, it was Stump who let go first.

I shook my wrist so as not to rub in who'd won our little contest, and said, "I need some work done on The Caddy, Stump. A chick put her boot into the right rear fender and it needs to be pulled out and touched up." Hoping to keep the costs down, I added, "Shouldn't be too much of a job."

Stump got a gleam in his bloodshot eyes and threw back the shot of rye that had been sitting on his desk. Wiping his chin on his thick right forearm, he replied, "I'll be the judge of that, Gabe. Let's go out and take a look."

Stump whistled through parched lips at his first sight of the fender, jabbed me in the ribs with his right elbow and said through a phlegmy laugh, "That was some sweet kick Esmeralda gave your Caddy, Gabe. You must have been a very naughty boy." Scratching his mop of unruly rust colored hair with his thick fingers, he exclaimed, "Ooh, baby, this is going to cost you! This honey is vintage, Gabe. I'll have to find the right shade of paint, pull out the dent slowly and carefully, make sure I don't make any scratches or swirl marks on the finish, buff it out primo, rewax, buff again, and maybe paint and buff again. This is one hell of a labor-intensive job, Gabe. It's going to take a while to complete, if you want it done right."

While Stump was running through his list of bullshit as to why he would soon have his hand in my pockets, I looked over at one of the empty bays and watched his help giving me the once over. Most of the guys working for Stump were Hispanic. They were the cheapest labor in The Hamptons and quite often the most reliable. Like most of their compadres, I was sure the guys working for Stump would work hard, learn their trade and then go off and start their own businesses. Surveying the McNamara Collision staff, it occurred to me that in twenty years most of the signs on the East End would either be bilingual or written exclusively in Spanish. I glared at the trio of amigos who were busy staring at me and figured that Stump had learned about my altercation with the Zombies and Esmeralda from his crew. Who the hell cared? He knew what he knew and it really didn't matter; he just didn't have to enjoy it so much.

I asked, "How much?"

"You got insurance to cover this?"

"I'd rather not get them involved."

Stump burped and said, "You might want to rethink that." Mumbling some numbers under his breath, he rolled his eyes back into his forehead, wrinkled his brow and announced, "Twelve hundred."

"Holy fucking shit!" was my response.

"Labor intensive," Stump replied.

I was pissed but what could I do? The Caddy needed work and I couldn't stand driving it around the way it looked. I figured if it wasn't Stump robbing me , it would just be some other collision guy. Go with the devil you know was something my dad taught me. *Fucking Esmeralda!*

I snarled, "Alright, Stump, when will it be ready?"

He answered, "Give me two days. Come back Friday morning just to be sure."

Stump was ripping me off, and although I knew his price always included a loaner, I barked, "Well, what have you got for me to drive, you thief?"

Stump's face lit up like a Christmas tree and he bragged, "I just finished working on a Z4 the insurance company let me have for peanuts. They declared it a total, but it wasn't even close. Took the boys a week to piece it together and another couple of days to paint and shine it. Looks as good as new. I can probably get thirty thousand for it. Its all yours until we finish The Caddy."

The thought of driving around in what I considered a toy didn't impress me. I'm pretty big and always felt tight in sports cars, so I asked, "Got anything roomier?"

Stump got all puffed up like a blowfish and through a drunken grin said, "Got an orange and gray ninety-six Taurus that drives pretty good. I've also got a seventy-two Pinto in the back, if that's the kind of shit you're looking for."

I replied succinctly, "Screw you, Stump."

"Love you, too, Gabe. See you on Friday."

I squeezed into the little BMW and was surprised to find it sat comfortably. There was ample room for my legs, my wide body fit into the seat and cabin nicely, and after a short drive, I found I still liked throwing gears. The red iridescent paint shone like it had its own sun under the finish, the tan leather interior was pristine and the burled walnut dashboard was a knockout. My Cadillac was big and sweet and comfortable and I loved her, but I never felt rich driving it, just strong. The Z4 felt rich, and to my great surprise, I liked it.

It was another beautiful Spring day, and with the Z4's top down and the wind blowing through my hair, I drove south, towards the great Atlantic Ocean, and pulled into the parking lot at Flying Point Beach. Leaving the car in the nearly empty lot, I walked past the gray clapboard comfort station, up the tight ascending wood plank walkway leading through the grassy dunes and turned when I reached its peak. Behind me was a sea of tall grasses in varying shades of green and brown, all floating and dancing in the crystal blue waters of Mecox Bay and its surrounding inlets. The air was filled with the calls of many different kinds of seabirds, each singing their mating songs above the sound of the crashing surf, and above it all was a cloudless and deep blue sky, the brass ball of a sun traveling slowly across it, illuminating everything around it with a clean yellow light. In the distance, on the perimeter of the bay, homes of many chimneys had been erected wherever the land was solid enough to support a mansion. I got a strange feeling that every magnificent, God-delivered thing surrounding me was my own personal property and said out loud, "You're a lucky man, Gabriel Fortuna. This is your home."

Getting back into the Z4, I started to drive around aimlessly and soon found myself on another Dune Road, this one in the village of Southampton, on the strip of road where The Infamous S.H.I.T. lived and where he was going to hold his annual Red, White, and Blue Ball. Because of supermarket tabloids and television, everyone out here knew about Sylvester Hightower, the man whose name appeared on the property deed of the forty thousand square foot mansion that was built before the law limited home sizes in Southampton Village to twenty-five thousand square feet. The price had been forty million dollars when he bought it, but recent word was that an anonymous Swiss banker had offered eighty million for it, making it the most valuable property on the East End. The estate held eight acres of subdivideable oceanfront land and the eighty million dollar offer was more than fair, but the hip-hop impresario wasn't about to sell. He'd done nothing but get richer since buying the place and had since become owner of not only a rapidly growing and internationally famous urban flavored music company, but also a high-end line of hip-hop clothing named HighWear, a lower-end line entitled Sh*tWear, four Mercedes Benz dealerships, five-star hotels in Monte Carlo, Cannes, Santa Barbara and New York, and a few hot pillow joints in Newark, Chicago, Detroit and Atlanta. He was also majority owner of Hipster Discount Airlines, and was in negotiations with a major media outlet to introduce his own nationally available cable television network, LIVIN' LARGE TV.

Dune Road, normally congested during the summer, became virtually impassable with the arrival of the gangstah contingent from New York. Outsiders from urban and suburban areas parked their cars along the narrow road to catch a glimpse of their hero, reveled in tearing up any parking tickets they might get from the local police and urinated frequently onto hydrangeas, dogwoods and bougainvilleas. Worse yet, the young urbanites often drove their cars into town, right down Main Street and in broad daylight. With their windows open and their tops down, they blasted away on double-woofered, twelve-speaker digital radios, assaulting well bred ears with synthesized screams of,"Fuck," "Bitch," or "Kill, muthafucka, kill." The townies might have been able to put up with all of it but worst of all, of course, was the fact that the Infamous S.H.I.T. was black.

I drove past what I knew had to be one beautiful oceanfront home after another, but nearly all of them were completely concealed from onlookers by hedgerows, or trees or stone fences, and when the owner had enough money and cared to show it to the driving public, all three. Most of what I saw behind the roadside blockades were the tops of houses, either widows' walks or cedar roofs, all angled and peaked as they ran their way along the two hundred foot lengths of house. It occurred to me for the millionth time that there was no end to the money out here. Dune Road was just another place that proved it.

After a mile, I came to what I knew was Hightower's place and pulled off onto the bay side of the road to scope it out. The driveway had a wide, cobblestone apron that ran about fifty feet into the property before it turned into crushed bluestone gravel. Two, six-foot tall stone columns flanked the apron and a large bronze word was etched into each slab: *Playthang.* A stone- faced guardhouse large enough to be a comfortable home for a family of ten was off to the side, its front set about ten feet behind the pillar on the right and shaded by four large elms. The house had dark green shutters, a wraparound porch, two chimneys and looked quaint enough to have come out of one of Grimm's fairy tales. There didn't seem to be anyone from the guardhouse controlling the entrance, and trucks delivering tables, chairs, napkins and whatever else might be needed for the weekend gala were driving in and out of the place every few minutes. A large flatbed arrived carrying several pieces of statuary, each a replica of a thin, eyeglass wearing Sylvester Hightower in various poses, and each with an American flag draped ceremoniously across his otherwise naked body. He wore granite smiles under the high Afro that had become his trademark, and at the bottom of each statue, on two-foot tall marble pedestals, was inscribed the words, GOD BLESS AMERICA! It made sense to me; where else in the world could a guy like Sylvester Hightower become as rich as a king.

In my driver's side mirror, I caught a line of approaching cars that could have been a presidential motorcade, the difference being that instead of the usual black limousines that made presidential caravans look like they were on their way to a funeral, this line of cars was all golden BMW convertibles with their tops down, and instead of *Hail To The Chief,* The Infamous S.H.I.T.'s latest hit, *Burn, Muthafucka, Burn,* was blasting out of every car's twelve speaker radio.

The first three open-topped 325's passed and all I got were nasty looks from the entourage seated inside them, but when the fourth car, a new 625csi passed, things changed. Driving that car was a block of black granite in a tuxedo and sun glasses. He looked straight ahead at the road, and with thick-fingered hands at ten and two, stoically steered the car towards *Playthang*. In the front seat beside the driver was a raisin-faced, Afro topped, slender black man in a purple cape. He was rocking and bopping and cutting out riffs in rhythm to the blasting music and occasionally threw his hands bombastically into the air when the chorus, "Burn, muthafucka, burn," blared from the speakers. He was in constant motion and it occurred to me that I was getting nervous just looking at him.

In the backseat was a very beautiful, dark skinned woman. Her eyes locked onto mine as the car passed and it didn't matter to me that she was wearing an absurd, short-cropped orange Afro wig, or that her feral eyes were surrounded by painted on tiger stripes, or that an incredibly low-cut scoop top was all that covered most of her magnificent breasts; she was one hundred percent, drop-dead gorgeous.

She stared at me as hard as I was staring at her and I caught a look of surprise and recognition play in her fiery eyes. Turning in the backseat and rising to her knees as the car made its left into *Playthang*, she waved me forward with a sexy gesture from her hand. I didn't know who she was or what she wanted, but a couple of seconds later I was racing up the gravel driveway and stopping in front of the pink and chartreuse mansion belonging to The Infamous S.H.I.T.

I stopped my car in front of the high-gloss pink, double-door entry and a young man in a single-breasted, HighWear, satin accented pink tuxedo opened my driver's side door. He didn't speak to me but held out his hand for the key, which I gave him without a question; after all, it wasn't the Caddy. He drove away and was disappearing behind the house when I felt a thick tap on my shoulder. I turned to find the large, hulking black man I'd seen chauffeuring Hightower. His six-foot six, three hundred and fifty pound frame was housed in a double-breasted black tuxedo, without pink accents, and high gloss patent leather black sneakers. His face was flat and spread out like it had been smashed with a shovel, and his eyes were perfect circles of black coal floating in bloodshot whites.

In the deepest voice I'd ever heard, he said, "This way, Mo'fo'."

I followed the big guy's lead and entered *Playthang*. Once inside the place, everything was different. The entry had a high-domed ceiling of glass, letting in enough sunlight to light the entire passage, and its wainscotings, moldings and walls were painted in varying shades of white, giving the place a neutral and peaceful backdrop. The artwork adorning the walls, mostly pastoral scenes of lovely East End settings, were easy on the eye, and four white marble rounded pedsetals softened the squared corners of the vestibule with lovely and calming individual glass sculptures of a cresting wave, a seabird in flight, a mother and child, and Ray Charles, not Hightower, with an American flag draped over his shoulders. The music that filled the open space was soft and gentle, mostly violins and cellos, making the place feel like a portal to heaven.

I was lead into a large, soft fern colored living room dominated by a series of lace-covered French doors leading onto a broad stone terrace. Layer upon layer of high-gloss white crown molding surrounded the ceiling of the great room, and oversized, Loire-Valley imported fireplaces were set on either end of it, turning the great room into a grand salon. Furnishings were antique French and huge matching gilt mirrors rested upon each marble mantel. In the center of the rectangular room was a large, dusty rose circular sectional couch with two circumferential openings allowing people the chance to enter and leave the seating area. Sitting on the section facing me was the slender, raisin-faced black man and the same beautiful woman I'd seen in the car. She smiled seductively when I entered the room, but the guy in the purple cape barely acknowledged my presence, choosing instead to fill his wine glass.

He said, "Let the muthafucka in, Romey."

Normally, I don't like it when a three hundred and fifty pound black guy sweeps his hands inside my legs and brushes up against my boys, but I was so taken with the gorgeous young woman smiling at me that I might have permitted a strip search. Romey finished patting me down, and when I didn't move quickly enough to his liking, gave me a light shove.

He said, deeply, "Go on in and sit down, Mo'fo'," and go in I did.

Reaching the circle of sofas, I entered but didn't sit. I stood still and eyed the ebon princess and found something familiar in her expression, but was still unable to place her. I paid no attention to the guy sharing the sectional with her, giving him, I hoped, a taste of his own medicine.

From his cushioned seat, he looked up at me and screeched, "You know who I am, Muthafucka?"

I don't like it when a guy talks like that in front of a woman, especially a beautiful one who's smiling at me. I figured the slim hipster had to be the owner of the place, so I answered, "You ought to watch your mouth, Hightower. It isn't good manners to curse in front of a lady."

"Oooooweee, so the muthafucka knows who I am."

Suddenly, Hightower jumped off the sofa and came springing at me like a skinny rabbit caught by Elmer Fudd in his carrot patch. Placing his shrunken, lilac-smelling face into mine, he said, "Listen, Muthafucka. I don't know who the fuck you is or what the fuck you be doin' camped outside my house, but Ro says she knows you and wants to thank you for something. I'm going to be right there, outside those doors, Muthafucka, so you better be righteous with my woman or else there's going to be hell to pay. Ooooweee! You hear me, Muthafucka? Hell to pay!!"

I was looking over Hightower's shoulder at the knockout who wanted to thank me for something I couldn't remember and was only vaguely aware of the reed of a man screaming into my face, but he was becoming annoying, so I leaned over and whispered into his ear, just so he knew where we stood, "Go fuck yourself."

"Ooooweee!" he yelped. "Muthafucka thinks he be one tough muthafucka!" Pressing my left bicep, he blared, "Muthafucka is strong, too."

Hightower had made the mistake of pressing the bicep that had been bruised by one of The Latin Zombies and a shot of pain ripped through me. I lifted my good arm and swatted him away like the annoyance he was and immediately felt Romey's strong grasp around my chest and arms, giving me a bear hug that came close to crushing the breath out of me.

Reflexively, I kicked my right heel back and caught Romey with a solid blow to his nuts. Snapping my head back, I butted him squarely on his nose, forcing him to loosen his grip just enough for me to get the room I needed to spin around and deliver a hard open palm to his forehead. That flat blow sent him careening backwards over a small, wooden antique chair and onto the floor. Unfortunately for the antique chair, it became antique toothpicks.

"That's enough, Muthafucka! That's enough!" Hightower hollered, his shrill shriek gone and in its place a mature male baritone. "That was an expensive chair, Muthafucka. Original Louis Quatorze. Shit man, why the fuck did you go and do that?" Turning to the young woman, he added, "Ro, you sure you want to be alone with this guy? He's one dangerous muthafucka. I can send in Conway and Bobby to keep you company. Elroy, too, if you like. What do you say, Ro, baby?" Hightower looked down at Romey, who was seated on the floor with a handkerchief to his bleeding nose. The Infamous S.H.I.T. said, "Doesn't look like Jerome's gonna be much help, though."

The black beauty on the sofa answered, "You can leave me alone with Mr. Fortuna. I'll be safer alone with him than I would be with any of the boys you'd leave to watch over me. I'll call if I need you."

Hightower stretched out a hand to Romey to help him up, turned and looked at me with a cross-eyed expression. Screwing up his little face, he screeched a fresh, "Muthafucka!"

Once on his feet, Romey dusted himself off and walked right up to me. His lazy eyes looked down into my hard ones and he said, "This ain't over, Mo'fo'."

Strike four!

The two men left the room and I turned to find the lovely young lady had left the sofa and was approaching me. Because I'd seen her only in a seated position, I hadn't noticed that she was wearing a pair of neon pink hot pants barely long enough to cover her privates, and that her legs were long and oiled and beautifully shaped, ending in perfectly turned ankles before slipping down into toe-ringed, sandal covered feet.

I caught my breath and asked, "How do you know my name?"

She answered, "I don't blame you for not recognizing me. It was a long time ago and I was only a little girl."

Meandering over to the corner bar and pouring some port into a cordial glass, she added, "I'm Roxanne Rosario, sometimes known as RoRo, sometimes Ro Squared, and almost always referred to as Sylvester Hightower's girlfriend. Want a drink?"

I answered, "No thanks, I'm not much of a morning drinker." I hesitated a moment and asked, "Which name do you prefer?"

She answered, "I guess you can call me plain Ro."

I replied, "I prefer Roxanne."

"You know," she responded through a smile, "so do I."

I approached the bar, stood close enough to lean over and kiss her and it took only a moment of that kind of closeness to realize I'd been right; she was as beautiful as anyone I'd ever seen, even more gorgeous than Teresa, if that were possible.

I asked, "You want to tell me what I'm doing here?" and quickly added, "Not that I wouldn't appreciate the chance to get to know you better."

Roxanne smiled brightly and answered, "I'm Roxanne Rosario from Eagle Avenue in the South Bronx. Fifteen years ago, you smashed through the door of my apartment and stopped some crackhead from killing my mother. Before dragging my mom into the bedroom, that freak told me to keep my mouth shut or I'd be next. He was stoned and didn't know I'd called 911, and two minutes later you came barreling through the front door and kicked that junkie's ass like you were his long lost papa. I never spoke with you after that night, not even in court when the trial came. You were this big, handsome white cop and I was this poor dark-skinned little girl from the projects. I guess I was afraid of you. When I saw you in that car today, it all came rushing back to me. I was so grateful to see you. I thanked God for giving me the chance to finally say, thank you."

Some people you don't forget, and Ernesto Garcia was one of them. I'd sent that lowlife to jail for the rape of Gladys Rosario fifteen years earlier, but I barely remembered Gladys' daughter. She was a little girl then, cowering in the corner of the living room with a blanket wrapped around her, crying, "Momma, Momma." After I took care of Ernesto and settled Gladys down, I picked that little girl up in my arms, hugged her and told her everything was going to be alright. It occurred to me that now the little girl was a grown woman and again I wanted to pick her up in my arms and hug her and tell her everything is going to be alright. It looks like some things never change.

I replied casually, "So, you're Gladys' little girl." Then, remembering her as a poor little kid living in a rundown ghetto apartment, I took a step back and tried to stop thinking about her legs, her ass, her breasts, and her perfectly moist mouth. Collecting myself, I asked, "How's your mother?"

Roxanne sighed, "Oh, Momma was killed about ten years ago by a different junkie. I was seventeen then and out of the house, but I hadn't yet made enough money to get her out of the projects. I felt guilty about her death for a while, but Sylvester explained to me that there was nothing I could have done to prevent it; I was still too young."

I said, "I don't know a lot about Mr. Hightower, but I can tell you that he gave you good advice about that. The Saint Mary's Projects were always a dangerous place. What happened to your mother could have happened to anyone living there. It could have happened to you. You're lucky you got out. No reason to feel guilty, Roxanne. There's no reason at all."

Roxanne finished her drink and placed the empty glass down lightly on the bar. She worked a long finger around its rim and said, "You know, when I saw you out there in your car it was like I saw you yesterday. You're still just as handsome, and from what you did to Jerome, I can see that you're just as strong as when you were a young cop on the beat. How do you do it?"

I examined the chiseled abdominals peeking out from Roxanne's midriff and answered, "The same way you do, Roxanne. I work at it."

Stepping out from behind the bar and sidling up to me, Roxanne looked deeply into my eyes and asked, "What were you doing out there checking out Sly's house? You don't strike me as being a Hightower groupie."

I laughed easily and answered, "I was just driving along Dune Road and enjoying the views until I came to this place. I had to stop and see what all the fuss was about."

She replied, "Sylvester is having a party this weekend."

I responded, "No shit," and then, embarrassed, corrected myself and said, "Excuse me, I didn't mean that."

Roxanne smiled brightly and said, "No problem, I'm used to that kind of talk." After a moment, she added, "How would you like to attend the party?"

I answered with a question of my own, "Is that an invitation?"

She said, "It could be. First, you have to have dinner with me tomorrow evening so that I can feel you out and see what kind of man you are outside your uniform. After all, its been fifteen years. Lots of things can change in that amount of time. Just look at me."

For the past twenty minutes all I'd been doing was looking at her, so I gratefully answered, "It's a date. I'll be here at seven."

Roxanne smiled sweetly, showing off a cute pair of dimples I hadn't yet noticed, and said, "That won't be necessary. I've got my own place off Wireless Way in Hampton Park. It's not as grand as *Playthang*, but it's all mine and I like it just fine." After planting a soft kiss on my cheek, she added, "Thank you for all you've done for me, Officer Fortuna."

"It's Gabriel," was my reply.

She wrote her address on a slip of pink paper and I left the room floating on air. A new tuxedo clad servant opened the front door for me and I couldn't help but see the sneer on his face as I passed him. Outside, Romey and the Infamous S.H.I.T. were standing and waiting for me at the Z4. They shot me hard stares and didn't seem to feel the need to speak, so I kept my mouth shut, opened the door to the little speedster and got behind the wheel.

Hightower, though, was not about to let me leave without a fond farewell. He leaned into the car and shrieked, "You better be good to Ro, Muthafucka! You hear me? Cause if you ain't good, Muthafucka, it's gonna be your ass and your balls and your muthafucka brains that get blown away. Oooooweee! Your muthafucka balls and your muthafucka brains. You got that Muthafucka?"

Romey didn't say anything. He stood stone still with his arms folded over his massive chest, frowning and confident that his day alone with me would eventually come.

I had other things on my mind besides dealing with a crazy rap star and his muscle. One of them was a beautiful young woman from the South Bronx who was great looking enough to help me temporarily forget about my problems. I threw the car into gear and peeled out of Playthang's driveway, showering the two gangstahs behind me with enough gravel and dirt to make them hate me even more. With my hand waving good-by from the open-topped car, I hit Dune Road and started back home.

12

I slid along the gravel in front of my house and came to a screeching halt inches before the rear of the late model, dark green Chevy Caprice that only cops drive. The feeling that something good was coming my way was replaced by a feeling that I was soon to have my ass busted, and upon reaching my door and seeing the post-it hanging just below the keyhole, I knew I was right to feel that way. I picked it off and read the feminine but scratchy handwriting, "Where the fucks are ju, Gabriel?"

Fucking Esmeralda!

I noticed that the door was ajar and pushed it open. Broken dishes were scattered everywhere, lamps were down, their shades crushed, chairs lay on their sides with their legs broken, cushions and armrests torn, my refrigerator and oven doors were open, every tray taken out and bent beyond repair, the picture window was smashed and through its broken pane I could see my deck furniture floating about twenty feet out in the still waters of Noyac Bay. Clothes were scattered throughout the room, hanging from broken light fixtures, over upturned table legs, and stuffed into the fireplace like so much kindling. The only thing upright was my couch, and that didn't look too good because Ledbetter and Stern were sitting on its knife-slashed cushions, wearing big smiles on their smug Fed faces. Reggie's painting was smashed, too, a twenty pound dumbell lying across its broken frame.

Ledbetter said, "Looks like somebody doesn't like you, Fortuna."

Stern cleverly added, "Looks like more than one person doesn't like him."

I picked up a shadeless brass tablelamp from the floor, smacked it threateningly into the palm of my hand and asked, "What the fuck do you guys want?" The smiles the Feds had been wearing vanished fast. They stood quickly and simultaneously rounded their hands into tight fists. Casting the useless lamp to the floor, I said, "Maybe you guys don't understand English. I said, what the fuck do you want?"

Ledbetter took a step forward and answered, "The place was like this when we got here. I don't want you to think we had anything to do with it."

I responded, "I never thought that," and then kicked a soft chenille throw pillow I'd picked up on a roadtrip to North Carolina through my broken picture window, raising my hands to signal a successful field goal when it landed beyond the deck and in the water.

Stern looked puzzled and said, "You don't seem too upset, Fortuna."

I snapped, "I'm plenty upset. There just isn't much I can do about it." With a menacing scowl, I added, "At least, not now."

Ledbetter tried to sound concerned, fulfilling the role of good cop, and asked, "Got any idea who'd have the balls to do this?"

Recalling that Esmeralda certainly didn't have any balls, I answered with a partial truth, "I've got plenty of ideas who'd like to do this, but I don't know anyone with balls enough to actually do it."

Stern, the bad cop, glared at me and said, "Listen, tough guy, I don't know who the fuck you think you are but you're going to listen to me and listen good. We weren't fooling around when we told you to keep out of this. It looks more and more like a terrorist group is involved and we don't need you making things more difficult for us. You get that?"

It suddenly occurred to me that one of the three stooges was missing and I asked, "Where's Gasper?"

Ledbetter forgot about his good cop routine. He entered the realm of the sarcastic cop and answered, "He's probably out giving someone a parking ticket. We don't want his help and he's been told so."

I said, "This is still a murder in Southampton. Are you telling me the local police are going to stand aside and make believe it didn't happen? Don't make me laugh."

Taking his turn at being the sarcastic cop, Stern said, "Maybe you don't hear so good, Fortuna. We said, keep out of this. Captain Dupree will be informed of what's going on with our investigation when the time is right, but he's not privy to information from Homeland Security. He'll be part of the prosecution when we get these bastards, and he's American enough to know when to step aside."

I wasn't going to tell these guys again that they were barking up the wrong tree. At The Drivers Seat, I'd told Gasper what I thought and that was as far as I would go, but it seemed that Gasper wasn't sharing my opinions with the Feds.

I said, "Get this straight, assholes. I'm not looking for any trouble with you guys, so don't come here threatening me. I'll keep out of your case so long as I'm not considered a suspect. As soon as I'm sure that's the way it is, I'll be out of your hair."

"That's not good enough, Fortuna," Stern warned. "You are a suspect. The local cops think that when anyone with an ex-wife as good looking as yours has sex with a murder victim, the ex-husband automatically becomes a prime suspect." The Fed added with a laugh, "You can't blame them for feeling that way. They've learned most of their policing techniques from watching episodes of *Law and Order.*"

I wanted to get rid of the bums without forceably throwing them out, so I calmy asked, "Will there be anything else?" After looking around at my ruined belongings, I added, "I'd like to start getting rid of some of this shit."

Ledbetter answered easily, "No, that's all," but couldn't help finishing off our meeting with a bad attitude, saying, "Just stay the hell out of it," with the perfect amount of snake venom.

I ignored the prick, let the Feds leave without further confrontation and went about taking inventory of my ransacked home. I was surprised to find that although nearly everything in the house was broken, it didn't appear that anything had been taken. Entering the gym I saw that my weights had been scattered haphazardly about the small room and that my big mirror had been smashed, flooding the floor with a thousand shards of glass. I didn't dwell on that for too long because my eyes locked on my gym locker. It had been broken open and the locked metal box from the bottom shelf had been removed. It lay open on the floor, its broken lock beside it. Raising the metal lid, I looked inside and whispered, "Holy fucking shit."

13

I began to collect my broken belongings, starting in the gym, then the bedrooms, working my way to the great room. All the while I piled the broken stuff outside my front door, I worried about who had taken my gun and what he, or she, intended to do with it. I questioned why, after only two days, Esmeralda would be so pissed at me that she'd have to trash my place, and then I thought of Enrique, whose face, the last time I saw it, was having a van door smashed into it. It would probably have given him a great amount of satisfaction breaking up my home, and an even greater thrill at finding and stealing my piece. I knew I'd have to have a conversation with, and probably have to teach another lesson to some of the Latin Zombies, and Enrique in particular, about the taking of someone's private property.

I was tossing the pieces of my shattered phone onto the pile of junk that had reached waist high outside my front door, when I saw Gasper pull up in front of my place in his Trailblazer. He looked tired, but was wearing a pair of crisp blue jeans, a tan linen shirt and a cordovan leather belt with a big, fancy buckle, the combination of which made him look a little less ragged. He hopped down from his high-riding Chevy and kept quiet as he walked over to me.

"Good afternoon, Gabe."

"Good afternoon, G," I responded.

Gasper took a forlorn look at the mountain of junk outside my door, sighed and said, "What the hell happened here?"

"Just a little misunderstanding between me and a new girlfriend."

I didn't want to tell Gasper about the theft of my Smith and Wesson yet. Lately, he hadn't been behaving like the good old buddy he was supposed to be, and anyway, I first wanted to find out why he was visiting me.

I asked, "What brings you around?"

Gasper answered, "I was upset about the way we separated the other day at The Driver's Seat. We've both been under a lot of pressure and I don't want this bullshit to come between us. I just wanted you to know how I feel."

I replied, "That's nice, Gasper," and was immediately aware that I hadn't called him G. I felt like a man who's been calling his wife Honey, or Baby, all their married life and suddenly finds himself calling her by her first name. Something is different, something is wrong, and something is over. It felt that way when I first started calling my ex-wife, Teresa, instead of, Lover, and it felt that way then with Gasper. Something was definitely over. I could see from Gasper's eyes that he knew it, too.

I said, "Just tell me how I'm supposed to feel when my long lost old friend tells me I'm a suspect in a murder case."

Gasper answered, "Do we have to go through this again? I've told you a hundred times, it's just procedure. We've got to follow leads even when we know they won't lead anywhere, even when we know they're bullshit. You were a cop. You know that."

I exclaimed, "Bullshit, Gasper! My word to you that I had nothing to do with it should be good enough."

Gasper looked resigned to the fact that I was going to give him nothing but grief, sighed and said, "It is bullshit, to me, but I'm responsible to the town police and I've got to follow up according to the book or I put my job in jeopardy."

Already used to calling my old friend by his first name, I asked, "What do you really want, Gasper? You don't expect me to believe you came here to bear your soul. There are some questions you want to ask, so why not ask them and get this bullshit over with."

Gasper put on the weakest smile I'd ever seen and confessed, "I guess you've got me, Gabe. I've got just a few more questions about you and Teresa and Al Shareef and what you were doing that night before we found the body."

I replied, "Fuck you, Gasper," and watched him twitch at the insult. Being captain of the town police and having someone tell him to fuck himself wasn't something he was used to, but he held his anger better than I held mine. From out of the blue, I added, "Let me have your cell phone."

A confused look swept over Gasper's face and he said, "There's no need to call your lawyer, Gabe."

"Fuck you," I repeated, and then added, "I want to call Norsic Sanitation to get rid of this pile of shit, Dave the Glazier to replace my picture window and Ralph's Hardware to get a new lock installed. If I do need a lawyer, you can bet I won't be calling him on *your* cell."

I made the calls and arranged for everything to be taken care of that afternoon. I didn't need to be home when the worker's arrived, this being a small town, I knew and trusted the guys who came to my home to do their jobs. Gasper asked me about my early and only conversation with Al Shareef, how I felt about seeing Teresa again, if I still had feelings for her, and if there was anyone who could vouch for my whereabouts when Al Shareef bought it.

I started each answer with, "Fuck you," and answered every one honestly because I had nothing to hide: "Fuck you. He told me he wanted a larger house and that you recommended me to provide the security for the party; Fuck you, I didn't really care who Teresa was fucking because she was always fucking someone and usually more than one guy a week; Fuck you, I hadn't seen Teresa in five years except in my imagination sometimes in the shower, where once in a while I did her for old time's sake; Fuck you. The only feeling I had for her was anger because knowing her had gotten me into this shit and because she was still great looking and as good a lay any man could want; and Fuck you. I can't tell you the names of anyone who could vouch for me because I was on the job and had kept pretty much to myself."

Gasper wrote most of what I told him down in a little black notebook, naturally leaving out all the, "Fuck yous." What I'd told him was a bunch of useless bullshit, but he now had a record of interrogating me and had covered his ass. Mine was still wide open to the wind and ready for a ramrod to be shoved into it.

After closing the notebook and sticking his pen into his shirt pocket, Gasper looked up at me with quiet eyes and said through a sincere tone, "I'm sorry about all this, Gabe. I'm just doing my job."

I replied coldly, "Sure, Gasper. I understand."

He said, "This is uncomfortable as hell, but I've got to ask it; is there anything else you'd like to tell me before I go?"

I thought for a second and came to the conclusion that now was as good a time as any and answered, "Yeah. You'd better take out that little black notebook of yours and open it to a fresh page. Somebody's stolen my gun."

14

I told Gasper everything I had on the S&W: its serial number, that it was loaded, that enough ammo to fight off the Taliban had been taken with it and that he might want to talk to The Latin Zombies about its disappearance. He looked at me cross-eyed when I told him that, like he didn't know from where it was coming, and I told him I'd had a little misunderstanding with the boys a while earlier and that they might be the ones responsible for breaking up my place and taking the gun.

"This isn't good, Gabe," he mumbled, nervously jotting down the information.

"No shit," I responded, thinking that Gasper was acting unusually uptight for a cop who'd been on the force for over twenty years and had probably filed missing gun reports a thousand times. He finished writing and we just looked at each other. We didn't shake hands, he left and I went back to throwing things on top of the junk pile.

Dave the Glazier and his assistant soon arrived and after looking at the rear window, he told me the job would take a few hours. I told him that Norsic and the locksmith would be there in a little while and he said, "No problem," and went off to smack out the shards of glass still stuck in the window frame.

I left my house, hopped into the Z4 and it took everything I had not to fly down Noyac and Deerfield Roads at a hundred miles an hour. As I drove, I imagined holding Enrique's head by the hair with my left hand and pounding his face into pulp with my right. Esmeralda entered my little fantasy also, and the things I did to her could have gotten me arrested by Oprah's Thought Police. I careened into the Princess Diner's parking lot, entered the diner and walked up to the register where owner, Katerina Constantinoupolous, was gorging herself on the free cookies normally reserved for the paying customers. There were crumbs all over her chins and covering the small counter where the register rested, and when I slapped my palms onto the glass, I heard and felt them crunch.

"Where's Esmeralda?" I bellowed.

Katerina jumped back a step, opened her mouth and half a cookie fell out. I felt bad at taking my anger out on the corpulent Mrs. C, but I was really steamed and snapped, "I'm sorry. I need to speak with Esmeralda. Is she working today?"

Katerina wiped some crumbs from her massive breasts, cleaned her mouth and cheeks with a swirling motion of a small and puffy hand and answered, "She's on a break, Gabe. You'll probably find her out back taking it easy."

I said, "Thanks, Mrs. C. You can go back to your cookies," and barreled out the front door.

I saw Esmeralda sitting on the green bilko door that opened to the diner's basement. She was talking with one of her friends, a new waitress from Guatemala named Josephina, when she spotted me tear-assing around the corner of the diner. She muttered something to the new girl, and the young Guatemalan flicked her cigarette into the rear parking lot before expelling an unusually large cloud of blue smoke.

Josephina had lovely green eyes and a nice high pair of sizeable breasts for a little girl, but as she walked past me she gave me the evil eye, like I was some Gringo who'd bayoneted her great great grandfather at The Alamo. My guess was that like most of the Latin newcomers to the East End, she was getting pissed off at having to work long hard hours for very little money and felt that every Anglo she met was trying to take advantage of her. I was sympathetic to her plight, but not enough to take my mind off the business at hand. I fastened my eyes on Esmeralda and bolted forward.

As I approached, Esmie sighed longingly and assumed a provocative pose on the bilko, arching her back and throwing her breasts upward and outward. She kittenishly called, "Ola, Gabriel, mi amor. Ju musts haves founds my notes on jour door. Or maybes ju coulds not waits to sees me. I gets off at seex. Why donts ju comes backs and takes me homes den. We can makes love all nights." Smiling sensuously, she finished her proposal, adding, "Ju likes?"

Fuming, I pushed my face into hers and exclaimed angrily, "No! I do not likes!" Esmeralda's sexy little kitten smile turned into a frozen mask of shock as I continued my harangue, yelling at close range, "What gives you the idea that you can come to my place and trash it just because I don't want to sleep with you? What gives you that right? Huh? What?"

Esmeralda's eyes filled with tears. Stunned and hurt by my angry outburst, she gathered herself and replied, "Ju means, mi amor, ju do nots wants to bees weets me?"

Esmie was a really great looking little Latin piece and we'd had a great time out at my place, so I was surprised to discover that she was right; I didn't wants to bees weet her.

I bellowed, "That's not what I'm talking about! I'm talking about you and your brother and his friends trashing my place! What makes you think you can get away with that? Huh? What?"

My little Hispanic waitress took a deep breath and rose from the bilko. Through a proud but sad expression, she said, "I deeds not trashes jour place, Gabriel. All I deeds was places a leetle notes on jour doors to reminds ju how much I cares for ju and how much I wants to be weets ju. I sees now ju do nots feels like dees for me. I has my prides. Ju weel no mores hears from me. Dees, I promises ju."

Normally, I feel bad when a woman cries when I won't go to bed with her, but I was still fresh from leaving my broken home and I asked in rapid fire action, "What about your crazy fucking brother? What about Enrique?"

Esmeralda answered soulfully, "I cannot speaks for Enrique, Gabriel. He does not loves ju." Taking a deep breath, she closed her eyes, clenched her fists and added, "My brother, he hates ju. When ju shuts the van door een his face, ju knocks outs two of hees fronts teets and he has to goes to the hospital for steetches. What he does now ees what he does. I promises ju dees, Gabriel; I weel not helps heem to hurts ju."

I tried to put the memory of my night with Esmeralda out of my mind and concentrate on what was really important, that being, someone out there was out to fuck me in a way that was very different from the way Esmeralda wanted to fuck me. Having been around the block enough times to know that Esmeralda was on the level, I knew she hadn't trashed my place, but that still didn't mean her crazy brother hadn't.

I said, "I'm sorry, Esmie. I didn't mean for it to turn out this way."

"Ju shoulds not sheets wheres ju eats, Gabriel. Please, do not comes heres agains. Eet weel hurts me toos much to sees ju."

I was quiet for a few seconds and then said what I had to say, "I'm sorry, Esmie, but the diner serves the best burrito in The Hamptons. I have to return."

She smiled softly and responded, "Ju weres my best lover, Gabriel. I weel hurts every times I sees ju, but what musts be, musts be. I knows. The burritos, they ees too goods."

My little senorita's shoulders were slumped as she rounded the corner to reenter the diner. I knew I would have loved to have spent some future nights with the lady, but she was too possessive and too volatile for me to take what I wanted from a woman and still retain my freedom. Any future dealings with her would have to be a life sentence, or a death sentence if I ever tried to leave her. Leaning against the back wall of the diner and collecting myself, I thought about Roxanne Rosario. She was certainly different from any other woman I'd ever been with, and unlike what most of the locals thought, different did not necessarily mean bad; it could mean exciting and great.

Returning to the diner, I sat at the counter, ordered my burrito and a Peconic water from a glowering Josephine and thought, if it wasn't Esmeralda who had broken up my place, how could I know for sure that it was Enrique who had? And if it wasn't Enrique, who could it have been? And worst of all, no matter who'd done it, they had my gun and that couldn't be good for anyone.

15

I left the diner and drove east on 27. The Watermill traffic light held me up as usual, but after a short while of drumming my fingers on the Z4's side panel I was on my way. I turned right just past the Milk Pail and got onto Mecox Road, heading south towards the ocean and cruising past what used to be magnificent farms and orchards but what was now a massive subdivision of fifteen thousand square foot homes on four-acre parcels called Ocean Estates at the Pasture, only there was no pasture, just a bunch of McMansions jammed together in cluster formation, and the ocean was still over a mile away.

Bearing left where the road bent sharply, I meandered along a more rural blacktop until I reached another Job's Lane where to the right, off the ocean, was still a working farm. Its sales hut was situated on the road, selling its freshly cut produce and artisan cheeses behind stacks of cubed straw and inviting scarecrows. Traveling past graying cedar mansions half-hidden behind recently trimmed hedges, I reached the end of the lane and made a right onto another Dune Road, this one in Bridgehampton. The houses here were close together and there wasn't any land to spare for lawns or tennis courts, but being on the ocean, there was no doubt that the properties were all valued in the millions. Teresa's place was about three-quarters of a mile down the road, only six beachfront houses from Cameron Beach, a beautiful public place open to all residents of Southampton Township who'd purchased a twenty-dollar seasonal parking sticker for their cars.

Reaching Teresa's house, I found three parked cars in the driveway. One, a soft-pink Porsche Carrera with the tags, REALST8, belonged to Teresa. The others, a late model black Rolls Royce with the plate, Shareef-9, told me someone from the deceased's family was paying a visit to my ex-wife, and the other, a twenty-something year old Mercedes Benz 280SL convertible with the plate SHMPTN-1, told me that someone who loved his town and received a heightened sense of self from others knowing it was also present.

I pulled in and parked behind Teresa's car, making sure she wasn't going to pull out and leave until I was finished with her. I noticed a set of golf clubs in the back seat of the 280SL, a place guys put their clubs when the trunk isn't big enough to hold them or when they are in a rush to go to or get away from somewhere. I saw that the clubs were a relatively new set of Calloways with graphite shafts and slipped a few out of the bag. Being a low handicapper myself, I nonchalantly took a few practice swings. I couldn't believe how the grips on each club had been worn down where a powerful thumb had been pressed into them, and noticed that the shaft of the nine-iron had a slight bend in it. There was also a small chip missing from the spot where the shaft had its tiny crease. The club was damaged and being curious about it, I figured, "What the fuck?" and threw it into the passenger seat of the Z4. The shaft slid to the floor, leaving only the clubhead visible to anyone who walked past.

I was checking out the biggest Big Bertha Driver in the world when the door to the Rolls opened and out stepped Mustafa. He didn't smile the way he had the last time we met but his eyes were dancing around in the same manner. I figured he was keeping his mouth shut due to some recent dental surgery, and not wanting to rub anything in, I kept my mouth shut, too. Sliding the driver back into the bag, I neatly rearranged the clubs in the Mercedes, waved a pleasant hello to the bodyguard as I walked past him and hustled up the small flight of steps to Teresa's front door.

I knocked solidly and a few seconds later the door opened, introducing me to a confident and smiling Teresa Fortuna. She was wearing a tight pair of crisp Levi's, the waistband cut away to help them look sexier as they rode low on her hips, and her blouse was loose-fitting white linen, the top three buttons opened, revealing all of her cleavage and most of her lovely, naturally rounded 36C breasts. I'd lived with that look and I knew that if a breeze came up or if she made any one of several seductive movements, one or both of her rosy pink nipples would be exposed and any man who might be looking there, and that meant any man with balls and a prostate, would be hers. At least that was what she thought. A soft breeze suddenly picked up and I saw one of those soft, pink buttons but I wasn't impressed. Things had changed, and by the way Teresa's smile left her face when she saw I didn't give a shit, she didn't like it.

Without any of the sexiness I was used to hearing from her, she asked icily, "What do you want, Gabe?"

I innocently answered, "Is this the same woman whose last words to me the other day were, 'Come over here and let's let nature take its course'.?"

"That was then and this is now. What do you want? I'm busy."

"Well, aren't you going to invite me in? I'd like to speak with you for a while. There are a few questions I need to know the answers to and I think you may have them."

Teresa crossed her arms over her chest and blocked the door, making it pretty obvious that she wanted me to get lost, but I stood in front of her like a block of granite and made it pretty clear I wasn't going anywhere. We traded dirty looks for a few seconds before a husky voice belonging to someone who'd sucked down too many nonfiltered cigarettes called from inside the house, "Is everything alright, Teresa?"

Placing her hands on her hips, Teresa sighed and looked down at her tapping bare feet as a man I'd recognized from a thousand photographs in The Southampton Press walked toward us. Southampton Town Supervisor, Armand Conforti, strode to the door with his short legs and ample waist stuffed into a pair of brown Sansabelt slacks. He stopped and stood possessively beside my ex-wife.

"Can we help you?" he asked through a phony smile, the same one he'd used for all those posed photos I'd seen in the papers. "I thought I heard Ms. Fortuna ask you to leave."

The fat tub in front of me had political power and was used to getting his way. I had no political clout, but was used to the same thing. I answered, "I never heard her say that. What I heard her say was, 'What do you want?' Maybe you should get your ears cleaned."

Conforti's ears didn't need any cleaning after the steam blew through them, but he might have needed a cardiologist if his breathing didn't slow. The guy had a short fuse; that much was apparent by the way he was sucking in air. I wondered how he was going to act when I told him to go fuck himself.

He asked, "Do you know to whom you're speaking?"

I gave Teresa a quick glance and she rolled her eyes, waiting for the inevitable.

"Sure I do," I answered. "You're Armand Conforti, hot shit in town government."

"And ..."

"And what?"

"And," Conforti repeated, apparently waiting for an 'I'm sorry' or some other sort of apology.

I looked at Teresa again, smiled, shrugged and said, "And go fuck yourself. Teresa is my ex-wife and I'd like to talk to her. I didn't vote for you in the last election and I won't vote for you in the next. Why don't you leave us alone for a while, take a good walk on the beach and burn off a couple of pounds? Look at yourself, you fat bastard. You've got more chins than a Chinese phonebook."

Conforti was about to explode and only Teresa placing her hand on his fat ass, stroking it and telling him to, "Calm down, Armand baby," prevented him from getting that ass whipped. He was still fuming, though, and I was waiting to see if he was going to make a mistake and take a poke at me when I heard the Rolls in the driveway turn over and begin to back out of the short driveway. I turned and saw Yousef Al Shareef in the passenger seat before the car backed onto Dune Road and took off. It occurred to me that Yousef must have left through the back door after he'd heard my voice. I turned to Teresa and gave her the most disgusted expression I could manage.

She said, "Fuck you, Gabe," and turning her attention to Conforti, mewed through a sad expression, "Armand, please leave me and my ex alone. He's a hardheaded asshole and he's got some things he wants to talk about. I know him and he won't leave until we get through this. Go home and I'll call you when he's gone. We can still have dinner later. Okay?"

Conforti gave me the once-over, sneered as if there was something he could do with me and said, "We can call the police, Teresa. I'm sure Captain Dupree can handle his friend."

I interrupted, saying, "You wouldn't want to put a wager on that, would you, Fatboy?"

Teresa placed her open palms on Conforti's chest and begged, "Please, Armand, go home. I promise I'll call you later. Please, go now before there's trouble."

Gallantly, the fat bastard asked, "You sure you'll be okay alone with this guy, Teresa?"

Exasperated, Teresa answered, "I'll be fine, Armand. Just go."

Conforti walked down the steps, got into his car and pulled away without looking at us or into my car where the nine-iron lay. I knew that someone didn't rise to his political post in one of the wealthiest resort capitals of the world and retain it for as long as he had without being tough, so I figured that from now on I'd have to watch my back for fat supervisors as well as lean Zombies. I walked past Teresa without waiting for an invitation, settled into an oversized and overstuffed leather armchair and gazed out a wall-sized window looking out over the ocean.

Teresa followed me into the living room and asked, "Alright, now what the fuck do you want, Gabe?"

"Teresa! Is that any way to speak to your ex-husband, someone who's been inside you several thousand times?" Through an obnoxious smile, I added, "Can't we all just get along?"

Teresa, trying her best to ignore me, walked over to the mahogany bar, took out a Baccarat rocks glass from the cabinet, and filled it halfway with a pretty amber liqueur. Lighting a cigarette, she took a deep toke, tapped the ashes into a lovely little crystal ashtray, and after taking a strong sip of her liqueur, felt relaxed enough to say, "Now, what do you want to know?"

I answered, "That's better," but remained seated, looking out the window, taking in the ocean and giving her time to worry. I was taken by a family walking along the surf, the twenty-something mommy and daddy holding hands as their two-year old toddler, laughing hysterically, kicked up fountains of water between them. I smiled at the perfect picture and said, "You've done well for yourself, Teresa. This place is beautiful. Finally have everything you want?"

"Not everything," she answered. "You're still here."

It took only that much for me to remember whom I was with and why I was there. I turned my attention back to Teresa and replied nonchalantly, "Well, if you answer my questions without trying to fuck me over I could be gone in a very short while. First, what's the story with you and Conforti?"

Taking on a suddenly smug look, Teresa answered, "We go out once in a while. What's it to you?"

Waving my finger in a childish, 'no-no', fashion, I sang, "If you want me out of here, you won't talk like that."

Teresa responded by blowing away some hair that had fallen in her face and by closing two buttons of her blouse, an obvious attempt at ruining my view, but we both knew that I didn't care. She blew at her hair again.

I continued, "He's not your type. He isn't rich and he isn't good looking. Judging from the size of his ass, I'd bet Mr. Happy couldn't be more than three inches."

Teresa lashed out, saying, "You're such an asshole, Gabe. You could never understand that there might be more to a man than looks or money."

I coldly replied, "I don't judge men except through their actions and you know it. I don't care what a guy looks like or how much bread he has. I always thought that was your criteria for a good catch. That's why I'm curious; what does this guy Conforti have?"

Teresa straightened her spine and snapped, "He has access, you asshole. Armand Conforti has access. As town supervisor he can get me involved in some of the richest land deals in The Hamptons, making me part of things I could never have gotten into without him. Armand is an important man out here and everything goes through his office. He can do things for me you could never do."

I smoothly asked, "Can he make you come ten times in a night?"

She curtly replied, "Don't flatter yourself. Most of those times I was faking."

Teresa proved once again that she knew how to get to me and I blurted, "You're full of shit!" and then seeing the curved smile that response brought to Teresa's lips, I breathed deeply and asked, "What about the kid?"

"What kid?"

"Yousef Al Shareef. You fucking him, too, or was he just here to watch?"

Teresa surprised me with a cruel laugh, threw back her shoulders and feeling more confident because of all the cognac she'd been downing answered, "You're such an asshole, Gabe. Of course, I'm fucking him. He's ten times better than his father was and hung like a stallion to boot."

I replied, "I'm sure his mother would love to hear your appraisal of the Al Shareef men."

"Up yours," was my ex-wife's trite response.

It was getting depressing being around Teresa, so I said, "My next few questions will be my last, so long as I know you're telling me the truth. Now, don't fuck around with me and be honest."

Teresa's answer to that was to pour more cognac into the Baccarat.

I asked, "Why were Al Shareef and Conforti here? You may have had a threesome going, and if you did, I don't want the details, but what went on before and after your little party? It wasn't just about sex. With you it's never just about sex. It's always about something else you want."

Teresa was drunk, and like the drunken tramp she was, she opened her blouse, took it off and threw it at me, hitting me with it in the face. I smelled her perfume and it was intoxicating as ever, but I wasn't buying. Dropping the shirt to the floor, I asked coldly, "What does the kid have to do with any of this?"

Teresa ran her fingers through her hair and slurred, "With his father's death, Yousef owns The Castle and all its property. The town wants to buy it and Armand is going to allow me to broker the deal. At four percent commission, that could be more than a million dollars."

I said, "I thought brokers got six percent," and a couple of beats later added, "You're becoming cheaper than ever."

Teresa responded with an incoherent scream loud enough to bring down neighboring property values a full ten percent, and then screamed quite coherently, "Fuck you, Gabe! Even at four percent there's enough money in it for me to suck a thousand cocks. Are you satisfied now?"

The murder suspect and whore panting in front of me like a trapped animal was a woman whom I once called my wife and the truth was I wasn't satisfied at all. In fact, I was pretty disgusted. There was nothing left to ask, so I silently got up, walked to the front door and, after leaving, shut it gently behind me. I'd walked down the front steps and was halfway to my car when I heard what must have been the Baccarat smashing against a wall and Teresa's final wail, "Bastard!! Lousy, fucking bastard!!"

Feeling low, I left her parking area to head home. I was sure that I'd found out what I needed to know; it *was* all about land and money, but I also had discovered that Conforti knew Gasper and I were friends.

Now, how and why would he need or want to know that?

There was still a question that I hadn't asked and it was one that only I could answer. Teresa was my ex-wife; what did that make me?

16

Being in no mood to head straight home, I drove to Sag Harbor, nosed the Z4 into a spot in front of Sylvester's Coffee Emporium on Main Street and stopped at the Conca D'Oro Italian Restaurant for a slice of pizza, something I rarely allowed myself because of the unusually high carbohydrate count of the thick slice sold there. John D'Italia, the owner of the place, was behind the counter, and not having seen him for a couple of months, we talked for a while.

He commented, like nearly everyone else who lived out here full-time, that the city people no longer came out only for the summer season. Many had stopped renting summer shares, and because of historically low interest rates, had bought their own second homes and were now coming out year round. None of the locals liked the crowded roads, the congested restaurants, or the near impossibility of getting timely tee times, even on public courses in Manorville, Riverhead, or Baiting Hollow, but John admitted he liked the money the newcomers freely spent, and like most of the merchants in the East End towns, he now kept open year round and made a much larger profit than he had only a few years earlier. After a short while, the place started to fill up, so I finished my slice, wished John the best and took off for home.

Reaching my place, I was relieved to find that Norsic had picked up my broken stuff and that the door had a new lock on it. Ralph, the locksmith, had left the latch open so that I could get inside without a problem and two new sets of keys were waiting on my butcher block counter. Dave, the glazier, had replaced the rear picture window with a new piece of hurricane-proof, triple-insulated glass that fit perfectly into the frame, and Reggie's broken picture was leaning against the wall beside the fireplace where I'd left it. I didn't know what I was going to tell her about its quick and sudden demise, hoped there was a way of getting it repaired without her knowledge and decided I'd have to speak with Greg over at the Grenning Gallery to see if he knew anyone in the area who could do a decent restoration. After going into the bathroom to splash some cold water onto my face, I felt the need for a bit of playful, verbal jousting and leaned out the window to give my friends next door a call.

"Hey, Carla! Reggie! You guys home?"

No one answered, which was unusual because I thought I saw Carla's car parked in front of her house when I'd pulled into my place.

"Reggie!" I called louder. "What's happening?"

Still, no answer.

I marched over to their place, hoping that they were out walking the beach because they were tired of me hassling them over their complete lack of exercise. Their front door was closed, but unlocked as always, and as I turned the knob and entered, I got a strange feeling that something was wrong. The place was neat, as it always was, but it was too still. There had always been a sense of energy in Carla and Reggie's home, something I felt even when they were away on vacation and I dropped by simply to water their plants. That energy was gone. I walked down the short corridor to their bedroom, opened the door and saw them lying in their bed, fully clothed and holding hands. Each had a small bullet hole in her forehead, and the pillows, where the backs of their heads rested, were saturated with drying blood. The room didn't smell, so I knew they couldn't have been dead for more than a few hours, but the place didn't need to smell for me to feel sick. I ran to the bathroom and heaved my guts before I went to the phone and dialed 911 for the Southampton Town Police.

A couple of minutes later, the first police car flew into the driveway. Tom Peterson, a cop I'd known for a long time, barreled into my friends' living room, saw me sitting in the chair with my head in my hands and asked, "Where are they?"

I pointed down the hall to their bedroom and Tom went in with his gun drawn. I heard him whistle before he said, "Holy fucking shit."

He came out of their bedroom white as a sheet and I pointed to where the toilet was.

Two more patrol cars rushed into the driveway before I saw Gasper's Trailblazer come to a sudden halt behind them. He rushed into the house and took one fast look at me sitting on the sofa before going into the girls' bedroom. He came out a couple of minutes later looking sad, worried and pissed. Walking over to where I was seated, he asked, "What do you know, Gabe?"

I told him I had just gotten home, was kind of depressed over my afternoon meeting with Teresa and wanted to have a little talk with Carla and Reggie because they were a lot of fun and always had a way of cheering me up whenever I was feeling low. I usually was able to reach them through our bathroom windows, but when they didn't answer my calls I went over to see what was going on. I found the front door unlocked, went into their bedroom and found them lying on their bed, dead. I dialed 911 and that was that.

Gasper asked, "When was the last time you spoke with them?"

"Sunday morning, after the party at The Castle."

"Did you notice anything unusual going on here recently?"

"What do you mean, 'unusual'?"

"You know, strange men, other women, stuff like that."

I answered bluntly, "As far as I know, I was the only man who ever went into their place. They had a lot of female friends. I didn't keep track of their social lives."

Gasper continued, "Have you heard any recent arguments between the two of them? Were they having any problems?"

I responded, "I never heard them argue, and to my knowledge they didn't have any problems. They were a happy couple who did good things for the community and minded their own business." Stiffly, I asked, "Where are you going with this?"

Gasper had been taking notes in that little book of his but closed it with my question. He placed it into his pocket and answered, "These girls were lesbians, Gabe. You know that."

"So? What of it? They were nice people. They were my friends."

Gasper eyed me suspiciously, something I'd never seen from him before, and he said, "It's just that it might have been the result of a lover's quarrel or a triangle affair gone bad. We've never had a double homicide out here, so I'm wondering if maybe it was a murder/suicide. That's a possibility, too."

I couldn't hide my sarcasm and said, "If that were the case, where's the gun? Did Reggie or Carla throw it into the bay after she blew her own brains out?"

Gasper reconsidered his previous statement and replied, "Whatever happened, it isn't good. This is the third murder in Southampton Township in less than a week and that's three more murders than we've had in the past six years. The curious thing, Gabe, is that you seem to be in the middle of all three."

I followed that tidbit of bullshit by immediately barking, "I'm not in the middle of anything. I don't know what the fuck you're getting at, Gasper, but I don't like what I'm hearing."

Gasper made sure I completely caught his drift when he raised an eyebrow and asked, "What were you doing at Teresa's place this afternoon?"

"That's my business," I answered, and followed that with a question of my own. "What was your boy, Armand Conforti, doing there?"

Gasper calmly replied, "That's not my business and not necessary for me to know, but you were told to keep out of the Al Shareef case. I wouldn't call going to Teresa to question her about her relationship with the dead guy and his son exactly keeping out of it. Would you, Gabe?"

I was past the point of giving a shit and responded, "Gasper, I don't give a damn what you, the Feds, or Conforti say. I'm going to find out who killed Al Shareef and what happened to those two poor girls in the bedroom. If you don't like it, that's tough fucking shit. Now, either arrest me or get the hell out of my face."

Gasper seemed more in control of himself than he was the last few times we'd argued and replied with a shrug, "Arrest you? Why would I do that, Gabe? I've got no reason to think you had anything to do with this, at least not until we take the slugs out of the pillows and the mattress and check to see what kind of gun they came from. I sure hope it wasn't a Smith and Wesson, because if it is, stolen gun or not, you've got problems."

I balled my hands into fists and would have slugged my old friend then and there if there weren't four other cops standing around us. Gritting my teeth, I asked, "May I leave?"

He answered, "Of course, Gabe. Just don't leave town. We might have some more questions for you to answer."

I turned to go and was on my way out the front door when Gasper called, "Just one last piece of advice before you go, Gabe; for your own good, stay away from Teresa."

Yeah!! Right!! Like that's gonna happen!!!

17

Sitting on my torn couch, alternating my stare between the empty fireplace and Reggie's broken picture, feeling sorry for myself and for my friends, I waited as time crawled by. I tried to figure out why The Latin Zombies would kill two innocent women just because they might have been seen breaking up my place and it didn't make sense. Neither did Gasper's idea of a love triangle seem plausible; Carla and Reggie were two women who were devoted to each other and had often criticized me for some of my wild scenes, continuously encouraging me to find someone to care about, to give love a chance and maybe get married again. I recalled how I'd laughed when they teased that I could be robbing the world of the great Fortuna gene pool. I told them not to worry and that there were probably plenty of little Fortunas already running around that I didn't know about. They didn't find my braggadocio funny, and after I thought about it, neither did I. The ladies weren't naïve, but they weren't runarounds and loved each other as much as any two people could. Something had happened to them for a reason I did not yet know, but it would soon come to me, and when it did, I was going to make sure that the people responsible paid.

Fighting my lethargy, I got off the couch and after showering and shaving, got dressed, fell into the Z4 and headed out for the Rolling Hills subdivision in Hampton Park. There were a few ways to get there, but I chose the most scenic and quiet route, driving with the cartop down, the windows up and the interior heat blasting through the chilly forest shadows.

I passed the quiet entrance to The Castle and a mile further ahead hung a right onto Edge of Woods Road, driving three more silent miles before hitting Wireless Way. At the two stone entrance pillars, I made a right and passed several large, but not ostentatious, cedar shingled, Hamptons-styled houses tucked quietly behind birch, beech, scrub oak and pine trees. About a half mile down the blacktopped roadway, I passed a mailbox with the golden reflector numbers 76 on its post and made a right onto a tan gravel drive. I continued up the serpentine path for a short distance until it opened into a small clearing where a comfortably modest cedar shingled home sat, a small lawn, some foundation shrubs and a few young specimen trees whose lower branches had been chewed by some passing deer surrounding it. The house was a modified saltbox, the roofline not quite so steep as the traditional East End style house usually was, and an addition had been placed onto where the master bedroom was normally located, suggesting it had been turned into the master suite that had become so popular among those who could afford one.

I parked in a small parking area at the end of the driveway, beside a purple Hummer that made the Z4 look like a Matchbox Car. A small family of white tailed deer passed through the woods barely fifty feet in front of me and I sat watching them as they slowly made their way along the trail. It was quiet around Roxanne's place and I would have normally felt very much at peace there, but I wasn't feeling normal, and in spite of the locale's serenity, I just couldn't shake the bad feeling that my two friends had been killed because of me. Unable to sit any longer, I left the car, reached the front door, wearily stroked the bottoms of my shoes across the cheery welcome mat, and feeling like a total piece of shit, rang the front bell.

From inside the house, Roxanne's cheerful voice called, "Just a moment. Be right there."

There came a shuffling of feet across an oaken floor, the door swung open and except for the brilliant and friendly smile on the young woman's face standing in front of me, there was little that reminded me of the sultry and alluring ebon goddess I'd met the day before. This pretty woman had relaxed honey highlighted brown hair hanging loosely to her shoulders, not a short cropped Afro wig from a Sixties Mod Squad episode, and instead of tight, over-revealing slut clothing, she wore an oversized navy blue Southampton sweatshirt, a pair of relaxed-fit Wrangler blue jeans and a pair of white Adidas tennis sneakers. Her only make-up was the mascara and black liner that framed her fiery green and oranged specked eyes, and a touch of pink lipstick that warmed her full and sensuous lips. She was incredibly beautiful, but in a more dignified and simple way than the flamboyantly gorgeous knockout I'd met at *Playthang*. I liked the way she looked. I liked it a lot and almost forgot my problems.

Leaning forward, I kissed her cheek and being honest, said, "Hi, Roxanne. I barely recognize you."

A quizzical expression swept across my host's face and she playfully asked, "Then, how do you know it's me?"

I answered, "Beautiful is beautiful. That's what you are and that doesn't change because of different clothes and different hairstyles. You're still you."

Roxanned cautiously replied, "Smooth talker," and added with a smile, "Come on in."

Roxanne's place was easy on the eyes, furnished almost entirely in tans and browns and beiges, surrounded by linen white walls. There was a minimalist, three slab limestone fireplace with a raised limestone hearth at the rear of the great room wall, flanked by two sets of French doors leading outside to a mahogany deck, the backyard and the black vinyl-lined swimming pool that was surrounded by irregular bluestone coping. In front of the fireplace sat a quiet grouping of two tan paisley club chairs opposed to a tobacco-brown leather couch. Between them was a square, bronze and glass cocktail table large enough for anyone seated around it to comfortably place his drink or hors d'oeuvres. A green and ivory Oriental rug, floating on satin finished, Number One oak floors, anchored the furnishings. Two skylights were built into the the angled roof, large enough to let in ample amounts of sunlight during the day and moonlight during the night, and a right-triangle picture window dominated the far right wall. It was framed above a rectangular cherry wood dining table holding eight Windsor chairs. The kitchen was off to the right also, just off the dining area, and a glass enclosed bay with another set of French doors attached it to a lovely little garden of late spring flowers and herbs. On the flip side of the house, a set of double interior doors led into a master suite. The doors were partly open and I was able to see into the bedroom, where a large champagne colored bedspread laid the foundation for many soft green, tan and pink throw pillows, all set on a dusty pink wall-to-wall rug. A staircase at the back wall and to the right of the doors led upstairs to a narrow, open hallway that looked down into the great room. The three doors along the upper hallway were closed and I figured they were the guest bedrooms.

Roxanne shut the front door and walking up beside me said, "Welcome to my humble chateau."

I commented, "Your place is beautiful. How long have you had it?"

"Oh, about two years. I bought the land six years ago when the subdivision opened, but with all the touring I wasn't able to start building. I was finally able to slow down a bit and broke ground about four years ago, and as simple as the place was to build, with all the town paperwork and bureaucracy, it still took about two years to get done."

Looking around, I said, "It was worth the wait. You're lucky to have it."

Roxanne surveyed her cozy home along with me and softly replied, "I like it out here. I've come to feel more at home in this place than I do in the city. It's quiet and peaceful. I can get in touch with myself."

I agreed with what she said and added, "I know what you mean. I feel the same way."

We were silent for a few uncomfortable moments and I found myself staring at Roxanne, hoping she would say something because I was at a loss for words.

Roxanne shook her head and laughed comfortably, men staring at her apparently something she'd become used to, and asked, "May I get you something to drink? Soda, water or some wine? I've got everything."

"Water will be fine," I answered.

She replied, "Make yourself at home, Gabriel Fortuna. I'll be right back."

Roxanne went into the kitchen and I took a tour of the downstairs living area to get a closer look at what she had on the walls. On the staircase wall were many small groupings of signed photos of Roxanne and famous black entertainers that even I recognized: Tina, Smokey, Whitney, Hammer, Prince, some young lady in a baseball cap, gold-toothed and glittery, whom I didn't recognize named Missy, and , of course, Sylvester Hightower, The Infamous S.H.I.T.

Above the fireplace mantle was an oil of Roxanne with a middle-aged woman I recognized immediately. In the painting, Gladys looked happy and proud of her daughter. It was sad to think of the hard life she'd had and how brutally it had ended. This set me to thinking about Reggie and Carla and the funk began settling back inside me.

Roxanne left the kitchen, cheerily calling, "Here you are. I hope you like a slice of lime in your Perrier." Reaching me, she must have seen the sadness in my eyes because she asked, "Is there something wrong, Gabe?"

I answered through a weak smile, "No. It's just that seeng your mother's picture on the wall brought back some unpleasant memories." Changing the subject, I added, "Your mom was a nice lady. She deserved better."

Roxanne sighed and said, "Thank you for saying that, Gabe. She was a good person who made some foolish choices. She liked you, though. She told me how you called her for months after the trial just to see how she was doing. Not even members of our own family did that. She always said you were a special cop and a special man."

Not feeling so special, I replied, "Thanks." Then, pointing at the wall, I asked, "What's with you and all the celebrities?"

Roxanne threw me a curious look and said, "You really don't know who I am, do you?"

I answered, "Aside from being a beautiful woman and a friend of Sylvester Hightower, no. Is there something else about you I should know?"

She smiled slyly and said, "Wait here."

Roxanne went into her bedroom and returned a minute later carrying a thick stack of magazines. She dropped them onto the cocktail table and I glanced down to view the cover of the top glossy, titled, '*Bling, Blam*'. I was greeted by a large headshot of the Roxanne I met at Hightower's place: short orange Afro wig, tiger eyes, orange streaks, the whole crazy trip. Below the first was another magazine, '*Hip Hop Jim Jam*'. It had a sultry Roxanne on the front cover, this time tressed in shiny black Jeri curls instead of a flamboyant orange wig, and provocatively bent over in a pair of low cut denim shorts, the backs of her oiled legs and her beautiful round ass covering most of the glossy page. The next cover showed Roxanne in a glamorous, low-cut, white sequined evening gown at The International Rap Awards in

Cannes. She was surrounded by a mob of French fotogs snapping her picture, while a bug-eyed Hightower and a gigantic Romey attired in matching hot-pink tuxedoes pretended to scoot them away. I recalled the mindless hours of lying on my bed watching television, a million clicks of the remote control rampaging through the hundred and fifty stations of 'nothing on' that Cablevision brought into my bedroom, and it came to me in a flash.

"You're RoRoRap!" I exclaimed. "Ro Squared!"

Roxanne laughed at my surprise and said, "I thought you knew that." Extending her hand, she added, "Nice to meet you, Gabriel Fortuna."

I took her hand, shook it lightly and said, "Holy shit! Excuse me, I mean, holy cow! I didn't realize. I mean, I don't go for that rap stuff and I just didn't put it together. Of course, you're RoRoRap." A series of flashbulbs went off in my head and I asked, "What the hell are you doing with me?"

Roxanne was clearly disappointed with my reaction and responded earnestly, saying, "I would have thought you'd know that a person doesn't have to be what he or she looks like, or even what she does for a living. I'm Roxanne Rosario, Gabe. RoRoRap is who I am when I perform or when I'm on photo ops. Are you always the same person?"

I answered through the vernacular of the day, "I'm Gabriel Fortuna twenty-four-seven, Roxanne, not very complicated." Picking up some magazines and flashing through a few more covers of RoRo doing her thing, I downplayed Roxanne's obvious cover girl sexuality and added, "You're very photogenic."

Some of the photographs were extremely revealing, leaving very little of RoRoRap to the imagination, and I was afraid I might have been caught ogling because Roxanne said through a worried expression, "I hope this doesn't ruin our night. I've been cooking all day. It's not often I get a guest."

I answered, "Hey, I'm just not used to spending time with celebrities." Placing the magazines face down to avoid further temptation, I added, "I can't believe you're a cook, too. This is almost overwhelming. The place smelled great when I came in, but I thought we were going out for dinner. What are we having?"

An easy smile washed across Roxanne's face and she said, "Veal Parmigiana, spaghetti in marinara sauce, classic Caesar salad and for dessert, a cannoli I bought at La Parmagiana on Hampton Road. It's the only thing I didn't make myself. I've got problems when I work with ricotta."

Thinking of my constant diet, I said, "Whew, that's a lot of food."

Through a sexy smile, Roxanne replied, "Don't worry. You'll work it off."

I found myself feeling great, looking forward to the dessert after the dessert and working it off with Roxanne's assistance when a wave of guilt came over me so hard I felt like I was drowning. The memory of Carla and Reggie in their beds with those little red holes in their foreheads attacked me and I had to reach out and grab the wall.

"Gabe, is everything olay?"

Roxanne was by my side with her arms around my waist, staring up into my eyes with a concerned expression in hers. She said, "You haven't looked right since you came into the house. What's going on?"

Normally, I don't like to open up and tell people my problems, but I felt overwhelmed and needed to share my story with someone. If I was going to be spending time with Roxanne, and I knew I wanted to, I also knew I'd better be honest with her and tell her what was happening. I stated coldly, "Two friends of mine were murdered today. I found their bodies this afternoon and called the police. They were nice girls and they were good friends."

Roxanne held my hand, guided me to the couch and sat beside me. I told her about The Castle, the Feds, Gasper, The Latin Zombies, Reggie and Carla, and the destruction of my home. I didn't tell her about my missing Smith and Wesson, though, figuring that what I was telling her was scary enough without mentioning my stolen gun. Her expression remained blank as I related my tale and she soaked it all up like a sponge, never stopping once to catch her breath or to ask a question. It occurred to me that growing up in the South Bronx, this was the kind of stuff she'd been surrounded by most of her early life. Being a cop in my previous life, I'd seen it all before, too, but this time it was different; this time, it was happening to me.

When I was done with my story, she said, "You're staying here tonight, Gabe."

I replied, "Thanks, Roxanne, but I don't want to impose."

"There's no imposition. I've got three guest rooms and you can take your pick." Smiling sweetly, and there were those dimples again, she added, "Come on, let's eat. Dinner is getting cold."

Roxanne led me into the dining area, lighted three aromatic candles she'd placed onto the table and turned down the recessed halogen lighting. She sat me facing the triangular picture window and went into the kitchen, returning with two large plates of thinly sliced veal covered in melted mozzarella and tomato sauce and two steaming sides of spaghetti marinara. Going back into the kitchen, she returned with a tray holding a couple of glasses of red wine, some grated Parmesan cheese and a piping hot platter of veal, in case I wanted seconds.

Roxanne sat across from me and placed an orange linen napkin across her legs. Turning her alluring eyes to me, she said, "Tell me something else about yourself, Gabe. You know all about me. I'd like to be on a level playing field with my dinner companion."

Most beautiful women I spent any time with I just wanted to take to bed and everything that came before was just laying the groundwork. It felt different with Roxanne. I didn't know why, and it made me nervous and glad at the same time.

I said, "I was born in The Bronx and raised in Queens, but most people I know out here think of me as a local. In the early Sixties, my parents bought a small cottage in Noyac, an area that wasn't very popular back then and which wasn't much more than a bunch of fisherman's cabins on Noyac Bay. We loved the place and spent nearly every long weekend and summer vacation out there, enjoying the beach, the weather, and the overall quiet and ease of life. The Bridgehampton Racetrack was around then, too. It was a glamorless figure-eight hidden high in the Noyac hills and if you weren't from around here, or a visiting racer, the only way to find it was by following the thunder of motorcycle mufflers. I loved hanging out there; it was a pretty cool place to grow up."

Talking about the old days in The Hamptons had excited me for a few moments and helped me to forget about my friends, but as I twirled my spaghetti I returned to my hapless condition and couldn't bring the pasta to my lips. It seemed easier to talk than to eat, so I placed my fork down and continued.

"Like those of our neighbors, our cottage wasn't much of a place, only twelve hundred square feet of plywood and planks making up three small bedrooms, a living room and a galley kitchen, but it was on Noyac Bay. With the back of the house facing west, the days were glistening and the sunsets were magnificent. My folks always called our place their little piece of heaven. I felt that way, too."

I stopped talking but still couldn't eat and took only a small sip of wine. The red felt good going down, filled in the tiny parched cracks in my throat and there was a slight burn in my empty stomach where it settled. Again, I raised my fork and twirled it in the pasta, but I still didn't feel the urge to eat and I dropped it into the plate.

Roxanne took a sip of her wine, and doing her best to ignore my disinterest in her dinner, said, "That's a beautiful description, Gabe. It sounds like poetry. Tell me more."

I felt a surge of anger, shrugged and said, "Today, most of the cabins are gone, replaced by ten thousand square foot McMansions with docks extending a hundred feet into the water. The racetrack is gone, too, morphed into some piece of shit called, Golf at the Bridge, another eighteen hole plaything where a membership fee of half a million dollars allows some lucky rich bastard the right to hit his little white golf balls into little round holes, while looking out over Sag Harbor and basking in feelings of well-being and entitlement."

Roxanne, troubled and concerned by the sudden change in my demeanor, interrupted and said, "You sound angry about that, Gabe. Is it the people, the golf, or just the way things have changed?"

I apologized, saying, "Sorry. Just cranky. It's been a long and terrible day."

"Well, it's just us now. Try and put the rest of it behind you."

I smiled weakly, placed a piece of veal into my mouth and would have chewed it if it wasn't so soft and delicious that it virtually melted on my tongue. Trying my best to get back into the swing of things, I exclaimed, "Hey, this stuff is great!"

Roxanne responded proudly, "Thank you, my good man, but there's no escaping my questions. I want to learn more about you. Tell me more about Gabriel Fortuna."

"There's not much more to tell. I graduated from Queens College, majoring in business and not Phys. Ed. like everyone meeting me assumes, but upon graduating discovered I really didn't care that much about making a boatload of money. I joined the army to find myself but all I found was trouble. A fat sergeant named Bitel had a way of pushing my buttons and abusing the rest of my buddies, until one day I couldn't take any more of his crap, and in a fair fight, just beat the shit out of him. I had to do some fancy talking to keep out of the brig and somehow got an honorable discharge. I became a cop because I was capable with my hands and my head and thought that the streets were a place I could do some good. I did fifteen years, two of them as a detective, until I became so bored behind a desk I asked to be demoted back to patrol duty. I retired early because of some trouble I had with the brass, but because I had information that could have caused the higher-ups some problems, still got a full pension. I'm not rich but I'm not poor and I love living on the East End of Long Island. End of story."

Roxanne nodded her head as I spoke, listened and slurped in her pasta until one strand buggy-whipped and slapped against her cheek, leaving a droplet of marinara sauce where it had struck. She wiped it away with a giggle and asked, "What about your family?"

I answered, "My parents were New York City public school teachers. They're in their late sixties now and a few years ago moved to Florida. They knew how much I loved it out here and left me their place in Noyac." After a sip of wine, I added, "I had a brother."

"Had?"

"He accidently drowned when we were kids. There was nothing anyone could have done. Nobody's fault. I miss him."

"I'm sorry, Gabe."

I said, "That's okay." Shrugging again, I added, "That's life."

Roxanne stared into her veal, built up some nerve and raised her eyes to mine. She asked, "Ever been married?"

"Once."

"Want to talk about it?"

"No."

"Friends?"

"Not many."

And that was that.

We finished eating, and Roxanne, noticing that I'd mostly just moved things around in my plate, said, "You didn't seem very hungry, Gabe. That's alright. I guess it's a lucky thing I forgot to serve the salad." Smiling warmly, she confessed, "I guess you can tell I'm not very experienced at this dinner date stuff."

I answered, "You did great, Roxanne. Dinner was delicious and you were a wonderful hostess. If there was anything wrong, it was in my spirit and not in your food."

Roxanne's face brightened with an idea and she said excitedly, "Hey, we can have the cannolis for breakfast." Standing, she tossed her napkin onto the table and added, "I'll clear the table. Why don't you go inside and start a fire."

I left the table and not finding any real wood, took a Duraflame log from a group of five lying to the side of the hearth. I placed it into the firebox, lighted it at the arrows, and sat on the sofa watching its paper burn towards the center before the entire chemical log illuminated with a sudden *'whoosh'*. Roxanne finished in the kitchen, sat beside me and asked if there was anything I wanted before she closed her eyes and kissed me softly on the lips. We sat there for a long while, looking into the orange and red flames of the fake log, and I felt a comfort I hadn't felt in too long a time.

Finally, she said, "Gabe, why don't you go upstairs and get some sleep. I'll see you in the morning after you get some rest."

From years of suffering a bad habit, I foolishly asked, "Aren't we going to sleep together?"

Roxanne looked at me through sparkling but sorry eyes and said, "I told you before, Gabe, a person is not necessarily what she looks like. I've been with only four men in my life, and one of them was an *uncle* my mother brought home because she was lonely. I was only fifteen and my mother never found out what that man did to me because I didn't want to hurt her. Sylvester was my last lover and I haven't been with him in three years. He's become more like a brother to me than anything and I don't sleep around no matter what the magazines say. You were my dinner guest. I like you because I know who you are and what you've done for me and for others. If I ever was to sleep with you, it will be on my terms."

Roxanne ran her long fingers through my hair and through a soft laugh, said, "You don't want sex now, Gabe. Go upstairs and get some sleep. I'll see you in the morning."

Never before had I been happy about leaving a beautiful lady without first making love to her, but Roxanne was right, I needed rest. I went up the stairs, stopped at the railing in front of the second bedroom door and looked down into the great room.

I called, "Thank you, Roxanne. Good night."

Roxanne craned her neck backwards, looked up at me and responded, "Good night, Gabe. I'll see you in the morning."

For a minute, I remained at the railing and looked down upon her as she sat still in front of the fire, her legs curled beneath her as she watched and listened to the iridescent chemical flames crackle and pop. I sighed and went into the bedroom, undressed completely and crawled under the white down comforter. Closing my eyes, I pulled the cover up to my chin and fought off the thoughts of all the bad crap that was happening. I concentrated on Roxanne: her lovely smile, her kindness and the way she excited me, and a few moments later, I was gone.

18

The next morning I awoke to the muffled sounds of people arguing outside my bedroom door. It took a couple of seconds to remember where I was, but once I did I hopped out of bed, threw on my short rise boxers and hustled out into the narrow hallway.

Looking over the railing and down into Roxanne's living room, I saw she was surrounded by a group of black men, one of whom was Sylvester Hightower. He must have felt my presence because he suddenly turned his head up and stared at me. A tight scowl was plastered on his seedy face, and his light blue contact lenses danced behind a pair of thick Armani faux designer glasses. Romey was there and he was looking up at me, too. His eyes weren't blue or dancing and he wasn't wearing glasses, but I could easily see the menace in their too quiet composure. The other three men in the group were young and merely looked up at me with blank faces, passively waiting for the order from Hightower that would have sent them careening up the stairs after me. I hoped Hightower didn't give that order because it looked like a twelve foot drop from the upstairs hallway to the hard oak floor below and those three boys would have been badly hurt when they hit.

"Ooooweeee!" Hightower began. "Muthafucka is coming out to greet us in his muthafucka drawers. Your legs ain't that nice, man." Covering his eyes, he screeched at an incredibly higher decibel, "Ooooweeee! Muthafucka, I can see up your drawers. You got one muthafucka ugly set of balls. Go back where you came from and put on some muthafucka pants."

I didn't give a shit what Hightower had to say, but I could see tears in Roxanne's eyes and that bothered me a lot. Pressing my legs together in case Hightower was telling the truth, I asked, "You okay, Roxanne?"

Hightower yelped, "Ooooweeee! Muthafucka's a regular Cyrano de Bergerac. Cyrano de Muthafucka mo' like it." Turning to Romey for some sort of maniacal approval, Hightower stuck out his hand for an appreciative slap and added, "You get that, Romey? Cyrano and Roxanne. Standing on the balcony. True romance." Again he screeched, "Ooooweeee!" adding a tight little dance standing in place and hunching his shoulders before saying, "I am muthafucka good."

Romey skinned his boss a light 'five' and looked up at me. Through his deep bass, he asked, "What do you want us to do with the mo'fo'?"

I wasn't about to wait for Hightower to make up his mind and decide he wanted me to get my ass kicked, so I called, "Roxanne, I'm going to get dressed. I'll be down there in a minute." Looking threateningly at Hightower, I said, "Keep your boys downstairs until I'm done or I'll throw them down on top of you." Turning to Romey, I added, "If I have to toss you over the railing, you'll probably put a hole in the floor, so stay the fuck where you are."

Romey glared up at me, fumed, "Mo'fo'," and I thought I saw a small puff of smoke blow from his ears before I turned to get my pants.

I left the bedroom door open to make sure I could hear what was going on and to make sure that if Roxanne needed my help I'd be able to get to her quickly, but it turned out that Roxanne didn't need my help at all. She was tough enough to stand up to Hightower and probably could have done well against Romey, too, if it ever came to that. The summit meeting downstairs turned out to be more of a family squabble than anything, but I still stood at the door, with my pants on, ready and waiting for anything that might mean trouble.

Roxanne said, "I want you to leave my house, Sylvester. I want you to leave now."

"First you explain to me what that man is doing here," Hightower demanded, no street accent from another planet anywhere in his tone. In its place was a mellifluous voice one might have heard on the radio selling mutual funds and disposable diapers to seniors.

Roxanne answered, "That's none of your business. I can invite whomever I wish into my home."

Whom! Nice use of grammar. The objective case. Better not let her fans hear this!

Hightower blustered, "Not my business!!?? Ro, everything you do is my business. Where you eat, where you sleep, what you wear and who you fuck is all my business."

I heard a loud slap and knew it was Roxanne delivering a blow to Hightower's face. I zipped my pants quickly, ran out of the bedroom and looked down to find the would-be empresario rubbing his cheek. Roxanne was standing directly in front of him and breathing hard. No one looked up to pay attention to me.

Pointing a warning finger into Hightower's face, Roxanne said, "Don't ever speak to me that way again. I will not have you telling me how to live my life. You've been good to me, Sylvester, but I've been just as good to you. You know I've stayed with the tour the last couple of years because I felt that I owed you, but I don't owe you anymore. I've put in my time and I've paid you back for everything you've done for me. It's my time now, and I'll do what I want with whomever I want. Do I make myself clear?"

Hightower rubbed his cheek and chirped, "Oooweeee, Romey, girl sure can hit." Finally acknowledging my presence, the rap mogul looked up to me and said in his radio voice, "You better be good to this girl, Fortuna. Cause if you're not, we'll be coming back. You hear?"

I answered easily, "I hear."

Turning back to Roxanne, Hightower suddenly turned into a businessman and said, "Now look here, Ro, you know I still need you. We've been together for a long time and I've got tours lined up all across the country and people want to see RoRoRap perform. You can't back out of our plans. Besides that, you know how much I care about you. I'm just afraid this boy is going to use you and confuse you and then you'll be no good to anyone, not even to yourself. You know what I mean?"

Roxanne lifted her hand to Hightower's cheek, stroked it gently where it still had to sting and said, "I appreciate all you've done for me, Sylvester, but what's best for you is not always what's best for me."

I wanted to puke when Hightower responded, "You know I still love you, Ro."

Roxanne took the bullshit better, and replied appreciatively, "I know, and I'll always love you."

Leaning dramatically backwards and forming a gigantic comma with his incredibly arched back, Hightower screeched, "Ooooweeee! You hear that, Muthafucka? RoRo still has it for S.H.I.T. You remember that, Fortuna. Treat her good or I'll be up your ass with a muthafucka bee's nest. You get me, Fortuna. A muthafucka bee's nest."

Hoping that the putz would soon be leaving, I calmly answered, "I hear you."

Hightower said, "Let's go Romey. The Infamous S.H.I.T. gots things to do. Best we be leaving this muthafucka love nest."

The entourage left the room with Romey trailing the pack, but before he followed the group out to their waiting cars, the huge bodyguard looked up to where I stood and nodded at me, throwing me one last scowl and one last, "Mo'fo'."

Roxanne, who suddenly seemed so alone, stood still with her arms wrapped tightly around her body, gazed sorrowfully up at me and said, "That was so embarrassing."

I replied, "He does know that nothing happened last night, doesn't he?"

Roxanne answered, "Sylvester has always been a forward thinker. He's got a keen view of the future and he's worried about what might happen. It isn't last night he's thinking about; it's tonight and the rest of the nights to come." A playful smile caressed Roxanne's face and she licked her lips before adding, "I wouldn't blame him for thinking that way, considering what you look like bare-chested."

I had been surprised about Roxanne's frank talk about our future and suddenly realized that in my rush to see that she was safe, I hadn't put on my shirt. My pectorals were trembling with an adrenaline pump, my arms were quivering with the need for action and everything was covered by a thin layer of perspiration that made my taut skin glisten.

I said, "I'll be right down," and went back into the bedroom for my shirt.

When I got downstairs, Roxanne was in the kitchen mixing a half-dozen eggs and some milk in a bowl with a whisk. She was sloppy with her work and her herky-jerky movements with the kitchen utensil had already spilled what appeared to be half the mixture onto the granite countertop, forming a bubbly yellow puddle on the ooba juba marble.

It was frustrating work for her and more than once I heard her blow away some relaxed hair that had fallen across her face.

She called over her shoulder, "I hope you like your eggs scrambled. If you prefer them fried, we've got a problem. I always break the yolks."

"Scrambled is fine," I answered.

I leaned against the dining room wall and quietly watched her work. She busily buzzed around the island to try and get things just right for me, paying little attention to anything save her chores except to cast an occasional smile my way. I was noticing everything about her, though. Roxanne was wearing a tighter pair of jeans this morning than she'd worn last night, a pair that better displayed the wondrous curve of her hips and the length and shape of her spectacular legs. I got excited when she reached up to get two mugs from an upper cabinet: standing on her toes, reaching, stretching the denim over her fine round ass, lifting and extending her arm, forcing her breasts to rub and rustle against her t-shirt, the shirt riding above her waist showing three inches of smooth dark skin, the narrow strap of a turquoise thong at the back of her waist, the outline of her bra against her back, a thin smooth line of cotton cloth without clasps that I could easily pull over her head and remove with the just the tips of my fingers.

After she'd gotten the mugs down from the cabinet and placed them onto the counter, she said, "Coffee's ready, if you'd like some. There's a carafe of it waiting on the table. It's hot. I hope you like decaffeinated. It's all I've got."

It was obvious to me that decaffeinated coffee was far from all Roxanne had. I silently left the wall, walked over to where she was still working, placed my arms around her waist from behind and slowly turned her from the stove. She lifted her face up towards mine and I gazed into her half-open green and orange eyes. Slowly, I moved my face forward and down to hers and kissed her warmly and deeply. She responded by letting my tongue search her mouth and by leaning her lower body into mine. She pressed into me, let out a low moan, and her right hand reached behind my head and drew me further into her mouth. I was about to remove a hand from her waist to cup one of her beautiful breasts but Roxanne must have felt what I was about to do and leaned away, breaking our hot kiss.

Breathing deeply, and with a flush to her cheeks, she said, "I liked that, Gabe. I liked that a lot." There was a sizzle behind her and she gulped in some air before adding, "The eggs are burning. Please, go sit. I'll bring breakfast."

Not wanting to do anything that might upset her, I kissed Roxanne on the tip of her nose, walked away and sat at the farm table under the picture window. I silently watched a couple of cardinals feeding at the birdfeeder Roxanne had hung on a tall metal pole outside the glass. The bright red male, trying to catch a mate through the lure of his flamboyant feathers, and the quieter female, gray and dull compared to the male who wanted her so badly nature had made him as bright as it could, pecked away at the feeding trough and spilled seed all over the ground, where a bunch of squirrels and chipmunk had gathered to eat what had fallen.

Roxanne entered the dining area carrying a tray on which were two plates of slightly burned scrambled eggs, another plate holding eight slices of rye toast, stacked high and dry, no butter of jelly, two large mugs for our coffee, and two smaler plates, each holding a day-old cannoli. Smiling, she placed a dessert plate in front of me and said, "Breakfast is served, Mr. Fortuna. We're doing everything backwards today. Let's make the eggs dessert."

We started with the cannolis and smiled a lot but didn't say much. Neither of us ate any of the bread, both of us counting carbs, I guess, and with the cannolis providing more than enough grams of that, we certainly didn't need any more. We both pretty much passed on the burnt, dry eggs, too, but the coffee was good and each of us had two large mugs with Half and Half. After clearing the table and placing things into the sink for washing, Roxanne took the bread slices outside, broke them into small pieces and scattered them on the ground below the feeder. She closed the French doors and found me at the sink scraping burnt egg from her non-stick frying pan.

Smiling, she said, "I'll dry."

We finished and didn't know what to do with each other, so we just stood around, shuffled our feet and felt uncomfortable. After a while, I said, "Well, I guess I'll be going."

Roxanne suddenly took on an unhappy expression and asked, "What are you going to do?"

I answered, "I've got some things on my agenda. You remember what I told you last night. Nothing has changed."

Roxanne wrung her hands a bit, looked around the room like she was searching for something and asked, "Would you like some company, Gabe? I've got nothing to do and I like being with you. If you wouldn't mind, I'd like to spend more time with you."

It occurred to me that Roxanne accompanying me was what I wanted most in the world. I hadn't had the courage to ask her, but I answered, "Sure, Roxanne. I'd love your company."

Smiling brightly, she sang, "Great, I'll get my things."

I watched Roxanne dance away and marveled at how beautiful she was and how kind and generous she'd been to me. I didn't know what I'd done to deserve being with her; it had to be more than being a good cop fifteen years ago, but I wasn't going to ask any questions.

19

The first stop was to my place. With Roxanne seated beside me, I cruised down Major's Path, made a right at its end and headed east on Noyac Road. It was already past eleven, a late start on the day for me, and when I hit the small shopping area in Noyac I pulled into the parking lot. Nosing into a tight spot directly in front of The Whalebone because most of the other spots in the small parking area were already filled by truckloads of mostly Hispanic workers stopping to pick up lunch at Cromer's, I saw Janet Maglie staring at us through the glass window of her store and the expression on her face was not a very happy one. Seeing me riding with a beautiful young black woman either made her realize her chances of coitis with me were gone or she was just totally disgusted. Either way, it was tough shit, Janet Maglie, but I threw her a neighborly smile and waved as she turned her sour puss away.

I said to Roxanne, "Come on. Let's get some lunch. How does a small bucket of fried chicken and some cole slaw sound?"

Roxanne heard fried chicken and put on the ghetto-black voice she must have used in her act, answering, "Cans we have some biscuit wit dat?"

I knew there were a lot of Sylvester Hightower concerts and record sales in her history, but I didn't like that kind of humor and said, "That's not funny."

Roxanne was embarrassed and replied, "I'm sorry. It won't happen again. I promise."

We entered the store and I said hello to Nadine and Jimmy, two long time employees who always worked the registers. We passed them and their incredulous stares and got on the long line at the deli counter where it seemed every Mexican, Costa Rican, Guatamalan, Honduran, Nicaraguan and Salvadoran landscaper's assistant and housepainter in The Hamptons was waiting to put in their orders for lunch. They looked at Roxanne and smiled to their buddies, saying things in Spanish I could not understand, and then looked me over, probably wondering what a near forty year old white guy was doing with such a great looking piece of minority ass. Roxanne ignored them, checked out the blackboard specials and took a firm hold of my hand.

She asked, "How long is this going to take, Gabe?"

I answered, "Be patient, Princess. The wait will be worth it."

Roxanne squeezed my hand, looked like she was about to cry and said, "No one has ever called me, Princess."

I replied, "Then you've been handing around with a bunch of idiots. Get new friends."

Rory, a star-struck teenager behind the counter, took our orders and got our small bucket in between moments of gawking at Roxanne. I thanked him, told him to close his gaping mouth before he swallowed a fly and paid the bill under the suspicious glare of Janet Maglie who had just come into the store under the pretrense of buying a family sized bag of Doritos. We returned to the car surrounded by the warm sweet smell of fried chicken and neither of us paid much attention to the twenty pairs of eyes that had rushed to the glass doors to watch us drive away.

Pulling into my driveway, I saw the yellow crime tape wrapped around Carla and Reggie's house and for a second felt like I was going to throw up. To make matters worse, Gasper's Trailblazer and the dark green Caprice were waiting for us in front of my place.

I turned to Roxanne and said, "Shit. Bad company."

We entered the unlocked door and found Gasper, Ledbetter and Stern gathered in my nearly bare great room. Standing by my new picture window and checking out the view of Noyac Bay, they turned when they heard us enter and each looked at me for only a moment before their eyes went to Roxanne. They looked her over for an inordinately long time and I noticed that only Gasper had a look of disgust upon his face. The two Feds were almost salivating, and the way Ledbetter suddenly cringed when Roxanne pulled her sweatshirt over her head, revealing a tight fitting pink t-shirt, I thought he might have come in his pants.

I wasn't ready for Roxanne to see my super nasty side yet; that could come later, after we knew each other better, so, trying my best not to sound too pissed off, I asked, "What are you guys doing here? I didn't know I'd given you permission to enter my place any time you want." Placing the chicken bucket and the bag of cole slaw on the counter, I impatiently added, "What the hell do you want now?"

Stern stepped away from the window, removed his eyes from Roxanne, put them on me and said, "We understand you visited your ex-wife again."

"That's right," I answered, keeping my reply short and sweet.

It then became Ledbetter's turn. Having recovered from undressing Roxanne with his eyes, he said, "We told you to stay away from her. Al Shareef has been dead for five days and we've had to talk to you about keeping out of it at least that many times."

I said with a shrug, "So? I don't take orders from you."

Stern uttered, "Wise guy," and then lashed out, "This is the last time we're going to tell you, Fortuna. Stay out of this. It's Federal business. Next time we come to you, it'll be to put you in shackles and you'll be spending time in a lockup."

I barked, "You can't do that. You've got nothing on me."

"Can't we?" Stern warned. "Just try us."

Ledbetter produced a slimy smile and interrupted, saying, "Who knows? Maybe if you'd minded your own damned business your friends next door would still be with us."

I walked across the room, and not wanting to bust up Ledbetter's face because that might have made even bigger trouble for me, punched him flush in the stomach with only half my strength. His eyes bugged and his tongue hung out of his mouth before he doubled over and began gasping for air. I turned to see if Stern wanted some of the same and found him standing beside the fireplace with his gun pointed at me.

He said, "You could be arrested for that," and glancing down at Ledbetter, who had dropped to his knees and was puking up some yellow bile, added, "but I guess he might have had it coming."

I figured there was no love lost between Homeland Security and the FBI and replied, "Get the hell out of my place."

Stern smiled cruelly and placed his pistol back into his shoulder holster. He and Gasper each took an arm of the downed Fed and helped Ledbetter to his feet. Some yellow bubbles were dripping down his chin and he wiped them away with the back of his hand before regaining some strength. Throwing off his cohorts, he warned, "I'll get you, Fortuna," and stumbled out of my house under his own power. Stern departed also, after throwing a wicked smile Roxanne's way, but Gasper hung behind.

The top cop stopped beside me and said, "I warned you. Stop looking for trouble." Turning his attention to Roxanne, he asked, "Who's the moulie?"

I answered through a deep, dark and dangerous voice, "Get the fuck out, Gasper. Get the fuck out and don't come back. If you do, what I did to Ledbetter will be nothing compared to what I do to you."

Gasper looked at me with eyes that were not so hurt as the ones he'd used to question my loyalty six years earlier when he'd advised me not to marry Teresa. I'd told him to get lost then, also. He was deeply hurt when I'd chosen pussy over him, but now his eyes told me he didn't give a shit. We were through. He smirked and left my place without looking back.

Roxanne approached and asked, "Who was that?"

I answered, "Two strangers and an old friend. The suits are federal officers investigating the Al Shareef murder. The guy in the khakis and flannel shirt is Gasper Dupree. He's a captain in the Town Police. He used to be my best friend."

Roxanne shook her head trying to get everything orderly and asked, "Used to be? What's changed?"

I answered, "Everything."

Roxanne looked at me quizzically and I decided to change the subject from policemen and broken friendships to physical therapy and said, "I've got to hit the the gym for an hour. Care to join me?"

She hadn't brought a change of clothes and wouldn't work in what she had on, a nice pair of semi-tight Polo jeans and an Italian knit t-shirt that the Feds had found so alluring, but came to the gym, sat on the flat bench and watched me do my thing.

I started with stomach work as always, doing the hundreds of crunches and leg raises, side twists and leg lifts on the Roman chair. Then, I hit the universal for three sets of fifteen repetitions of pyramiding military presses with weights from one hundred to two hundred pounds. Roxanne was nice enough to spot me when I struggled with the last couple of reps at the heaviest weight, just putting her fingertips beneath the bar to help me to lift it. I did my lateral raises to work the outside of my deltoids and finished with straight arm raises to work their fronts. I threw smiles at Roxanne in between sets and she seemed to enjoy watching me, but I felt self-conscious doing this stuff in front of her, acting like I was Mr. Cardinal and this is what I did to lure my mate. I did my best to shrug off my sense of foolishness and hit the leg press, again doing three sets of fifteen, this time with weights from three hundred to four hundred and fifty pounds, and then went to work on my quads with leg extensions, the backs of my leg with hamstring curls and finished up with calf raises holding fifty-pound dumbells in either hand. My shoulders already felt sore but my legs didn't hurt. That, I knew from experience, would come tomorrow, when I might find it difficult to walk.

When it was clear I was finished, Roxanne said, "Whew, you are one strong mother."

Toweling myself down, I replied, "You should have seen me ten or fifteen years ago when I was really an ox."

She responded, "Have you forgotten? That was when we met, and you were the most handsome ox I'd ever seen."

I walked over to Roxanne and kissed her softly on the lips. She responded by closing her eyes and keeping them closed even after I pulled away.

I said, "Wait here, or on the deck, or wherever you like. I'm going to take a shower and then we'll have a little picnic. There's someone I want you to meet."

I finished showering, got dressed and entered the great room to see Roxanne in front of the fireplace examining Reggie's broken picture. Although she threw a happy face my way, she quickly returned to the torn artwork and said, "This is really beautiful. Who would do such a thing to something as lovely as this?"

I answered darkly, "I don't know, but when I find out they're going to be sorry they were ever born."

Roxanne shot me a worried look and said, "I don't like that kind of talk, Gabe. It scares me. It reminds me of when I was a little girl and everything was settled with somebody getting killed. I can't have that in my life."

I understood her trepidation and replied, "I'm sorry, Roxanne. I'm just angry and venting. My friend painted that picture and gave it to me just before she was murdered. I won't let that anger get the best of me again. I promise."

After grabbing the bucket of chicken, the cole slaw and the soda, I took Roxanne's hand and sang, "Picnic time." Happy to see her troubled expression disappear and her glad smile return, I led her out of the house and we walked down Noyac Road.

Roxanne asked, "Where are we going?" and I answered, "I told you I wanted you to meet someone."

Stopping behind David's bench, I said, "David, I'd like you to meet my friend, Roxanne. If you like, you may call her RoRo."

Roxanne read the bronze inscription, and after a sensitive stare directed towards me, looked back to the bench and said, "It's nice to meet you, David. Please, call me Roxanne."

Roxanne and I took our places on the bench, looked out onto Noyac Bay and had a perfect lunch. The chicken was still warm and not greasy, and the cole slaw had the perfect tang. We shared the two-liter bottle of Diet Coke by passing it back and forth because I'd forgotten to bring along cups, and we each laughed after Roxanne let out a small burp because the soda was warm and the bubbles too effervescent. After finishing, I threw our mess into the tall garbage cans that lined the beach, and returning to the bench, I sat beside Roxanne and placed my arms around her shoulders. We just sat there, wordlessly enjoying the fresh salty air, the natural sounds of sea-birds and shore-lapping water, the laughter from those already soaking up pre-summer sun, and the teal blue color of Noyac Bay. During one especially peaceful moment, Roxanne turned and gave me a soft kiss on my neck. She snuggled deeper into my arms and we sat there a while longer, the three of us: my new friend, my bother and me.

20

Normally, I wasn't the cuddling kind, but it was comfortable on the beach with Roxanne in my arms and it wasn't until it started to get a little too crowded with sun worshippers that we realized the passage of time and decided to leave. Back at my place, Roxanne picked up Reggie's picture from the floor, reexamined it and said, "Gabe, why don't we see if we can get this fixed. It's too beautiful to leave broken." I knew she was right, that the painting was special and that the more time you wait to take care of something the less likely you ever are to fix it, so with the top down on the Z4 and Roxanne holding the painting over her head as I drove, we coasted into Sag Harbor at ten miles per hour and dropped it off with Greg at The Grenning Gallery to see if there was anything he could do with it.

We left the gallery and cruised up Sag Harbor's Main Street, passing the quaint old storefronts, the neon lighted Sag Harbor movie house, several nautically themed antique stores, and Ned Parkhouse's classical music palace. Leaving the commercial part of the village, we were suddenly surrounded by large shade trees and big old captains' houses from the nineteenth century. Topped by numerous widow's walks, where forlorn wives had anxiously paced while staring out to sea for ships they knew might never return, they were still the highest points in Sag Harbor. The size of the architecture gradually whittled down and Main Street turned into a tree-lined fantasy of more modest, cedar shake and shingle homes, their original construction dates often going back over two hundred years. White picket fences formed the perimeter of the old houses and red and white geraniums, blue tulips and yellow daffodils grew through the freshly painted white pickets as early sprouting peonies of assorted colors drooped over their tops. After a few blocks of historic buildings, The Whaling Museum and the old Jermaine Library sat proudly across the street from each other, signaling the end of the village.

After fifteen bucolic minutes of driving past centuries old farms, tree nurseries, open corrals, carpenters framing ever new and bigger McMansions and open fields of wildflowers, I reached The Castle and was surprised to find several cars already parked in the small parking area to its side. I recognized them immediately: Teresa's Porsche, Conforti's old Mercedes, Gasper's Trailblazer, and pissing me off big time, The Caddy. I parked my loaner Z4 to the side, allowing anyone who wanted to leave an open exit, and went to inspect my car.

"Kind of big, don't you think?" Roxanne asked as I examined the rear fender for swirl marks. "Who would want a dinosaur like that? It's such a throwback."

I looked at her from where I kneeled beside my ding-free fender and answered with a crooked smile, "It's mine."

"Oh."

"Come on," I said, slapping dirt from my knees. "There are some people I have to see."

We crossed the drawbridge and I pressed the bell. Immediately, we were greeted by Mrs. Al Shareef's voice.

"Yes, Mr. Fortuna. What can I do for you?"

"I'm sorry to trouble you, Mrs. Al Shareef, but if you wouldn't mind, I'd like to speak with you and your son again."

"But I do mind, Mr. Fortuna. When last you were here, you said you would not be returning. The authorities have advised me not to speak with you and that you are nothing more than a problem for them. Why should I allow you entrance?"

I stared into the camera above the door and said with conviction, "Because I think I'm close to discovering who murdered your husband."

A few seconds passed before the doors began their silent retreat. When they were fully opened, I saw Mrs. Al Shareef waiting a hundred feet away at the head of the great room. Wrapped from head to toe in bountiful folds of black silk, she stood with her hands clasped calmly together at her chest.

Roxanne and I walked across the square room and Mrs. Al Shareef never moved to greet us. There were no niceties or introductions and when we were standing before her, the wife of the mudered Muslim movie producer coolly asked, "What information do you have concerning my husband's death?"

I answered, "There are some things I still can't reveal. It's too early in my investigation and too dangerous for you to know the information I've acquired, but I will tell you this, your husband was not killed by terrorists.

Mrs. Al Shareef reflected for a few moments and replied, "This is not the belief of your government. Your intelligence officials are convinced that those who wished to silence Binyamin'a appeals for universal peace and tolerance killed my husband. Are you suggesting they are wrong?"

I answered, "Governments are often wrong. We've discovered that governmental intelligence is almost always wrong. I can't tell you what I think happened to your husband because I still need proof. Right now, all I have is an idea of what happened, but it's a good idea. Until I get something real, you just have to believe me when I tell you it was not terrorists who did this thing to your family."

Mrs. Al Shareef studied my face and said, "Mr. Fortuna, I do believe you. I also do not believe my husband was killed by his own people. It is not Allah's way to murder a good Muslim because one does not agree with his films. I, too, am of the belief there is more to his death that no one as yet sees." Looking to my right, she raised an eyebrow and asked, "Who is this woman you bring to my home?"

Roxanne opened her mouth to answer but I broke in and said, "This is my niece, uh, Lois Antonelli. She's from my father's side of the family, from a mixed marriage with my Uncle Vito. She's visiting from the city for Memorial Day Weekend and I'm driving her around, showing her the scenery. I hope her being here isn't a problem for you."

Mrs. Al Shareef responded, "You Americans, so free in your ways, whom you marry, where you go, how you dress and what you believe." Raising both her eyebrows, she said, "You are a very dangerous people."

I knew she was right, but not for the reasons she gave and asked, "May I please speak with your son? It's important."

She hesitated and I guessed she was still not completely sure I could be trusted. I knew that if I were in her shoes I would feel the same way, and then, she said, "Come with me. I will take you to Yousef."

Mrs. Al Shareef turned and led us down the corridor leading to the rear of the house and the stone terrace. When she was far enough ahead of us, I whispered to Roxanne, "No one has to know who you are. It's safer for you and it's safer for me. Trust me and keep quiet."

We followed the widow out onto the terrace and when we reached the railing she pointed to the white marble pool house where Yousef, Teresa, Conforti, Gasper and Stump McNamara sat laughing it up around a round mosaic and stone table. I noticed that Teresa was seated directly on the kid's right and that her left hand was hidden under the table. The way her shoulder was moving around in tight little circles, it looked to me that she might have been very close to closing a deal.

Mrs. Al Shareef said, "Yousef is there, speaking business with some people from your town. I do not think you need me any longer. I believe you know how to get to the pool." Turning to leave, she had taken only a few steps before she stopped, turned and added, "Good luck, Mr. Fortuna. Please, keep me advised." Then with a rustle of very expensive cloth, she was gone.

Roxanne looked at me incredulously and said, "Lois Antonelli? Your cousin from a mixed marriage? Uncle Vito? Is that the best you could do?"

Taking her hand, I answered, "I was under pressure. Come on, let's go, and remember, keep quiet. Nobody has to know who you are."

The little band of five watched us approach, and although they all stopped talking and took notice, each reacted to our appearance in a distinctly different manner. Yousef turned to Teresa, wearing a sour and pissed expression; for him I was little more than an intrusion to what looked like an approaching happy ending. Conforti carried an angry scowl; he had obviously not mellowed since our last meeting at Teresa's place. Teresa's eyes shifted between Roxanne and me, measuring us both and realizing that I was with a woman at least her equal in sexual attraction; she'd lost whatever power she might have had over me and knew it. Stump was scratching his rusty hair, wondering what I was doing there, and when I saw a surprised look suddenly cross his face,

I knew he realized I had seen The Caddy and that he had better come up with something fast. And Gasper, well, he just stared at me without batting an eye, looking like a hard-hearted stranger. I wasn't happy to see Mustafa and two of his friends standing on the other side of the pool house, protecting the little get together from danger. From the way he regarded me, I could tell he wasn't too happy at seeing me either.

Reaching the table, I said, "Good afternoon, everyone." Nodding towards Roxanne, I added through a friendly tone, "This is my cousin, Lois, from Brooklyn. She's here for the weekend."

The only one at the table with stones enough to speak was Teresa, and raising her hand from Yousef's lap, she scornfully said, "Sure, she is, Gabe. I remember her family. They were from the African branch of the Fortunas, weren't they?"

I did my best to ignore Teresa, smiled like a traveling salesman with a bridge to sell and said, "Well, I don't mean to be disturbing anything important, so why don't all of you just continue. I'll just stand here and stay out of the way. Make believe I'm not here." Taking a step back, I added, "Please, continue."

Armand Conforti slid his wrought iron chair back from the table, stood tall and puffed out his chest. After throwing Teresa a sideways glance to make sure she was aware of his tough guy routine, he petulantly asked, "What are you doing here, Fortuna?" Hiking up his pants, he came into my face like he was a wise guy from The Sopranos, daring me to do something.

Trying my best not to teach the fat slob the lesson he deserved, I answered innocently, "Who me? I just came by to ask Yousef some questions. You see, I've gotten together with a few friends and we wanted to know if the young man was at all interested in selling The Castle to a consortium of local investors. We could break it up and build quite a subdivision. We'd call it, The Castle at Deerfield. Probably keep this place as the clubhouse. What do you think, Conforti? Pretty good idea, right?"

Town Supervisor Conforti took a quick breath, turned a sick shade of red and placed a shaky hand on top of the table for balance.

I looked at Yousef and asked, "Any interest there, Mr. Al Shareef?"

Yousef answered, "You are too late, Mr. Fortuna. I have already come to an understanding with the Town about the property. Ms. Fortuna will handle all the necessary paper work. If you had come earlier with your idea, there might have been a chance for you and your friends, but as my father wished, the Town already has a commitment. My word is my bond."

Gasper shuffled in his chair and gave Teresa a look that told me they'd been doing more in the past couple of years than I'd given either of them credit for. I couldn't blame him. Teresa was a great piece of ass and if he could get himself some of it, well, that was the way nature meant things to be, but watching them made me wonder if his early advice not to marry her was an attempt to protect me, or if he was only looking out for his own interests. The memory of our years not speaking with each other woke me up and I knew it was the second.

Gasper shrugged off whatever discomfort he might have felt and said, "What are you really doing here, Gabe? Whatever friends you might have don't have enough money to buy a half-acre lot in Flanders. You were told to keep away from the Al Shareefs. You're really looking for it, aren't you?"

I gave Gasper a hard stare and said, "I don't know, Gasper. I'm not sure I have to look for anything. I think I may have found it."

Silence surrounded the table for a few seconds and I could see Teresa's face take on a new and unfamiliar expression, one that displayed more than a hint of fear. I'd seen something like that look on her only once before, the night six years ago when I caught her in bed with a cattle baron from Texas who'd contracted through her to buy one hundred acres of Montauk land to build a seaside ranch. I'd clocked him with one punch and then stood over her with a balled fist. She looked up at me with the sheets pulled up tightly under her chin, trembling and wearing a look similar to the one she was wearing at the table. I didn't hit her then and she had to know I wouldn't hit her now; so, why did she look so goddamned afraid?

"I think you can leave now, Mr. Fortuna," coughed the smoky voice.

It was Supervisor Conforti again. He'd regained his composure and was again trying to act like a big man in front of Teresa. He took the few steps to where I was standing and committed the error of placing his hand on my left arm, mistakenly thinking that his title and his touch would be enough to send me on my way.

I ripped my arm out of his grasp, said, "Don't ever put your fucking hands on me again, Fatboy," and pushed him hard.

Conforti retreated a few stumbling steps and flailed his arms, struggling for balance before falling backwards into the pool. For a fat guy, he didn't make too much of a splash. He wasn't very buoyant either.

I turned to the small crowd that had universally risen from the table to see if they were going to have to help the gasping supervisor and said, "I give that dive a four."

"Gabe?" Roxanne gasped.

I stared at her crossly and scolded, "You mean, Uncle Gabe, don't you?"

Gasper separated himself from the small crowd of gawkers and said, "Alright, that's enough. You're coming with me."

I snapped, "I'm not going anywhere. Your boss put his hands on me first. Even if you won't back me on it, I've got witnesses." I nodded at Roxanne, Mustafa and Mrs. Al Shareef, whom I'd spotted watching from a second floor window. Feeling out an old friend, I asked, "How about you, Stump? You saw what happened. You going to back me?"

Watching Conforti take his dip and paddle around the pool with his clothes on had obviously brought the collision man an unexpected treat. Wearing a big smile on his round red face, he said, "Sure, Gabe, you know me. I'm on your side."

I replied, "Sure, you are."

Still smiling, Stump said, "I guess you saw The Caddy out there."

I answered, "Yeah, I checked it out, too. Nice job."

He said, "Well, I was able to get my hands on the paint faster than I thought." Rising from his chair and dangling the keys from his thick fingers, he added, "The boys worked hard on it and were able to finish a day earlier than planned."

"So I see. I guess that means they didn't have to work so many hours. My cost must have come down dramatically."

Stump laughed hoarsely and said, "That's what I like most about you, Gabe. You just don't give a shit." Pointing a dirty thumb at Roxanne, he lost his smile and asked, "Who's the darkie, Gabe; and don't give me any of that Lois Antonelli stuff."

I answered succinctly, "Go fuck yourself, Stump."

He shook his head, grinned like he'd just been defeated in a game of horseshoes and said, "You always was a man of few words, Gabe. Sometimes, they're even the right ones. I guess from your point of view I deserved that, but then, you aren't standing in my shoes." Extending his thick arm, he asked, "You want your keys?"

I answered, "Sure do." Reaching into my pocket, I produced the Z4's. "And you yours."

Gasper fished Conforti out of the pool. The fat bastard shook like a seal when he was on dry land and stared at me with fiery eyes that said he would try his best to get even with me, maybe even do more than get even.

Yousef was laughing and looking at Teresa like a puppy, beaming at the fox standing to his right with only one thing on his mind, and it wasn't his dead father, The Castle or me.

Teresa was different, though. She was staring at me, looking like a lost soul who had finally gone too far and was afraid of eternal damnation. I knew I'd need to talk with her again, but that would have to come later, when we were alone.

Mustafa and his boys were still beside the pool house, apparently keeping out of things unless it was the kid who was threatened. They were laughing among themselves and enjoying the sight of Americans acting like fools. It didn't look like I was going to have any trouble with him, so when I caught his eye I nodded his way, and he nodded in return.

Roxanne and I turned to leave the patio and I glanced up at the second floor window to catch the eagle-eye stare of Mrs. Al Shareef. She'd watched everything and nodded at me in much the same manner as had Mustafa. I couldn't be sure, but I got the distinct impression that I now had some allies on which I hadn't counted.

21

I pulled Roxanne from the patio, through the house and past the portcullis. I didn't want to talk about anything having to do with The Castle or any of the people we'd just left until we were far away from them, so I kept up my quick pace towards the car and called over my shoulder, "We'll be in the car in just a moment, Lois. In a little while we'll be in town and Uncle Gabe will buy you some ice cream at Saint Ambroeus. Just be patient, dear."

We reached the parking area and I tore open the passenger door to The Caddy in an ungentlemanly and ununcly fashion. Roxanne got in with an unamused expression plastered onto her face and I raced to the Z4, pulled the bent club from where I'd hidden it in the narrow space behind the sport car's bucket seats, and scampered back to The Caddy, tossing the nine-iron into its cavernous rear seat.

Roxanne was shaking her hand, trying to get some circulation back into it, and asked, "What are you doing with that golf club?" As I piled into the car, she added, "The next time you want to drag me somewhere, just say, 'Let's go'." Staring into her palm, she concluded with, "Uncle Gabe, I think you might have broken it."

I turned over the engine and said, "I'm sorry if I hurt you, but we had to get out of there. As for the club, that's an important piece of evidence. If what I think is true, it's the key to everything that's been going down. We've got to get to the hospital."

Roxanne laughed, "Hospital? Why do we need to take it there? Is it bleeding?"

I answered, "No, but it is bent and has lost a piece of its shaft. I hate it when a shaft is damaged, don't you? Now, hold on."

I barreled into the emergency parking lot at Southampton Hospital, leaving a cloud of dust as I braked hard in the dirt-covered, rural parking area. With the nine-iron in one hand and Roxanne in the other, I charged into the place and found a few people sitting around the waiting room, mostly young men with their arms in makeshift slings and their girlfriends seated silently besides them with tears in their eyes. I told Roxanne to take a seat and wait for me, and with nine-iron in hand, sped quickly down the hallway towards the staircase doors leading to the morgue. I swung the interior door open and was surprised to find an obviously peeved and uptight Chief of Staff, Doctor Eliot Sanders, standing before me, blocking my way.

"Mr. Fortuna, I assume," he said flatly.

I answered, "Yes," and not wanting to divulge my true reason for being in the hospital, got right to another point and only partially lied, "I'm a friend of Nurse Nichols. I need to speak with her right away."

"I am Chief of Staff, Dr. Eliot Sanders, Mr. Fortuna. There is no need for you to wait for Nurse Nichols; she has been put on disciplinary probation and is not here. When the appropriate period has passed, she will be summarily transferred to another hospital, if not forced to resign completely from her nursing career. As a matter of fact, her professional demise is being discussed with her union right now. Breaking hospital rules is a very serious offense, Mr. Fortuna. Unless you are suffering from some sort of injury, I'm afraid I must ask you to leave the hospital grounds now."

I couldn't stand the pomposity of the guy, but he was probably right for someone living in his world. After all, you just can't have people coming in off the streets asking to view stiffs who've just been murdered and autopsied. I knew that and so did Stacy. There were consequences that came with breaking rules, but this guy's attitude was something I couldn't stand.

Hiding my contempt, I asked, "What about Dr. Greenberg? Is he around?"

"Dr. Greenberg is also on temporary probation and that is more than I need to tell you. Now, what is it that you want, Mr. Fortuna? It's possible that I may be able to help you and then you may leave. If I cannot help you, you may still leave."

Sanders stood in front of the doors, blocking my path to the morgue. He crossed his arms dramatically over his chest to show me he wasn't going to budge, glanced down at my side and noticed the nine-iron in my hand.

He asked, "What are you doing with a golf club in my hospital?"

Time was tight, so I held the nine-iron up to his face and said, "This is why I'm here, Doc."

"I don't understand you, Mr. Fortuna. I'll repeat; why are you here with a golf club? In fact, why are you here at all?"

Not feeling any great need to answer any of his questions, I asked, "Is Binyamin Al Shareef's body still in your morgue?"

"That is no concern of yours, Mr. Fortuna."

"Please, Dr. Sanders, I must know. It's very important that I see the body."

Sanders turned as red as a Bridgehampton tomato and cried, "That is absolutely out of the question. Why, that would make me as criminal as Nurse Nichols and Dr. Greenberg." Through a previously hidden sense of gallows humor, he tried to smile and asked, "And what would you do if I foolishly showed you Mr. Al Shareef's body? Would you smack it in the head with your golf club?"

I almost laughed and wanted to answer, "That's pretty much it, Doctor," but this was too serious a matter for laughs and jokes, so I did something I rarely did; I begged.

"Please, Dr. Sanders. Please, may I see the body of Mr. Al Shareef?"

Whatever humor Sanders had was used up with his one-liner and only his upper class superiority was displayed as he scolded, "Mr. Fortuna, you've been told that that is against the law and yet you persist. Either you leave the hospital this minute or I shall be forced to notify the police that you are becoming a menace and a danger to the well being of patients awaiting treatment. If you do not leave this very moment, I shall see to it that you are arrested."

I showed Sanders what I thought about his bullshit threats by throwing him a tight scowl. The look I threw would have been enough to make most men cower, but Sanders surprised me and trumped my scowl with an incredibly high-arched right eyebrow. I had no choice. I gave the doctor a short, crisp uppercut and caught him on the way down, out cold.

I took off through the double doors leading into the hospital's interior, raced down the staircase leading to the basement, made for the morgue door, and finding it unlocked, entered the tiled room and ran to the wall of drawers. I yanked open Number 8, pulled back the sheet and again found myself face to face with Binyamin Al Shareef. His color hadn't improved since my last visit, and if anything had changed, he looked as if he'd lost some weight, his eyes having sunk a bit and his cheeks having caved into his face, but that deep crease across his forehead was still there, exactly as it was just a couple of days ago. I placed the nine-iron across his forehead and it slid into the slot perfectly. Then, I heard the door behind me open.

I said, "Alright, Dr. Sanders. I'm sorry I had to clock you and run in here without authorization, but I had to see the body."

Turning to face the doctor, I found myself twice as sorry because Gasper was standing in the doorway with his gun out. He was pointing it at me, and from the angry expression in his eyes, I could tell he was thinking about using it.

I said, "What are you going to do, Gasper, shoot me for murdering a dead guy?"

He answered coldly, "Put down the golf club, Gabe, and step away from the body."

I always do what I'm told when someone is pointing a gun at my head, so I gently laid the club down and stepped to the side. Nodding at the short iron, I said, "That's what was used to kill Al Shareef."

Gasper didn't reply, but went to his belt and removed a pair of handcuffs.

My hands were raised over my head but my mouth wasn't gagged, so I continued, saying, "I took it out of Supervisor Conforti's golf bag when I went to Teresa's house."

Gasper didn't seem too impressed by what I was telling him; he just sort of gazed at me with a weird expression, like he didn't know what to do with me. Not wanting him to do anything rash, I added, "Doesn't that make you even a little curious?"

Gasper approached me, his gun pointing at the center of my chest, which is a lot less threatening than one pointed at your face, and said, "Shut up, Gabe, and put these on. I'm arresting you for breaking and entering. I told you to keep out of this. Now, just get those on and keep quiet."

I took the cuffs from Gasper and was about to place one loop around my left wrist when I noticed the morgue door begin to glide open. Roxanne slinked silently into the room, holding the kind of sap you see in *film-noire* movies from the Forties. She took a few quiet steps, crisply smacked the leather sock across the back of Gasper's head and must have known what she was doing because the moment she rapped that thing against his noggin there was a dull, *thud*, and Gasper began his tumble. All I could do was slow his fall on the way down, deposit him in a curled heap on the floor and cast an astonished eye at Roxanne.

She returned to the morgue door, looked down the hallway and said, "We'd better get out of here. There'll probably be others coming soon."

She didn't have to say it twice. I retrieved the nine-iron and in another moment I was at her side, taking hold of her hand and racing to the basement exit. Opening the door to the ouside world, I peeked out onto the street and was surprised to find it quiet, without a trace of waiting police.

Concerned about Roxanne's sudden involvement in my problem, I said, "You shouldn't have done that to Gasper. As much as I appreciate what you did, smacking a cop in the head with a blackjack is a criminal offense."

Roxanne smiled cutely and said, "But, Uncle Gabe, I thought that man was going to hurt you." Turning her cute, little girl smile into one of mature concern, she added, "I believe in you, Gabe, and I'm willing to take my chances where the police are concerned. Anyway, that'll teach him to call me a *moulie*."

It was comforting to know I was with a beautiful woman who could handle herself onstage and off and pointing at the sap, I asked, "Where'd you get that thing? You have to know they're illegal."

Roxanne answered, "The sap was a gift from Sylvester. All the girls in the show have one. He told us you never know when you might have to fight off an overzealous fan. This wasn't the first time I've used it … and I'll bet it won't be the last."

Kissing Roxanne on top of her head, I said, "God bless Sylvester Hightower," and in avuncular fashion, added, "Now, hold on, Lois, and let's get the hell out of here."

22

I prayed that no one had seen and reported a fire engine red, top-down Cadillac El Dorado careening down Major's Path and onto Wireless Way at sixty miles per hour. Racing up Roxanne's driveway, I pulled the car into the parking area beside her house and jammed it to a halt beside her humongous Hummer, hoping that the length of her flag lot, the shielding of her trees and her outrageous purple truck would prevent anyone from seeing it from the road. Running inside the house, I locked the door behind us and stationed myself at the window, pulling aside a curtain like Bogie did in *High Sierra* to see if Gasper or anyone was following.

After an anxious minute, Roxanne tapped me on the shoulder and said, "Gabe, why don't you sit down and relax. I'll put up some water for tea. You can start a fire, if you'd like, and we'll take it easy for a while. It's been a long day."

Roxanne went to prepare some herbal tea and I threw a Duraflame log into the fireplace. I put a match to it, but was far more interested in watching Roxanne puttering in the kitchen than I was in viewing a chemical fire. She'd already changed her clothing, removing her long and loose fitting sweatshirt and replacing it with a gorgeous blue blouse. She'd tucked her tight top into the waistband of her tan corduroy dungaree jeans and I watched it gently pull across her chest nearly every time she moved. By the time Roxanne placed the tray of steaming tea and sweeteners on the cocktail table, the fire in the hearth was not nearly as hot as the fire inside me.

Sitting beside me on the couch, she looked earnestly into my eyes, placed her hand on top of mine and asked, "What do we do, now?"

I didn't know what to say but I liked the way she was looking at me as much as I liked her eyes, her mouth, her skin, her lips and her legs. There was nothing about her I didn't like. Leaning towards her, I placed my hand beneath her chin and lifted her face to where I could more tenderly reach her mouth. I was relieved when she did not lean away and I kissed her fully and softly on the lips.

Roxanne's body trembled, her breathing quickened and she opened her moist mouth a bit wider to accept my tongue. Her hand reached for the back of my head and she pulled me forward until my mouth pressed hard against hers. Breaking free from her lips, I brought my mouth to her neck, where I planted many soft and sweet licks. She pulled me closer and repeated my name gently and softly, before calling me "Darling" and "Sweetheart," terms I'd never been called until I heard them from Roxanne.

My passion climbed and with trembling fingers I opened the remaining buttons of her blouse, spread its halves apart and thrilled at the weight of her sweet brown breasts as they tumbled into my open palms. Each received their share of hungry, wet kisses before I began to swirl my tongue in tight circles around her aureoles. Roxanne's nipples grew tighter and harder, her chest began to heave and again she whispered, "Darling," this time the word leaving her lips in a rush like the wind.

Roxanne pressed my mouth onto her breasts and allowed me to feed on her hard, brown raisins. With a gasp, she pulled my head away from her sweet flesh, gazed into my eyes and panted, "Let's go into the bedroom. I want to make love with you in my bed. Please, Gabe. Let's go now."

We kissed our way across the great room, through the double doors and onto her bed. I laid her gently down, but my fingers worked fast at undoing the buttons to her jeans and she helped me out by lifting the small of her back from the mattress. I pulled gently at the waistband and her pants slid down her legs as easily as a droplet of water trails down a glass. Tossing aside her pants, I knelt to kiss her on the inside of each thigh, where her skin was especially smooth and silky. Her legs began to quiver with excitement and I inhaled the deep, funky aroma of her sex. Leaving her trembling thighs, I gazed down at the soft green cotton thong that hid her privates. I couldn't resist cupping her there, over the soft fabric with my open palm. I pressed ever so lightly with my heel on her pubic bone and let the tip of my middle finger touch the cloth above where I knew her opening must be. Her dampness seeped through the soft cloth and I pressed my fingertip into her ripe passage.

Roxanne bolted upright with excitement, threw her arms around my neck and kissed me voraciously. I returned her urgency but soon broke my lips from hers and worked my hot mouth down her long and silken neck until I again found her swollen breasts. I took her hardened nipples into my mouth, one and then the other, nipped at them and bit them and then released them to the air for a quick kiss and lick.

Roxanne moaned and rocked on the bed, her hips swirled in greater and greater circles and her breasts heaved like volcanoes set to erupt. I removed my mouth from a ravaged nipple and closed it over her yearning mouth as my hands swept her undulating body. My fingertips hit, lingered and then ran from her most sensitive places. She sucked on my tongue with a hard passion and my mind swirled in a whirlpool of heat and flesh. Her hunger and excitement were so great they enflamed me and I feared I would come before I had the chance to bring her to ecstasy.

I brought my hands to her waist and the light green thong came down swiftly and easily, its departure revealing her soft patch of matted brown fur. My lips floated to her naked and exposed mound and I kissed her there as I slid two fingers inside her wet, pink pussy. Roxanne groaned violently and arched her back as my fingers slid slowly in and out of her soft vagina, and I dug deep, exploring her most secret places. I brought my mouth down to her, found her saturated slit, and pushing aside her labia with my probing tongue, I searched inside her silken igloo as if on a search for buried treasure. A low, guttural moan and a more rapid quivering at the interior muscles of her sleek thighs brought my mouth to again kiss at the inside of her thighs, but it wasn't long before I returned to her sopping pussy, where I licked up and down with deep, full lappings. I moved my tongue further and further up her slit until it reached its ultimate destination, stopping directly upon the little pearl that had grown large and pink with excitement.

Roxanne lifted her vagina, forcing her clitoris deep into my mouth. I licked at it ferociously and then placed my entire mouth over its dome and sucked deeply until I felt as if I was pulling the small piece of flesh from her body. Her clit grew more and more swollen under my tongue, and suddenly, I changed my manner of loving it. Instead of sucking on her pearl, I began to violently beat at it with rapid movements of my stiffened tongue. Roxanne emitted a rapturous wail and I removed my tongue from her inflamed clitoris. Thrusting it deeply inside her saturated pussy, I lapped at the juices flowing from her sex as if I was a man dying of thirst, and all the while I drank of her love, I kneaded her clitoris with the tip of my thumb to drive her into a greater sexual frenzy.

Roxanne's body trembled and her vagina quaked violently with the arrival of an ardent climax. She spent luxuriously, calling my name and grinding her sweet wet love onto my face and fingers. She began weeping with the delirium of sexual release and I delicately removed my fingers and lips from her electrified body and sat on my knees above her, between her legs, panting and watching her writhe in ecstasy.

Slowly, Roxanne's breathing subsided, and when she was able to open her eyes, she whispered, "I never knew," and reached out for me.

I lay down beside her and slowly Roxanne's hands traveled down my body. Reaching between my legs, she took me gently in her hands and began her lovemaking by rubbing her thumb slowly over my hard knob, spreading the droplets of precum that had leaked from the small hole at the tip of my penis to lubricate the head of my cock with its own fluid.

After a flurry of soft kisses, my dark angel left my lips and with a gentle push, laid me on my back. Floating between my legs, she began to lick and kiss me along my shaft. Wave after wave of extreme pleasure coarsed through me as Roxanne worked her mouth over and around my swollen head. She sucked hard at the bulbous end of my stiff cock and brought her hand to my testicles, gently squeezing them. I was completely at her mercy and I thought I might die when she tightened her grip on my balls to the point of pain, but magically, she relaxed her hand at the perfect moment and I found I had to fight to stop myself from coming.

Roxanne continued to squeeze and release my balls to a rhythm that matched the pulse of my throbbing meat, and when she suddenly took my seething cock fully into her mouth, giving me the deepest deep-throat I had ever had, I emitted a howling gasp that was new even to me. She slid my saliva-coated, hard-as-a-rock rod in and out of her mouth at a lightning pace, moaning in time with every suck and stroke she gave me. Through half open eyes, I watched her head bob up and down and I placed my hand at the back of her head to aid in her frantic cock sucking rhythm. She brought me along like that until I felt the pressure build inside me and I could not hold back.

I cried, "I'm going to come, Roxanne."

In response, Roxanne grew even more excited and sucked deeper and harder. Her palm cupped my testicles, her fingernails teased my anus and I moaned like a wounded lion as I unleashed a torrent of love ink into her hungry mouth.

Roxanne drank deeply, and as I softened she kept a delicate hold of me, pleasing me long after my cries of orgasm had passed. There were times, when my body had calmed and I lay still that she would lean over and deliver a sweet soft kiss to my knob, where a few glistening love drops would sometimes leak. That move never failed to deliver a silent thrill and those drops were always gone when she lifted her head. A lick over her moist lips told me where they had gone.

With Roxanne stroking me and kissing me and cupping my testicles, it wasn't long before I was hard again. I kissed her neck and breasts, slid two fingers inside her vagina as my thumb kneaded her still engorged clitoris and the two of us writhed on our conjugal bed, our fingers the flames licking us to higher passions.

Rapturously looking into my eyes, she said, "I need to feel you inside me, Gabe. I need to feel that more than anything."

It was the moment I'd been longing for. I turned Roxanne from her side and onto her back and again kissed her magnificent pussy. She let out a soft moan and her reflexes momentarily brought her knees together before she was able to open them wide.

Roxanne whispered, "Please, Gabe. I need you. Make love to me now."

It was hard for me to believe how much I wanted to kiss her warm pink opening. I wanted to shower it with affection, to taste it and love it and make it mine forever, but even more, I needed to do what Roxanne wished. I brought my face up to hers and kissed her, letting my hard cock search between her legs on its own. In a few short heartbeats, it found Roxanne's moist sex and easily slid inside her. She gasped with the first inch I gave her, and then I slowly brought my weight onto her, pushing the rest of my cock deliberately into her yearning cunt. We enjoyed every inch of the thick ride: me, inserting myself inch by inch until I was embedded deep within her, and Roxanne, wantonly accepting me as she rocked her head back and forth on the pillow, gasping and moaning unintelligible words as she matched my downward plunges with upward thrusts of her own.

Gripping my back with her two strong hands, she pressed me tightly to her breasts, and wrapping her long taut legs around my waist, she pulled me more deeply inside her. She groaned and then sobbed, "You're so big, Gabe. I can feel you so deep inside me. You're completely filling me. I love how you love me. Please, Gabriel, don't stop. Just love me. Please, fuck me. Please, fuck me harder. Oh my God, I can feel you in my throat."

I thought my head was going to explode and I began to stroke Roxanne's pussy with faster and faster thrusts until she moaned, mewed and quivered. Her warm flow cascaded down her vagina and covered my hard cock and testicles with her come, driving me further insane with lust and bringing me to unleash a pounding of cock more intense than I had ever unleashed before.

We were both delirious and Roxanne's eyes had begun rolling inside her head. She begged, "I want you to come inside me, Gabe. I want to feel your hot stuff filling me. Please, Gabe. Please, come for me."

I didn't need another invitation and a few more hard strokes inside her warm and beautiful box was all I needed to send a rushing torrent of love down my shaft. As I came, I let out a long loud wail, and Roxanne grabbed me and held me close, calling my name loudly as she came as well.

Timeless moments passed, and completely spent, my body ceased its spasms. I lay on Roxanne, my cock buried deep inside her, and every few seconds she would tighten her vaginal muscles to squeeze out the last of my come drops, until finally, I grew too soft to remain inside her and I fell from her body. The two of us lay silently, wrapped in each other's arms, enjoying our common afterglow, feeling our hearts slow to more normal rhythms. I felt tears in my eyes and couldn't understand where they'd come from, but I knew it was good.

Roxanne found the strength to whisper, "That was the most incredible experience I've ever had. For a while, I didn't know where I

151

was." Gazing into my teary eyes, she added, "I didn't know it could ever be like that. Gabe, could I be in love with you?"

I wanted to tell Roxanne not to confuse great sex with love, but what had just happened to the two of us was different from any sex I'd ever had, too. I wanted to tell her it felt like love, but I didn't think I knew what the hell love felt like and I didn't want to lie. I kept quiet, deciding it was the honest thing to do. After a few minutes of silence, when the only noise in the bedroom was the sound of our slowed breathing, I sat up and kissed Roxanne on her lips. My left hand found the still hard nipple of her right breast and I gently kneaded it with my thumb. Roxanne shivered and I felt a rush between her legs and I knew she had come again.

"Oh, Gabe," she said, quivering and burrowing her face into my chest.

I held her tightly snd waited for her body to calm and soon she was able to raise her eyes. She looked at me longingly and said, "Gabe, what do we do now?"

I closed my eyes and kissed Roxanne deeply. Petting her softly above her love-soaked sex, she moaned in delight, and then, after she opened and spread her beautiful come-covered legs for me, I did her as slowly as anything I'd ever done, and when we were both spent, we fell asleep.

23

I woke up to light passing through the spread bedroom curtains and the aroma of bacon and eggs wafting through the house. Glancing at the clock on the nightstand, I saw it was only six-fifteen, unusually early in the morning for me to rise, but for a change I was waking up with a good feeling instead of a sense of doom, and the early rising only worked to make me feel like I would have more of the day to enjoy. My clothes were in a sloppy pile at the side of the bed where I'd dropped them, and when I got up to put them on, I suddenly felt a little woozy and had to reach out to the nightstand to collect my balance. It occurred to me that my evening with Roxanne had taken more out of me than I'd realized, and feeling too loose and dizzy to get dressed, I draped myself with the champagne comforter and left the bedroom.

Roxanne was in the kitchen finishing up what looked like a breakfast feast. The beginnings of French toast, scrambled eggs, waffles and maple syrup and coffee were already set on the kitchen island, ready to be placed onto the cook top the moment I made my appearance, and Roxanne was working on the counter near the kitchen sink, finishing up what looked like an apple pie.

Dressed in a loose-fitting, powder blue sweatshirt, a pair of snug dark blue denim jeans and thick old sweat socks, the kind you only find at New York City street fairs, her back was to me, and although I may have looked and felt like a conquering Caesar after a night with his concubines, I snuck up slowly on her, like a thief in the night. As she scalloped the edges of our pie, I laid a sweet kiss at the back of her neck and felt her shoulders rise to the chill that ran down her spine. My arms went around her waist and my hands moved to the front of her baggy sweatchirt and then under it, traveling upwards until they found her two magnificent breasts. I cupped them and felt a renewed urge to merge fly through me like a lightning bolt.

Roxanne turned and threw her arms around my neck. She kissed me hard on my mouth with closed lips, her teeth putting up a white picket fence when my tongue tried to reach beyond them. After a few seconds, she moved her face back a few inches from mine and I saw the fine lines of mascara-laced tears running down her cheeks. She raised the back of her hand to her face to wipe at her eyes and the fine black lines turned into broad, dark smudges.

"What's the matter, Roxanne? Did I do something wrong? Have I hurt you? What's the matter, Princess?"

Roxanne buried her face into my chest, and said, "Everything is alright, Gabe. That's what's wrong. I never felt anything like last night. I'm afraid."

Gently lifting her face away from my chest and staring into her beautiful green and orange eyes, I said, "You've got nothing to fear from me, Roxanne. I promise I'll never do anything to hurt you. Last night was special for me, too. I've never before cried with a woman; that's something you did for me and I'm grateful to you for it. I don't know how, or why, but making love with you was really making love. It was beyond sex." After kissing her lightly on her upturned lips, I added, "Don't cry, Princess. Let's just relax and see where this takes us."

Roxanne wiped away some new tears, pushed me lightly away from her, and after examining my appearance, fought back a laugh and said, "Look at you. You're ridiculous. That's a three thousand dollar silk comforter you're dragging around the floor, and I can already see a stain where your little man is poking out his head to say hello."

I looked down and saw that my erection had broken its way through the thick folds of cloth and somehow found an opening in the fabric. It was staring at Roxanne and salivating and I couldn't blame him.

Looking at my new lover, I said, "He likes you."

Roxanne reached down and tucked my penis back behind the folds of silk. Standing on her toes and kissing me lightly on the tip of my nose, she said, "Gabe, as much as I'd like to go back into the bedroom and make love with you, I can't. I'm all sore and can barely walk. Please, understand."

Like most women, Roxanne did not know that the only thing that comes even close to actually making love to a beautiful woman is for that woman to tell you she's too sore from already making love with you to possibly continue. Although there was nothing more I wanted to do than to kiss Roxanne and take her back into the bedroom, her entreaty to refrain from lovemaking that morning was enough to leave me feeling satisfied and cocky.

Holding back my enthusiasm, I replied in a concerned fashion, "I'm sorry if I hurt you."

She responded, "Don't worry, it's a good hurt. Now, take off that stupid toga and get dressed. Breakfast is just about ready."

I got dressed in my previous day's clothing, left the bedroom and found Roxanne seated at the table with our breakfast feast neatly laid out before her. Her eyes sparkled as I walked in and I leaned over and kissed her.

Roxanne breathed deeply, smiled contentedly and didn't say anything. I went to my seat and filled my plate with bacon and eggs and French toast. I hadn't completely realized, until I sat at the table and smeeled all that good, hot breakfast food how the previous evening's lovemaking had virtually exhausted me. I would never have admitted it to her, but I was actually glad she was too sore to make love. I didn't think I could have gotten through another session without having to retreat to an iron lung.

While holding a piece of bacon by one end and chewing it down on the other, Roxanne enthusiastically asked, "Well, what would you like to do today, Gabe?"

I answered, "I can't go home because Gasper would probably have an officer planted there waiting for me. These are the only clothes I have and I can't wear them forever, so if you wouldn't mind, maybe I could stop off somewhere and get some new stuff."

Spooning some scrambled eggs onto her plate, Roxanne said, "That's easy enough." After placing a fresh strip of bacon into her mouth, she added, "I've never been so hungry in my life. What have you done to me?"

I confidently answered, "You can be sure that it's nothing bad."

Coyly, she replied, "I'm not so sure of that."

I was feeling pretty great and was pouring about eight ounces of maple syrup onto my stack of waffles as I said, "Anyway, we'll have to use your car. The Caddy is hot and obvious. We'd be spotted and stopped before we hit Bridgehampton."

Sighing in a satisfied manner, Roxanne replied, "No problem. Mi caro es su caro," and after downing a six-ounce glass of orange juice in one mighty gulp, she voraciously attacked a fresh stack of pancakes.

We finished breakfast, did the dishes and placed them into her dishwasher just like any happy couple that lives together does. It was the most comfortable thing in the world to work beside her, and as we did our jobs, one, and then the other, would quietly and suddenly deliver a soft kiss to our mate on a neck or a back or a cheek, any place we could reach, just because we couldn't help it.

When we were finished in the kitchen, I became concerned that Roxanne was too recognizeable from our trip to the hospital and was at risk if the authorities spotted her. After Gasper got slugged by the sap, he most likely got descriptions of the woman who was with me from the patients in the emergency room. Remembering Roxanne from the confrontations at Al Shareef's and back at my place, he would put two and two together and come up with a pretty good idea of who had slugged him and probably had his men out looking for Roxanne already.

I asked Roxanne, "Do you have anything to wear with which you could disguise yourself?"

"Disguise myself? What on earth are you talking about?"

I explained my fears to Roxanne and she nodded her head in agreement. Telling me to wait on the couch, she retreated into her bedroom and returned ten minutes later wearing an outfit that sent me reeling. The Technicolor gargoyle standing before me could certainly never be confused with my new lover, Roxanne Rosario. This poser at the fireplace was dressed far more flamboyantly than even the young black goddess I'd seen riding in Sylvester Hightower's convertible and might even have needed to undergo DNA testing to prove she was from this planet if she ever was to want a civil service appointment.

Standing on a pair of six-inch, stiletto-heeled, thigh-high turquoise leather boots, she was wearing a shocking lavender, scoop-topped latex t-shirt snug enough to flatten and force most of her magnificent braless breasts over its plunging neckline. This risqué shirt lay under a neon-purple, leather fringed vest, the fringes of which appeared to be contrived from scores of baby rabbits' feet dyed a rainbow of colors. Her leather skin-tight pants were screaming yellow, with broad strips of brown fur trim running up the outside of each leg, and when she turned, I could see that her ass crack had created a perfect equator between each of her spectacularly semi-circular butt cheeks. She turned to face me and I could easily see the crease where her long and athletic legs ended and met her torso on either side of her protuberant sex mound. A four-inch wide belt of large metal hoops circled her waist, separating her torso from her legs, reminding me of old Isaac Hayes videos, where the Seventies rock star came onto the stage chained to his piano. Her face was covered with some kind of high-tech metallic stage make-up, giving it an unnatural and coppery shade of café au lait, and with either a pencil or a crayon, she had colored her eyelids a vivid orange, so that they appeared to be those of a haunting tigress. Yellow streaks extended from the corners of her eyes and tapered outwards until they disappeared into her hairline above the many piercings that invaded the circumference of each of her ears and tiny lobes. Glitter of gold and silver was sprinkled on her high cheeks, giving her a bit of an expression of a dancer from *CATS,* and all of this was set under a preposterous, chartreuse Afro wig that stood at least eight inches high at its zenith. She was outrageous.

I took in this kaleidoscope of colors and shapes with a wide open mouth and the only time I was absolutely sure it was Roxanne was when she smiled at me and said, "Gabriel Fortuna, say hello to RoRoRap." To my eye, she was undoubtedly grotesque, but I have to admit I never wanted anything so badly in my life. It wasn't really Roxanne standing before me, the lovely, charming, giving young lady with whom I had just spent a night of coital bliss. In her place was an even more incredibly sexual and sensual animal placed on this earth for one thing and one thing only, and believe me, it wasn't to rap music.

Catching my breath, I said, "Very attractive, Roxanne. Do you think anyone will notice you?"

She giggled and replied, "Don't be judgmental." Then, tossing me another Afro wig, a red and gray one only about twenty inches tall, she added, "Here, put this on."

I responded, "You've got to be kidding me."

Through laughter, she said, "Put it on, Gabe. If I'm in disguise, you're in disguise."

I put on the wig, looked at myself in the mirror and felt like a complete fool. Then, I figured, what the hell, hunched my back and put on a *gangstah* scowl. Turning to Roxanne, I asked, "Well, what do you think of your homeboy, now?"

Roxanne covered her theatrical face, laughed out loud through her fingers and when she caught her breath, called out, "You go, boy!"

We got the rest of our act together and at ten o'clock left Wireless Way for Easthampton. Roxanne drove and I asked RoRo (I refused to call her Roxanne in her getup) to first stop at the Bridgehampton Commons off Snake Hollow Road and Route 27, where I could sneak into The Big K and get some of the things I needed. Roxanne pulled into a spot not far from the entrance to the store and I said, "I'll only be a couple of minutes. You stay here and wait for me."

Leaving the truck, I caught my reflection in the side-view mirror and was stunned. It had been fun for a while to play dress-up with Roxanne, but being seen with this thing on my head in public was just too much. I tore the wig from my head, tossed it into the backseat and complained, "I can't wear this thing. I don't care if I get arrested and put into jail for a hundred years for something I didn't do; I will not be seen in this wig."

In a few minutes, I had my shopping cart filled with underwear, sweat clothes and a couple of pairs of jeans. Leaving the store, I headed towards Roxanne's waiting truck with an eye out for any Southampton Town Police cars, and when I got close to the truck, I saw the bright colored rainbow waving at me from behind the windshield. Getting used to the look of the wild woman at the wheel, I smiled and waved back.

I opened the passenger door, tossed my bags into the backseat and was just about to boost myself into the truck, when I heard the roar of an engine and the screeching of tires behind me. A white cargo van came to a sudden and jarring halt in the vacant spot at my side. Its panel door was flung open and six Latin Zombies tumbled out and surrounded me. Two of them I immediately recognized from the encounter at my house; one even had the fading remnants of a GF still planted above his swollen, purple eye. The Zombies formed a semi-circle around me and slowly began tightening it. I pressed my back against the Hummer and was plastered against the truck when the front passenger door of the van swung violently open and out jumped Enrique.

He was wearing black jeans, black boots, and a black mesh t-shirt, but what really caught my eye was the heavy gauze bandage drooping from his jaw. It was stained with pus and blood and was, in general, not a very pretty sight. Apparently, the slamming of the van door into his face had done more damage than Esmeralda had told me because Enrique was also sporting two black eyes and a butterfly bandage across his nose.

"MUTHAFUCK!" he screamed.

I looked at Roxanne and saw that no amount of make-up could hide her expression of fear, her once glittering, café au lait cheeks turning a shade of purple to match her vest. Not wanting to further unnerve her, I calmly called, "I'll be just a moment, Roxanne. Please, stay in the truck and keep the doors locked."

Turning back to the Zombies, I saw that this time they weren't fooling around with sticks. Each was carrying a blade: six-inch, double-edged knives with carved ivory handles and sharpened points that glistened in the sunlight of The Big K parking lot. I knew I had to get Enrique first and I had to get him fast. My only chance was to pretend that I didn't give a shit and bait him into charging.

Coolly, I said, "Hello, Enrique. I didn't know you shopped at K-Mart. I figured a class guy like you would do your shopping at Saks. What's the matter, did you lose your personal charge card?"

"MUTHAFUCK!" was his rather high-pitched reply to my query.

It occurred to me that Enrique might have a limited vocabulary, and feeling the vise of The Zombies tightening, I decided to change my style of attack. Extending my hand in a friendly fashion, I said, "Maybe we can talk this over."

Enrique howled, "Talk it over?! MUTHAFUCK! Ju weel never talks again. I am goings to cuts ju up, man. Prepares to Fuckeeng dies."

There was no use talking to these guys; their minds were made up and it had to be either them or me. I had my fists balled into maces and was about to deliver one to Enrique's enraged and bandaged face when a booming voice came from the rear of the truck, causing everyone around the van to tremble and then freeze.

"What the fuck is going on here, motherfuckers!?"

After the initial shock passed, Enrique looked to the rear of the Hummer, and not at first sure of what he saw, but still in awe of what might be, gradually lowered his blade. The rest of the Zombies took a few steps backward, destroying their tight circle and foolishly giving me room to operate. I was ready to level the first one to my left when I made the mistake of taking a gander at the rear of the truck to see who had come to my rescue.

There stood RoRoRap: her hands petulantly placed on her hips, defiantly bent at the waist, her magnificent breasts thrust forward. Leaning her big and beautiful painted face insanely forward, her incredible angle of attack threw it a good two feet in front of her ripe and bootilicious body.

Bootilicious???

Roxanne roared, "I said, what the fuck is going on here, motherfuckers?" Turning from the Zombies and eyeing me with the hard-eyed edge of a ghetto queen, she acidly asked, "You know these motherfuckers, Fortuna? Who the fuck these motherfuckers be?"

I couldn't form an answer, having been momentarily frozen by my multicultural Medusa, but Enrique found a way to stammer through his gauze, eloquently saying, "Jou're RoRoRap." Pointing his finger and smiling around at the startled Zombies, he explained, "That's fuckeeng RoSquared, man."

Ignoring me, Roxanne directed her words at the Zombie leader and blared, "That's right, motherfucker, RoRoRap. Now, who the fuck you be?"

Enrique's peanut-head kept turning from Roxanne, to me and to his boys, trying to figure out what the connection could possibly be between me and his ghetto heroine. Sheepishly, through his gauze, he asked, "RoRo, you knows dees fuckeengs guy?"

Roxanne placed one mighty leg in front of the other, and with her hands still braced solidly at her matchless hips, pitched her yellow, leather covered box at the Zombie crowd, forcing them even further away from me. Then she barked, "Know him? Who the fuck you think been lovin' me since I been out here? Yo momma? RoRo needs it at least twice a day or she can'ts perform, motherfucker. Now, gets the fuck away from my man before I call the Harlem Boys Choir to come out here and fuck you up good."

Enrique cried, "I'm sorry, RoRo. I deedn't knows. I would nots do anytheengs to hurts the mans who is fuckeeng RoRoRap."

The frustrated and enthralled Zombie turned to me and said, "I understands now, man." With eyes begging forgiveness, he added, "Why woulds you fuck Esmie whens ju gots the queen een jour bed? Forgeeves me, man. I promise nots to bothers ju again. Eets all a beegs mistake."

Roxanne was quietly standing with one foot ahead of the other, angrily and anxiously tapping a quick time on the pavement with her turquoise boot. Her tongue was traveling all around the inside of her mouth like she had a gigantic wad of something in there and declared to those watching what it was when she impudently spat out a humongous puddle of phlegm that hit the ground with a loud and angry, *thwack!*

Whoa!!! Fucking Roxanne!!!

"Well, is we through here, motherfuckers, or do I have to kick some fuckin' Latino ass?"

With a defensive shrug of his narrow shoulders, Enrique repeated, "Si,si,si," and closed his knife. Placing it into his back pocket, he shook his head at his great good luck at meeting the great rap star and said, "Holy Mother of Fuckeeng God, fuckeeng RoRo." Trying his best to smile, he said to me, "Muthafuck, ju one lucky muthafuck. Ju weel leeves to haves RoRo in jour beds another days."

I was speechless; I mean, what the hell was I supposed to say, "Thanks?"

Enrique went into his other back pocket, took out a linoleum wallet and removed a bunch of small white cards from one of the stiff folds. Recalling my punching range, he kept his distance and reached out to hand me the cards. He tried to smile, but couldn't, and finally winced with pain. Pointing to the cards, and placing a palm to his aching jaw, he indicated that I should read one.

It read, ENRIQUE SANTIAGO. Under his name, in smaller print, were the words, LATIN ZOMBIE, and below that, his telephone number.

He moaned through the stained gauze, "Anytime ju needs somethings: a paints job, some plumbings, landscapes, Falls cleanups, just geeves me a fuckeeng calls. I geeves ju the best fuckeeng price in the Hamptones."

Then, after a bow to RoRo and a quick flick of his head to the van, Enrique hopped into its front seat and hollered, ""Gets me to my fuckeeng dentist!" The crew piled into the rear and left as they'd come, with a squeal of balding tires and the roar of a heavily worked on engine.

Turning, I saw Roxanne leaning against the back fender of the Hummer, her outrageous ass covering much of that auto body part. I called, "You okay?"

"No," she answered flatly, trying to decompress and return from the land of RoRoRap. When that failed, she snapped, "You didn't tell me The Latin Zombies were trying to kill you."

I shrugged and answered truthfully, "I forgot."

For the first time in our short relationship, I saw that Roxanne might have been a little upset with me. We silently returned to our places inside the truck and I knew that I had to do something to break the tension between us. Reaching into the backseat, I retrieved the wig, placed it upon my head and adjusted it to my thick Caucasian skull. Roxanne turned over the engine as I tried to initiate a dull, homeboy glaze over my eyes.

From under the huge 'fro, I asked, "Harlem Boys' Choir?"

Roxanne turned to me, threw a ghetto shrug my way and answered, "Hey, whatever works." Trying to hold back her laughter, after a few struggling seconds she found she could not and guffawed at my sorry attempt at turning ghetto. Holding her sides, she managed to say, "You look ridiculous."

I retaliated, "And you don't?"

We pulled away from the Big K, and as I was adjusting my wig in the rear-view mirror, I saw a Southampton Town Police car barrel into the lot from Route 27. I ducked under the dashboard with the top of my 'fro sticking up over the glove compartment like a startled raccoon, but the cops passed us without a look. They chomped at their coffee break doughnuts and drove on to the Big K, answering a call from the store management about six belligerant Latinos and two unidentifiable flying Afros.

24

Being the Friday morning before Memorial Day, we found ourselves mired in stop-and-go traffic the moment we hit the six-block long village of Bridgehampton. Movement was especially slow at the blinking yellow light in front of The Candy Kitchen and at the traffic light stationed at the windmill at the intersection of Route 27 and Ocean Road. We managed to crawl through town and eventually reached the light at the windmill where I ordered Roxanne to hang a right onto Ocean Road. Heading south towards the Atlantic, in less than a mile we reached Bridge Lane, leaned a left and raced across the south of the highway side of Bridgehampton.

Roxanne and I began traveling through some of the most expensive real estate in The Hamptons, and that meant some of the richest real estate in the world. We were surrounded by farmlands, stables, mansions, private golf courses, private tennis clubs, shooting ranges, orchards, vineyards, magnificent subdivisions of Hampton's style homes, and off in the distance, on the dunes of the Atlantic Ocean, the Rennert Mansion, the largest private residence in the United States.

The scenery made it abundantly clear that there really was something special about living south of the highway. It wasn't just some shit from a privileged landowner who happened to own a piece of the coveted land or a trusty sales line used by ambitious agents to perspective buyers. And even though the mere words, south of the highway, did raise the value of houses situated there, the light really was different, the natural grasses and streams and coves really were outstandingly beautiful, and the great ocean really was always just a short walk or bike ride away. Add to that the millions, no, make that billions of dollars estate owners had poured into their private worlds of luxury and opulence, and anyone with eyes would have to admit that this was one spectacularly precious piece of earthly paradise.

We flew through Sagaponack and Wainscot and reached the entrance to Easthampton Village where Montauk Highway turned into a mature tree-lined boulevard of tall, thickly trunked and fully leafed maples, gingkoes, oaks and elms. Continuing past the renowned Easthampton Jewish Center, where celebrity Hebrews often congregated on Saturday mornings before their afternoon golf matches, we hit Lily Pond Lane and the bucolic grace of Easthampton Pond. Its family of white swans floated languidly on the still pond waters and greeted us with majestic silence, their beauty and grace further enhancing the promise of 'the good life' the word Hamptons insinuated. On a quiet and natural slope was the old village cemetery. The centuries old stone markers had been worn by rain, snow and wind and the names of those who lay beneath the grass could often not be read. It was tranquil and serene, telling nothing of the vibrancy and trendiness of the commercial district that began only four blocks down the road.

Reaching the heart of the bustling village center, I told Roxanne to make a right hand turn down the small lane immediately past the movie theater. We parked in the Citerella parking lot and were lucky to get a spot because the village was as alive as an ant colony, filling up with locals, summer renters and year-rounders hastily buying supplies for their Memorial Day get-togethers. We got out of the truck and made for Main Street, blazing a trail through the growing crowd that surrounded us, and saw across the wide street Dreamland Properties, with what appeared to be a long line of people waiting at its door.

I turned to Roxanne and asked, "You sure you want to come?"

She answered, "We're a team now, Gabe."

"It's just that Teresa is my ex-wife and I don't want you to feel uncomfortable."

"When was the last time you slept with her?"

I answered honestly, "Six years ago." I didn't think I needed to mention all the times in between that I'd wished I'd been sleeping with her.

Roxanne replied, "I'm fine with that. Let's go."

We pushed the pedestrian crossing button at the intersection of Newtown Lane and Main Street but still had to wait five minutes for the light to change to allow us to cross safely. The cops standing in the middle of the street trying to control traffic weren't any help because they weren't cops at all, merely local teenagers who'd gotten high-paying summer jobs because their parents lived in Easthampton, knew someone on the town board and were able to call in some favors and get their kids summer work. Nobody really listened to them, but their bodies served well to separate opposing lanes of traffic.

During our ride, I must have gotten used to Roxanne's disguise and my own questionable appearance, but no one in town had spent the necessary time to adapt their small world views to allow for the two urban invaders presently attacking their town. The shocked expressions on most of the blond tennis racket carrying women spread to the brunettes in coulottes and capris and then to the redheads in jeans and cargo pants. The lascivious grins of the many bald, cigar-smoking land barons, and the disapproving glares they received from their wives and girlfriends, told me, as I'd expected, that Roxanne's disguise was not going to go over so well in this not-so-quaint Hampton's village one hundred miles east of Manhattan.

The kids enjoyed us, though. Lots of them were pointing fingers and mouthing, 'RoRo', as if it couldn't possibly be her walking past their Starbucks. It occurred to me that Roxanne probably would have been less conspicuous dressed as one of the Seven Dwarfs, but it also occurred to me that the costume she wore had saved my ass when the Latin Zombies came knocking at my door.

We broke through the line of startled and entitled young wannabes and entered Dreamland Properties. As I expected, the waiting room was already filled with a humming crowd of people, the multitude sitting with clipboards on their laps, filling out questionaires that would inform the Dreamland agents just how much money their clients were looking to spend on a hot Hampton's property. We approached the once-bored receptionist who'd developed a more superior attitude than she had just a few short days earlier because she was working in a busy office, one into which people were flocking with the mad desire to spend a couple of million dollars for a weekend plaything. She was determined to prevent anyone from seeing an agent without first getting through her, but I wasn't looking for her permission when I told her I was going

165

to visit Teresa; I was just being nice. I could see from her expression that she nearly recognized me from my visit the other day, but my wild Afro confused her and she couldn't be sure.

Pointing at Roxanne, she asked, "Are you expecting to see Ms. Fortuna with that?"

I answered, "That's right, with her. You got a problem with that."

The receptionist surveyed the crowded room of potential buyers who had stopped filling out their questionaires and were now staring at the two refugees from Sly and The Family Stone. She turned back to me, and being a much better receptionist than I had given her credit for, defiantly answered, "Yes, I do have a problem with that."

I instructively replied, "Then you can go screw yourself," and once again grabbed Roxanne by the hand and pulled her through the shocked crowd of property seekers.

Passing through the slack jawed crowd of big spenders, we made it to the end of the corridor and Teresa's office. I threw open the door and was surprised to find my ex-wife seated alone behind her desk, a bottle of Johnny Walker Blue Label in front of her for company. Her makeup was smeared and her hair was in her eyes, but she still managed a crooked grin when she recognized who was standing at her door under an antique Afro. That drunken smile quickly morphed into a scowl when I pulled Roxanne into her office and shut the door behind us.

Teresa slurred, "What the hell did you bring that thing for? I got a business to run. Someone sees that and no one will be buying. Get her the fuck out of here."

I wanted to kick Teresa's ass for saying that and for a million other reasons, but there were things I needed to find out from her first. I asked, "What's with the morning drinking, Teresa? Someone might think you were afraid of something."

She eloquently responded, "Fuck you, Gabe," and followed her clever retort with a quick sip.

I smiled confidently, shook my head and said, "Never again, Sweetheart, but let's not talk about the past. Instead, you're going to tell me all about the Al Shareef murder."

Teresa shot me a hate-filled look, took a larger hit of her scotch and said, "Why don't you tell me. The police are pretty sure it was you who did it." Moving her drunken eyes to Roxanne, she matter-of-factly told my new girlfriend, "They think Gabe killed the Arab because Al Shareef was fucking me. Tell her, Gabe. Tell her I was the best piece you ever had,"

I shot back, "You're pathetic, Teresa. Just look at yourself. You're in way over your head and you know it. You aren't a murderer; you're a whore. Killing Al Shareef was something you never counted on; I know that. I could tell that much when I saw the frightened expression you were wearing at The Castle. Why not come clean and let the authorities know what happened? You'll get less time that way."

Teresa shrugged and gave me the finger.

Classy girl!

Pouring another hard drink, Teresa made believe she was considering what I'd said and belched, "Up yours, Gabe. If anyone goes down, it'll be you. I'm not taking the fall for Al Shareef so long as you're around."

I blasted, "Forget about Al Shareef! What about my two neighbors? You knew those girls, Teresa. They were always nice to you. Who killed them? I want to know why they had to die!"

With the mention of Reggie and Carla's murders, Teresa's expression changed. Although I'd seen she was afraid at The Castle, this was the first time I could ever remember her being close to tears.

She groaned, "I didn't know that would happen. You've got to believe me, Gabe. I never wanted to see Carla and Reggie get hurt."

"Well, they were hurt and hurt bad; they're dead. If you don't talk, you're going to go down for that, too."

Teresa nervously ran her fingers through her hair, pushed away her glass and said, "I've had too much to drink. I can't talk this way. I don't know what I'm saying."

Rushing to her desk, I slammed my hands on its top, leaned into her face and said, "Give it up, Teresa, and save yourself. I know who did it, at least I've got a good idea who did, but I haven't got the proof I need to make it stick. I'm still the fall guy. I need you to come forward and tell the authorities what really happened so we can put this behind us. Come on, Teresa. You've got to talk."

My ex-wife stiffened in her chair and said, "Fuck you, Gabe. I don't have to do anything, especially in front of this nigger. I want her out of my place, now. If you want to talk to me, you come to my place tonight at six, after I'm closed and this shit I've been drinking wears off. Get rid of her and come to my place and maybe I'll tell you what you want to know. Or maybe we won't talk at all. Maybe you'll change your mind about things and we can go to bed and do the things we used to do."

I straighted my spine and said, "That's not going to happen, Teresa."

Her eyes filled with tears, fears and memories and she said, "You told me I was the best lover you ever had. Don't you remember. You told me you loved me."

I softened and said gently, "Alright, Teresa, six o'clock at your place. I'll come alone and we'll talk. If that's what you want, that's what we'll do."

Teresa answered through a vacant expression and a hollow voice, "That's what I want."

Leaning over her, I whispered into her ear, "Stop drinking, Terri. Your answers aren't in the bottle. You know what you have to do."

Using the name I called her when we were lovers snapped Teresa out of her reverie. Sniffing in some snot, she wiped her upper lip dry, shot nails at me through fiery eyes and screamed, "Fuck you, Gabe! I'll do whatever I have to do, just like I've always done, and I don't need you or your advice to figure that out."

I was pissed at myself for suddenly going soft on someone who had helped set me up for murder, but I kept my anger to myself and calmly agreed, saying, "Alright, Teresa, tonight at six out at your place. I'll be there. You just be ready to talk."

Turning to leave, I was following Roxanne out the door when Teresa gently called, "Gabe? We had some good times, didn't we? It was fun for a while. We could have had something, the two of us. You should have stayed with me. None of this would have happened."

I turned and looked at Teresa and almost felt sorry for her, but all my love for her was gone. She was just a past; a past for both of us, but a past with which I still had to deal, if only for a short while longer.

I said, "I'll see you at six, Teresa," and shut the door behind me.

25

Roxanne and I left Dreamland Properties and the crowd on the street parted as if I was Charlton Heston taking a stroll through the Red Sea. I wasn't in the mood to care what anybody thought about our appearance, though, and I looked at Roxanne and asked, "Hungry?"

She felt my distress and asked, "You okay, Gabe? That was quite a scene in there. Nobody would blame you if you were upset."

I said, "I'm okay, but I'm starving. We haven't eaten in hours and I need to get some fuel." A second later, I copped to what she had figured out and added, "I'd just like to get out of here."

Roxanne replied sweetly, "Whatever you say, Gabe. I'm with you."

We crossed the street, got back into the Hummer and again headed east on Route 27. We had more than four hours to kill before my six o'clock meeting with Teresa and I wanted to get as far from Southampton as I could to insure no surprise visits from Gasper or any of his officers. That meant Montauk for a late lunch, and I couldn't think of a more comfortable spot for two people wearing sky-high Afros and skin-tight leather leggings than Cyril's.

Getting off Route 27, we hit Egypt Lane, backtracking a short distance to relax and to see a few more of the gorgeous estates located behind Easthampton Village and closer to the ocean. We drove past some formidable mansions and landscapes and then came upon Maidstone Golf Course, another of the old East End golf clubs whose membership list read like the Fortune Five Hundred. Its perfectly set

169

stony clubhouse was on a hill overlooking the ocean, its fairways and bunkers were manicured to perfection, and the soft ocean breezes sent the varied grasses at the fairway edges of the dancing to a perfectly synchronized natural choreography.

"What's with this place?" Roxanne asked, alluding to the entire East End and not particularly Maidstone. "Is everything out here about golf?"

"No," I answered. "There's fishing, boating, hiking, beaches, kite flying, water skiing, wind sailing, great scenery, wildlife, magnificent sunsets, theater, art galleries, great restaurants, beautiful people and that wonderful light that helps make everything appear clean and sharp." Breathing deeply, I thought of Teresa and Al Shareef and added, "But I think golf is what it's all about as far as the mess I'm in is concerned. And if I'm right, it's just too damned strange to believe."

A few miles east on Route 27 brought us to Amagansett, the beginning of the East End that is almost exclusively devoted to the beach and the ocean. Never ending dunes, ocean grasses and row upon row of expensive and modest beach houses of varying sizes, shapes and materials lined either side of the two-lane, sandy, black top that Montauk Highway had become. The cedar style homes of Southampton and Easthampton were not in vogue at the far eastern end of the island. In this part of NeverNeverLand, anything went, and during our Long Island Odyssey we came upon sections of the island devoted almost exclusively to beachfront motels, something that did not exist back in Southampton Township or Easthampton Village, where nearly all the oceanfront property was privately owned by individuals whose goal was to keep people away from the beach, not to lure them with the promise of a romantic hideaway.

Throngs of easygoing people out early for their Memorial Day Weekend were slowly riding their bikes in lanes along the shoulder of the highway, and we traveled among them for a few miles, passing LUNCH, the now famous seaside restaurant with the blue striped awning that everyone in the Hamptons had to visit at least once each summer, and the small sign advertising Montauk Downs, the state-run links-style golf course popular with non-club and golf club members alike. A couple of sandy miles further on we reached the small, ramshackle restaurant/bar with the outdoor flag bearing the name, Cyril's. Roxanne made a left, pulled into the poorly maintained parking lot and we jumped out of the truck.

Cyril's was a roadside place that had become very popular the last few years because of the quality of its spicy Jamaican style cooking, its lively evening bar action and the more relaxed way people from the eastern end of the Hamptons chose to live. Although I was still coiffed in my ridiculous Afro and Roxanne was dressed like a total outrage, we got only quick looks and bright smiles from the swim suited and tank-topped diners who filled the restaurant. Sitting at an outdoor table under an open umbrella, we checked out the specials from a smallboard and a few minutes later a pleasantly smiling black kid with a strong Jamaican accent came by to take our orders.

He said, "The lobster salad is good today," and after checking its price on the blackboard, I responded, "It better be."

It suddenly occurred to me that I actually might be what a local was, someone who looked at the prices on a menu.

Roxanne smiled at the waiter and said, "I'll have a burger, the jerk fries and a diet coke."

The kid said, "Sure thing, RoRo." Turning to me, he asked, "And you, sir?"

I said, "I'll have the same, but no coke. Bring me a Long Island iced tea."

He walked away and I said to Roxanne, "Looks like the kid knows you."

Roxanne replied, "There aren't many places a black woman can go to eat in the Hamptons without feeling conspicuous, especially if I'm out with a character like Sylvester. He likes the attention but I don't. The people out in Montauk are more mellow, not so celebrity conscious as the folks in South or Easthampton. Anyway, I know the owner. He's a nice fellow and makes sure I don't get bothered. No big deal."

I was still in a funk about Teresa and Roxanne felt it. We ate quietly, with me getting my thoughts together, and I appreciated how she left me alone to do that. I brooded for a while longer and finally she said, "You know, Gabe, you're not going to Teresa's place without me. We're in this together."

I answered, "It could be dangerous. I'd rather you weren't there."

Roxanne responded, "Gabe, when I saw you sitting in your car outside of *Playthang*, it was like I'd been given a second chance. I may have been a kid when we met, but I'm a woman now. I'm not going to let you get away from me again." Through a sexy smile, she added, "Especially not after last night. I'm not through with you yet, mister. Not by a long shot."

I smiled and said, "Teresa's not going to like you being there."

Reaching across the table and placing her hand on mine, Roxanne replied, "Well then, Teresa can just go fuck herself because I'm going to make sure she doesn't get a chance to fuck you."

I told Roxanne, "That wouldn't happen. I'm with you now."

Roxanne replied, "And I'm with you. And that's the way it's going to be."

Finished with our small talk, we mapped out what we would do when we met with Teresa at her place on Mecox Bay and I was glad Roxanne was included in the plans. She definitely had some good ideas and I was glad to know I finally had someone on my side. In the background, Jimmy Cliff came on the jukebox and wailed the soundtrack from an old art house movie, The Harder They Come, and as we finished our lunch, I hoped he was right when he sang, "The harder they fall."

The Jamaican kid arrived at our table to take the plates away, asked if we'd like anything else and through a toothy grin informed us that lunch was on the house. I knew the freebie wasn't being given to us because of my good looks and was impressed with Roxanne's pull because I'd been coming out here most of my life and nobody had ever given me anything for free except trouble. Recalling how Roxanne had sapped Gasper, saving me from jail time or worse, and how she'd taken everything in bed that I could deliver, I knew that no matter how troubling my recent fortunes had been, I was still luckier than most guys could ever dream of being. We rose from the table and I placed an arm around her waist. Drawing her to me, I kissed her cheek.

"What was that for?" she asked.

I answered, "That's for everything you've done for me." Pulling her closer, I kissed her firmly on the mouth and fed her the tip of my tongue. Our lips parted and I added, "And that's for everything you're going to do."

We left the retaurant, and with more than two hours to kill before our meet with Teresa, I made a left and headed towards the Village of Montauk. Here the traffic was light and we buzzed past

Montauk Downs, Hither Hills State Park and Gurney's Seaside Inn before reaching the beachside town named after the Indian tribe of the same name. Rows of wood-paneled Chevy station wagons from the Sixties, surfboards sticking out their open tailgates, lined the six-blocks of commercial district, with bait, tackle and reel shops, fisherman's clothing stores and a myriad of pancake houses and pizzerias making up most of the stores. We left the village and after a couple of leisurely miles of dunes and ocean grasses came to Montauk Point and the Montauk Point Lighthouse, an over two hundred year old structure commissioned by George Washington signaling the approach of land after a long Atlantic journey.

Parking the truck in the visitor's lot, we walked around the lighthouse on the huge stepping-stones that had been dropped at the edge of the cliffs to prevent further erosion taking the lighthouse into the sea. We stopped at a spot where the waves crashed, sat on our own boulder in the ocean and removed our shoes. Gulls and water and fishing boats and sky were the only things we could see. I remarked that three thousand miles away was Europe and that between that continent and us was nothing save the never-ending ocean.

I said, "Makes you feel small, doesn't it?"

Roxanne answered with a light kiss to my neck.

I placed my arms around her shoulders and pulled her close. She nestled into me and sighed. It was good.

26

We made great time traveling against traffic, and except for one ancient Ford Pinto that nearly caused an accident as if flew out of Mecox Road and onto 27, it was easy going. Pulling into Teresa's driveway fifteen minutes early, we camped the Hummer down beside the only other car parked in front of the house, my ex-wife's pink Porsche. I jumped from the truck, climbed the short flight of stairs and was surprised to find the door ajar. I knew Teresa was expecting me and might even have been planning something special for the two of us, considering that she thought I was coming alone, but I hadn't expected her to be this inviting.

Roxanne must have been thinking along the same lines because she came up beside me and said, "Seems like Teresa doesn't want anything to slow you down. If that woman is in her bed, naked and under the covers, we're leaving until she puts something on. You got that?"

I got it, but I knew Teresa's ways. She liked to answer the door naked when expecting a lover, subtlety never having been her strong suit.

I gently pushed open the front door and we entered the silent house. The sprinkler system hissed on early for its six o'clock watering and was enough of a surprise to send Roxanne leaping into my arms. Even in my precarious situation and her outrageous costume, touching her was enough to bring back a vivid stream of memories from our recent lovemaking. I folded my arms around her waist, squeezed and joked, "Don't be so pushy Roxanne." Then, relaxing my arms from around her waist, I let them fall to her round, leather bound butt. I pulled her into me again and a light sparked in her eyes that told me she was remembering last night, as well. Her breath came shallow and fast and I teased, "There'll be plenty of time for that later."

Roxanne broke away from my timid resistance and turned her attention to the interior of Teresa's place. Checking out the entryway, the living room, the fabulous ocean views and the fine furnishings, she unenthusiastically said, "Nice place." Turning to me, she added, "Please, don't do that again, Gabe. What happened last night was special. Don't make me feel cheap, as if I was just another one of your girls. I won't have it."

Roxanne was right and I was just about to apologize when I noticed the trail of dark impressions in the carpet. They led to the master suite, but weren't footprints; they were the kind of marks that heels make when a person is pulled along a thick rug. I got a bad feeling and followed them into Teresa's bedroom. The door was closed, but unlocked, and I opened that, too, with a gentle push.

From the open doorway, I saw Teresa's bed was unmade and sloppy, the comforter and sheets scattered about as if two people had recently made violent love on top of them. I completed my visual observations with an olfactory one; the unmistakable odor of recent sex filled the room. It occurred to me that if Teresa had been intending to use me for a wild fling, then she had first used someone else as a warmup, a nasty thing for her to do knowing how much I detested sloppy seconds. My mind switched to thoughts of Fatboy Conforti giving it to her and I shivered. Making sure not to touch anything, I entered the bedroom, carefully walked past her antique furnishings and glanced into her cavernous master bathroom. What I saw made me want to puke.

Teresa was in her tub, surrounded by millions of tiny pink bubbles and sitting as upright as a dead person in a filled bathtub could sit. Her head was arched back onto the porcelain, so that her long and lovely neck was fully exposed, and each of her arms was stretched above the water, her hands resting on the sides of the tub, palms up, giving her the appearance of a martyr on a white porcelain cross, but there was no cross and Teresa was certainly no martyr. Her wrists still dripped red and tiny scarlet rivers flowed awkwardly down the side of the tub in a zigzag pattern, pooling where they met the marble floor. In the middle of the puddle lay a double-edged razor. It occurred to me that when

I'd told Teresa, "Come clean," she might have taken me too literally. It further occurred to me that when I make observations like that, someone ought to kick my ass.

Roxanne had trailed me into the bathroom but wasn't prepared for a scene like this and sceamed, "Oh, my God!"

I ordered, "Don't touch anything. Whoever set this up might have left something behind. The police will go through the place with a microscope and we don't need anything of ours corrupting the crime scene."

Roxanne cried, "Crime scene?" Looking sicker with every moment, she implored, "Look at her, Gabe. You saw her this afternoon. We knew she was afraid, but how could she kill herself?"

I walked over to Roxanne, placed my hands on her shoulders and guided her out of the bathroom. Back in the bedroom, I turned her face up to mine and said, "Teresa didn't kill herself. She wasn't the type to wash away her dirty blues with bubbles and a razor blade. That's what men were for. She's dead for only one reason. Somebody killed her."

Roxanne burped sourly and said, "I think I'm going to be sick."

I responded, "There's a powder room on the second floor. Go do what you have to do and when you're finished we'll leave. I'm going to look around down here for a while longer. And remember, touch nothing."

Roxanne placed her hand to her mouth and rushed off to find the toilet. I went back to the bathroom and sorrowfully looked at Teresa.

Avoiding the slowly spreading pool of blood, I approached my ex-wife and gave her a quick examination. The underside of one of her arms had small bruises where someone would have grabbed her if he'd wanted to drag her across the living room floor. There was also a small hickey on the left side of her neck, something she certainly wasn't sporting when we'd visited her place earlier in the day, and a couple of her finger nails had jagged ends where they'd recently been broken. I recalled that Teresa insisted on having weekly manicures and I would have bet a lot of money that pieces of her broken nails could be found either in the bed or bedroom carpet or floating in one of the scarlet pools on the bathroom floor. Wherever they were, it was clear to me that Teresa had not gone down without a fight.

"Step away from Teresa, Gabe, and put your hands where I can see them."

Raising my hands above my head, I turned and said, "Hello, Gasper."

Once again, my old friend was standing in a doorway with a service revolver pointing at my head. Taking a quick look over my shoulder at Teresa, a shadow passed over his face and he said, "I'm going to walk out of here backwards, Gabe. You're going to follow me. Don't make any sudden movements. If you do, I swear I will shoot you. Do you understand me?"

Noting the dark aspect to my old friend's eyes, I knew he wasn't lying; Gasper would definitely have put a couple of holes in my well defined pecs if I didn't do exactly as he said. I nodded my head up and down in agreement, and with my hands raised I followed him out of the bathroom.

Gasper had known Teresa a long time, going back to when she was a teenager in Sag Harbor and he'd first become a cop. Back then, he'd never spoken to me about her, but I'd often heard her name bandied about in local bars. I decided to find out what all the fuss was about and dropped into The Espresso House on Henry Street, the place she worked on weekends making sandwiches and serving coffee. She looked great in her white apron and the second I saw her I wanted to be with her. She was responsive to my come-on and we arranged a date for the following Wednesday evening. That night, we began enjoying each other's company. It occurred to me that the locals were finally right about something; Teresa was spectacular.

Gasper warned me to stay away from her, telling me that she was bad news, that she hung out with the wrong crowd and that she'd been arrested a few times for minor offences and would probably end up doing time for major ones. Of course, I didn't listen to him. I told Gasper to mind his own fucking business, that I could handle any young lady with an ass like Teresa's without his advice and that it was time he found something regular for himself. The months passed without my being with another woman and I figured, this must be it, so I asked Teresa to marry me. Gasper dropped me the day I asked him to be my best man. Teresa and I got married in City Hall in Manhattan without anyone I knew at my side. My old friend and I didn't speak for years, and then, one day, years after Teresa and I were through, he called.

Fool me once, shame on you. Fool me twice, go fuck yourself.

I said, "I bet you never thought it would end like this."

"Shut up, Gabe. I don't know what you're talking about. Please, don't give me an excuse to kill you."

"Why not? I mean, isn't that the idea? You killed Teresa, set me up to look like her murderer and then arrived before I had a chance to leave. My guess is your report will say you had to shoot me as I tried to get away."

Gasper tightened his lips and said, "Just shut the fuck up, Gabe. I would never hurt Teresa. We were lovers before you came into the picture. Sure, there were always other guys with her, but there were always other women for me, too. Somehow, Teresa and I always ended up getting back together. It was different with you, though. She liked your big city ways and your big muscles and told me that I could take a few lessons from you in the sex department. You know how she was, cheap trash talker, but it was all a front. Inside, she was soft."

Even looking down a gun barrel I couldn't help myself, and I replied, "Gasper, the only thing soft about Teresa was her box and you know it."

Gasper breathed hard and looked past my shoulder to where Teresa lay lifeless in her tub. He returned to me with colder eyes and said, "You know, maybe you're right. Maybe I ought to kill you right now and end it. You'll either pay for this in court or you'll pay for it now. It's up to you."

I figured it was time to stop pushing my luck and said, "Don't do this, Gasper. You don't have to shoot me. You know I haven't killed anyone. Let me go."

Gasper grinned and replied, "I don't know anything except that wherever you go there are dead people. That's not good, Gabe. It makes you look guilty." His grin turned into a wicked leer and he added, "By the way, where's that *moulie* I saw you with? She was damned good-looking for a black chick. As long as she's taking white meat, I wouldn't mind giving her some of mine."

I answered, "You know how I am with women, Gasper. That black chick is already history."

"Maybe," Gasper replied suspiciously, "but you're still driving her Hummer."

"It's not the first time I've borrowed a chick's wheels and it won't be the last. She's just another piece."

"Yeah, that's the way you always was, Gabe, except for Teresa. She got under your skin." Smiling evilly, he added, "Why'd you have to go and kill her?"

I protested violently, "That's bullshit! You know I didn't kill her!" Seeing Gasper's gun hand twitch at my outburst, I calmed myself, took a step back and added, "Why don't you cut the shit and just let me go? I want to find the man who did this as much as you do."

Gasper gave a tight-lipped laugh and said, "Sorry, old buddy, but no can do. I think I've already got the guy who did it. You're either going to jail or dying right here."

Roxanne had been tiptoeing her way from the upstairs powder room as Gasper and I exchanged words. She was directly behind him when he said, 'Sorry, old buddy', and the sap was moving towards the back of his head when he said, 'dying right here'. This time when he pitched forward I didn't ease his fall and his head hit the side of the bed frame with a solid, *crack*. I wasn't worried about him, though. Gasper was always hardheaded. I just hoped it would hurt.

I looked up at Roxanne and saw that her eyes were sparkling and her chest heaving. Reaching out to her, I said, "Now, I owe you twice." Nodding at Gasper, I added, "Gasper owes you twice, too. Let's get the hell out of here."

I pulled Roxanne out of the bedroom by her sap-holding hand and we ran out of the house without bothering to close the front door. Clamboring into the Hummer, I checked my watch, saw it was only just then six o'clock and wondered if our arriving early had aided in our escape. Gasper was no fool, though, and I was sure that he wouldn't have tried to take me in by himself and that there must be a squadron of Town Police cars headed this way. Ordering Roxanne to step on it, we raced down Mecox Road and reached Route 27, where it felt like an eternity before someone slowed his SUV enough to allow us to cross over into the westbound lane of traffic. I waved my hand in the customary Hampton way to show my appreciation and we raced to Deerfield Road, made a right to Edge of Woods and finally got to Roxanne's place.

I knew we couldn't stay there. It was my guess that when Gasper went to Teresa's and saw the Hummer in the driveway, he'd radioed in the plates to headquarters. He would be sure to be leading a cadre of officers this way as soon as he woke up. I told Roxanne to pack a few things she might need and to do it fast. Pacing the living room floor and trying to figure things out, I stopped outside her bedroom doorway and caught a few seconds of her rmoving her rap star outfit. She was standing by the dresser, wearing only her thong and a lacy black cotton bra, and my impulse was to throw her onto the bed and make wild love to her but I knew there was no time for fun and games, or even for love, and gave up on the crazy idea in spite of how hot the sight of her body made me.

I ran into the bathroom and threw some cold water onto my face and jumped back when I saw the startled, Afro-headed, ridiculous white man staring back at me. Ripping off the wig and tossing it to the floor, I finished washing my face and left the room. Throwing some of my stuff into a bag, I called, "Are you ready?"

Roxanne was about to zipper her own bag shut when she noticed the blinking red light on her answering machine. She pressed the button for the caller's message and the taped response said, "You have one message." A moment later, Sylvester Hightower's voice erupted from the machine like he was Sam the Sham on acid.

He cried, "Get your ass over here, Ro! Someone's shot Romey!"

27

The Hummer had to be hot so there was no reason not to drive The Caddy. Roxanne had proven herself to be a good driver and had done pretty well at keeping us safe, touring the area and keeping us on time, but I knew how to drive if the going got tight. If anyone started chasing us, I wanted to be the one behind the wheel, so we threw our things into the Caddy's trunk and headed out, trying our best to avoid the police or anyone else who might recognize my car.

Somehow we reached Hightower's place without being stopped and we were waved into *Playthang* by one of four gate attendants dressed in double-breasted pink tuxedoes. I sped up the rocky driveway and came to a gravel-spitting halt in front of the high-gloss pink double-doors that now had large American flags attached to them, the one on the left, a replica of Betsy Ross' 'Old Glory' with thirteen stars in a circle on a field of blue, and the one on the right, today's present day flag of fifty stars. Another tuxedo clad servant appeared and quickly opened the passenger door for Roxanne, ignoring me completely. He followed Roxanne into the house and it didn't seem like anyone was going to take my car, so I placed the keys in my pocket and followed.

The place was like a funeral home. People were padding around worried and whispering as if they were afraid to wake the dead, but that tranquility came to a sudden halt when I heard the by-now familiar, high-pitched wail coming from the living room.

"OOOOWEEEE!!! Ro's back! Everything's gonna be fine, now!"

I'm sure that's what Hightower thought when Roxanne walked into the room. Then, I appeared in the doorway.

He saw me, recoiled in horror and painfully shrieked, "What the fuck you doing here, Muthafucka?"

I noticed that for the holiday, his hair was done in tight cornrows, fixed in place by a mutitude of red, white and blue beads, and he was wearing a white karate outfit with a blue belt and red trim, obviously a new level of expertise in the martial arts world reserved exclusively for patriotic and myopic *gangstah* rappers. His faux, red framed Polo glasses covered his bright blue contact lenses and I must have been getting used to him because neither his voice nor his appearance seemed to have any effect upon me. Looking around the large room, I saw Romey seated on the couch with a four-inch square of white gauze at his shoulder and his left arm in a sling. Roxanne was seated beside him, one arm draped across his massive back, and he was looking up at me with huge cow eyes.

"Mo'fo'," Romey said.

I took that as, hello, and entered the room.

Having me penetrate his inner sanctum must have driven Hightower to another level of discomfort because he squealed again, as if I hadn't heard him the first time, "What the fuck you doing here, Muthafucka?"

This time I did find him annoying. I was in no mood for his tired old shit and I had several good reasons why: I'd just left my dead ex-wife, had almost been shot by my ex-best friend, other people wanted to kill me before I could screw with their plans, and I wasn't at all sure I would get out of the mess I was in. The only good thing in my life was Roxanne, and she was sitting on the couch, comforting a gigantic bodyguard who should have been employed by the Worldwide Wrestling Federation, but had instead threatened to beat the crap out of me and referred to me only as, "Mo'fo," and not even as Mr. Mo'fo'.

I wasn't going to let my situation bring me any further down and I certainly wasn't going to give that asshole, Hightower, any satisfaction at all, so I answered, "I'm here with Roxanne. If you don't like it, take it up with her. Personally, I don't give a shit what you think."

Hightower bent at the knees like a limp noodle and yelped, "Is that true, Roxanne? Is Muthafucka with you?"

Roxanne, playing Nightingalesque attention to Romey, caressed the top of the big guy's huge head with slow strokes that started at his moony eyes and traveled along his tight haircut until they reached the back of his thick neck. He looked like he was close to purring when Roxanne answered softly, "Yes, he is, Sylvester, but don't you think you should be worried about Jerome and not my relationship with Gabe?"

Hightower began moving around the room quickly, as if he was warming up for The PotatoHampton 10K scheduled for that Sunday morning at the Bridgehampton Community Center, and said, "Ro, ever since you met Muthafucka, we ain't had nothing but trouble. I bet Romey getting shot had something to do with him, too. I wouldn't put it past him to have shot Romey himself. He knew Romey didn't like him. Romey said he was going to get him. Told him right to his muthafucka face. We all heard it. Why, I ought to get one of the boys to cap him right now."

A fire flashed in Roxanne's eyes and she pointed a quivering, malevolent finger at the would-be impresario. In a tight tone I hadn't before heard from her, she ordered, "Calm the fuck down, Sylvester. I don't want to hear any more shit about anyone getting capped. Gabe has been with me every minute of the last two days and he couldn't have possibly shot Romey without me knowing about it. Do you understand me, Sylvester? When I say every minute, I mean every minute."

"Every second?" Hightower screeched. Realizing Roxanne was not going to answer, he added, "That doesn't mean at night, too, does it Ro?"

"It means just what I said it means, Sylvester. Now, you can take that however you want, but Gabe and I were together all the time and that's the last time I'm going to tell you."

Romey stared down at the carpet, shook his head and groaned, "Mo'fo'."

Hightower raced into Roxanne's face and squeaked, "Gabe? Gabe? You mean Muthafucka, don't you?" Spinning to me, he shrilly called, "I told you not to fuck with Ro, but you couldn't keep away. There ain't enough white women out there in the world for you to fuck with; you gots to put your pecker into my girl."

Roxanne roared, "That's it, Sylvester! That's enough!" Leaving a dismayed Romey at the couch, she approached Hightower as if she were a gunfighter in a spaghetti western and warned, "I told you not to mess with my life. I told you if you did I would leave. Now, either you accept Gabe and apologize to him for the way you're behaving, or I'm out of here."

Hightower yelped, "Apologize? Me? I should apologize? What the fuck did I do?"

Crossing her arms and angrily tapping her foot much as she had when we'd confronted The Latin Zombies, Roxanne slowly gave her instructions, saying, "Sylvester, you heard me. Apologize, now."

Hightower squealed like a begger, "But, I'm only looking out for you, Ro."

"Apologize, Sylvester, or I'm gone."

With heavily lidded eyes, Hightower turned to me and said, "Sorry, Muthafucka. If Roxanne says she was with you all the time, then you couldn't have shot Romey." Turning back to Roxanne, he asked, "Satisfied?"

Roxanne answered, "No, but it's a start." Looking at me, she asked, "You okay with this, Gabe?"

I answered, "I'm okay," and turning my attention to the emasculated rap star, I asked through a broad grin, "How did Romey catch it?"

Hightower puckered his face in response, recovered his composure and answered me in his radio voice, the shrill S.H.I.T. gone, "Why should I tell you anything?"

I answered, "Because I used to be a cop and I know things. Like, whoever did this wasn't trying to shoot Romey; he was aiming for you."

With his eyes dancing in their sockets, Hightower blared, "What??? Muthafucka, how you know that? What makes you think someone wants to shoot me?"

Hoping my response would bust his ass, I answered, "You're ruining the neighborhood, Sylvester. By killing you, they could take care of two birds with one bullet. You'd be dead and your estate would sell *Playthang* to the highest bidder, which most certainly would not have been a black *gangstah* rap star, and I could be accused of shooting you because I was after your star performer and girlfriend, RoRoRap. The story would go that she liked me and you wouldn't let her go, so I took things into my own hands and got rid of you. At least, that's what they'd say. According to the law, I may have already killed one man over a woman; why not make it two? And it might've worked. After all, my trial would have been held here in Southampton and no one's going to go to too much trouble to find the real murderer of someone like you."

"Muthafucka," Hightower whispered.

"Mo'fo'," Romey groaned.

"Gabe," Roxanne sighed.

I winked at Roxanne that she shouldn't be overly concerned with my performance and asked the suddenly overwhelmed gangstah rapper, "You were standing next to Romey when he was shot, weren't you?"

Hightower turned to me open-mouthed and replied, "That's right. We were walking down the path leading to the beach so I could take my morning constitutional. I leaned down to pick up a pink flower from the beach grasses and a shot rang out. Romey fell on top of me, covered me with his body and said, 'Don't move man. Somebody out there's got a Smith and Wesson'."

I turned to Romey and asked, "How do you know it was an S&W?"

"I know a mo'fo' Smith and Wesson when I hears one, Mo'fo'."

I responded, "I'm sure you do," and returning to Hightower, added, "That was probably my gun. Whoever shot Romey may have used it to kill my neighbors. He's trying to make it look like I'm some kind of crazed serial killer."

Hightower whined, "You mean to say that because of you someone *is* trying to kill me?"

I calmly answered, "In a manner of speaking, I guess that's so."

Hightower returned to his female star and railed, "See, Ro, I was right. Muthafucka is nothing but trouble. He's trying to get me killed and doesn't even know it."

Ignoring the little man's tantrum, I stepped between him and Roxanne and asked, "Did you call the police?"

He replied nervously, "Of course, I did." Twisting his spiteful little face into mine, he added, "Police captain was here in five minutes."

I said, "That was Captain Dupree, correct?"

Romey answered from the couch, "Yeah, that's right. He came out and asked some questions and left without doing much of anything. Mo'fo' acted like he didn't give a shit."

I replied, "That's because he doesn't. By the way, Romey, how come you're not in the hospital?"

The giant proudly answered, "Take more than one shot in the shoulder to put me down. Anyways, I gots Sylvester to look after."

I said admiringly, "You are one tough dude, Romey."

He smiled back and responded, "Thanks, Mo'fo'."

Returning to Hightower, I asked, "Did you see anything before or after the shooting that looked suspicious?"

Staring at me crosseyed, he answered, "Just what I told the police, Muthafucka. I'm taking my walk, bend down and pop. Romey falls on me and that's that."

"Did anybody else see anything?"

"Nah, just the usual shit: rich, old white guys driving their convertibles down the road looking for young pussy that be jogging or biking in their bathing suits. Some of my boys said they saw the Town Supervisor driving by a little while after the shooting. Conway said he was traveling with some bigheaded white guy with rust colored hair. The redheaded guy was doing the driving. My boys said he was wheeling an old, orange and gray Taurus and yelling at the supervisor as he drove." Hightower thought for a moment and added, "They shouldn't let old pieces of shit like that Taurus on the road. This is supposed to be a high-class neighborhood with high-class vehicles. I told all this shit to Captain Dupree and he said he would speak with the suervisor and ask if he'd seen anything."

I wasn't surprised to hear about the presence of Conforti or the bigheaded white guy, but I was curious how any of Hightower's boys would know who either of them was.

I asked, "How would your boys know the supervisor?"

"That muthafucka? He's been here plenty of times. Doesn't appreciate someone like me owning *Playthang*. Told me that to my face. Wants me to sell real bad. Dumbass Muthafucka! Don't he know I ain't going anywhere? This is my home, at least one of them, and I ain't leaving. Of course, that can all change if someone comes up with the right price. I'm a businessman, and money talks, Muthafucka. Money fucking talks."

So does a bullet, Asshole!!! So does a fucking bullet!!!

I was sure Conforti had seen plenty of what had gone down on the beach, but I was also sure he wasn't about to talk to me about it. Things were falling into place, though. I was pretty sure I knew who committed the murders, and why, but it was still hard for even me to believe, so how was I going to convince anybody else? The next night was Hightower's Memorial Day Red, White and Blue Ball. Only a week had passed since Al Shareef's party, and it had been the longest week of my life. It was time to draw things to a close, but I couldn't do it by myself.

"Mr. Hightower," I said, trying to give the man some *respeck* and maybe get him on my side, "I've got a plan and I'm going to need your help."

28

Dinner was set for nine on the beachfront terrace, giving us about an hour to go to our rooms, wash and change for dinner. Hightower had given me my own fantastic guest suite overlooking the ocean, while insisting in a private conversation that I, "Keep the fuck away from Roxanne." I told him that as long as I was in his house I would respect his wishes, no matter how stupid I thought they were. I figured that he was hiding me from the law and placing his own life in jeopardy, and even if he didn't care what happened to me and was doing it all for Roxanne, what did that matter? The way I saw it, he could have made a phone call without my knowledge and had me arrested before I knew what hit me. I owed the man my freedom. You've got to respect someone for that, no matter how much you can't stand him.

I showered and shaved with the toiletries Hightower provided, toweling myself dry with the biggest and softest bath sheet that had ever caressed my skin. There was a hot pink, crystal atomizer resting on the limestone bathroom vanity countertop containing a few ounces of Hightower's private cologne, S.H.I.T. For Men. I picked it up and gave a couple of quick deep squeezes to the neon purple bulb attached to the end of the narrow and flexible connecting tube. A light mist flew out from the silver nozzle at the top of the bottle and my face puckered like a ten-year old raisin when the strong and familiar scent hit me. I said, "Muthafucka," in a voice too reminiscent of my host, dashed back into the shower, and after drying myself with another luxurious bath sheet, sprinkled on some nice clean talc I'd found in the medicine cabinet. Finally feeling refreshed, I got dressed.

Being punctual, at eight fifty-five, I opened the door to my room and was met by Conway, the same skinny black guy who had driven off with my car the first time I'd paid a visit to *Playthang*. Leaning against the wall with his arms folded across his chest, he was dressed in an expensive suit that had to have been hand tailored in Italy, and it occurred to me that as big an asshole as Hightower was, he treated his people well and seemed to have their complete loyalty.

"This way, man," Conway said, and without so much as a backwards glance to see if I was agreeable to his order, he began his slow, round shouldered, bopping walk down the hallway.

I followed the lithe servant down the long, many-doored and crystal-sconced corridor unti we reached a broad flight of pink marble steps. Slowly descending the wide radial staircase, we came to its end and faced a series of French doors leading out to the terrace.

I said, "Thanks, Conway, but I can handle the rest myself," and without waiting for a reply, passed him and entered a perfect Southampton night.

The terrace I walked was fashioned from irregularly patterned fieldstone, conservatively measuring from my layman's eye, eighty feet wide by a hundred feet long. The round, white cloth-covered tables had already been set for the next evening's party, except for the silverware and flowers, and there looked to be enough chairs stacked to the side to sit five or six hundred people. Hightower and his entourage occupied only two of the tables, the ones at the far end of the veranda, the ones overlooking the ocean. He, Roxanne and Romey were already seated at one and I assumed the empty chair with its back to the ocean was reserved for me. The other table held six of his flunkies and their girls. Except for their fine threads, the guys weren't much to speak of, but the girls were all young, well-dressed and very good-looking.

Reaching my host's table, I said, "Good evening, everyone," and walked over to where Roxanne was seated. I leaned over and kissed her lightly on the lips, and she smiled and returned my affectionate gaze. Done with my fond hello, I ungraciously turned to watch Hightower fume. With a nonchalant air, I sat in my chair and unfolded my large white cotton napkin, giving it a crisp sideways snap before placing it on my lap.

Smiling at my host, I said, "This is one hell of a beautiful place you've got here, Hightower. I've seen a lot of homes in Southampton and I've got to admit, this one takes the cake."

"Tell me something I don't know, Muthafucka. And by the way, no kissing at the table, neither."

"Sorry," I replied. "I'm still learning house rules."

"Well, learn 'em fast. I don't likes you and I wants you out of here."

"Sylvester," Roxanne warned.

"Sorry, Ro," Hightower responded to his star performer's unspoken threat. "I forgot myself." To me he added, "Wine, Muthafucka?"

We had salmon carpaccio for an appetizer. Conway filled a Baccarat globe with a chilled white wine that was way too expensive for my budget and better than anything I was accustomed to drinking, even at Red Bar. Medallions of local venison, local asparagus, and mashed fingerling pototoes served on white Rosenthal China chargers with eighteen carat gold trim was our main course. The wine presented with that was a California merlot, again served in Baccarat, the bottles from a vineyard Hightower had recently bought in Mendocino. He smacked his lips with every sip and quite often said, "Man this is good shit." Roxanne rolled her eyes with nearly every one of his comments and once in a while, Romey groaned. I couldn't tell if his somber sound was a response from the pain in his shoulder or the idiotic statements his boss made.

Everything about the place, except its owner, was beautiful, especially Roxanne. She was dressed casually in a pair of tan corduroy jeans and a long- sleeved black crewneck shirt. Once in a while, I would catch her staring at me, and even from six feet away I could feel the heat from her eyes. Once, after Roxanne and I had made some unusually salacious eye contact, I caught Hightower glaring at me and I could feel the heat from his eyes, as well.

Salad was served after the main course, "Like they do in Europe, Muthafucka," and a bottle of thick, dessert wine from Wolffer's was served with sweet, sweet slices of a Marie Antoinette cake purchased that morning from Tate's Bakery in Southampton. By ten-thirty, we were finished with one of the best meals I had ever eaten.

"Want a cigar, Muthafucka?"

"No, thanks. I don't smoke."

Hightower and Romey lit up a couple of illegal Cubans and I took the opportunity to ask Roxanne if she'd like to take a walk along the beach. She looked as happy as a young girl at her Sweet Sixteen and rose gracefully from the chair.

Taking my hand, she announced, "We'll be back in a short while," and although Hightower's eyes were dancing in fits and starts like a pair of marionette's legs, we turned and left the table before he could object.

Roxanne and I walked down a set of stone stairs leading from the veranda to the gunite vanishing pool and bluestone patio. There were many tables set there, too, supplying enough seats for at least another couple of hundred guests. I pulled Roxanne under an opened beach umbrella so that we were shielded from anyone on the veranda's view, and releasing her hand, I put my arms around her waist and slowly pulled her into me. She lifted her face to mine and I saw the moon reflected in her eyes just before she closed them. Her arms wrapped around my waist and held me tightly, and I leaned forward and down. Our lips touched, my tongue entered her mouth and I reached up to cup one of her magnificent breasts. Roxanne moaned lowly and pressed her sex into me and I returned the intimacy. Remembering my promise to Hightower and how I still needed his help, I pulled my mouth from Roxanne.

"Come on," I said breathlessly. "Let's take that walk."

Roxanne was gazing at me with half-closed bedroom eyes that were almost hot enough to make me forget Hightower and my pledge, but that was almost. A wicked smile spread across her face when my erection poked at her thigh and I whispered into her ear, "I promised Hightower I wouldn't start anything and I still need his help. It wouldn't take much for you to make me a liar. Please, let's just walk."

Roxanne and I left the patio and strolled along the planked walkway leading to the beach. Low dunes and natural beach grasses surrounded us, and in the moonlit night, with the ocean breezes moving them in silent undulating swells, the beach grasses put on a beautiful and erotic ballet. The ocean's waves crashed on the shore in precisely timed sequences, one after another in perfect measure, providing a natural beat for the fluttering grasses and matching the thunderous rhythm of my aching heart. At sea, the moonlight streaked its ghostly white fingers along the ocean's rippling black-glass surface, and every now and then, a night bird would fly across its cratered, yellow-white face, patrolling the waves in a nocturnal search for food.

Looking out to sea, I said, "Isn't it beautiful?" and Roxanne answered, "It's enough to make you question everything."

We stood silently for a while at the water's edge, and then, when the beauty of it all began to become painful, I said, "Roxanne."

She whispered, "Don't say it."

Unable to hold back, I responded, "This can never last."

She sighed and said, "I know that, Gabe. It's just so beautiful, though."

"I'm talking about us, Roxanne."

"I know that, Gabe. I am, too. I just knew it before you did."

The waves crashed a few more times before Roxanne turned to me. Through watery eyes, she said, "I don't think I ever truly felt like a woman before I was with you and I'll always love you for giving me that, but I know we come from two different worlds. Southampton is beautiful and I've come to love the time I spend here, but I'm a rap star with a message to share with millions of young brothers and sisters. Its grown to become a bigger message since I met you. I've got a lot more to say and I'm going to share it with my people. I know we can't last. It's just too bad. What woman wouldn't want to share her life with a man like you?"

I could have given her a list of several hundred but I didn't think there was any good reason to spoil the moment and do that. Instead, we stood with clasped hands and silently faced the ocean. Once in a while, a wave would crash close to us, sending a salty spray against our faces and our clothes, but except for a slight hunching of our shoulders when the cold spray hit, we remained still. Standing there at the foot of the ocean and holding Roxanne's hand, I had an epiphany. Roxanne had become more than my lover; she was my friend. After a few more minutes of blissful solitude, we returned to the terrace and found everyone gone except for a dozing Romey and a nervous Hightower.

Anxiously, he'd watched us climb the stairs, and when we reached his level, he said, "You two were gone a long time. Muthafucka, I hope you didn't try anything."

"Sylvester," Roxanne issued her one name warning, but I stopped her from continuing with just a hand to her shoulder and said, "You don't have to worry about us, Hightower. I promised you I wouldn't start anything with Roxanne and I didn't. I'll keep my word to you; I just hope you keep yours to me."

"Don't worry about me, Muthafucka. I'll keep my end of the deal. Nobody takes a shot at The Infamous S.H.I.T. and gets away with it."

After wishing Roxanne beautiful dreams, I walked away alone, without Conway or any other member of the entourage as an escort. Reaching my suite, I undressed, lay on the bed, and stared up at the twelve-foot high tray ceiling for at least an hour. Unable to relax, even though I was lying on the most comfortable cashmere-covered mattress in the world, I got up, opened the windows wide and allowed the full bright light from a pre-Memorial Day moon and the cool ocean breeze into my room. Exhausted from the day's insanity and unsure of what was to unfold the next day, I got back into bed and pulled the thick white silk duvet up to my chin and finally fell into a deep and dreamless sleep.

I don't know how long I was out, but I became aware of someone climbing into my bed. I thought I might be dreaming, especially when a gentle and familiar hand took hold of me, sending shivers down my spine. I recognized the grip and realized it wasn't a dream. The sensation of my lover's long fingers around my hardening pole sent me gasping for air.

I whispered, "Roxanne."

She softly responded, "Gabe."

There was a rustle of silk and a moment later Roxanne was kissing me sweetly on my mouth. Her hand, which had been gently stroking me, moved down and cupped my testicles. She kneaded my eggs, one and then the other, loving every nook and cranny of them, and I moaned with indescribable pleasure.

Biting my lower lip, I protested weakly, moaning, "I told Hightower I wouldn't start anything," but when the nail-tip of one her fingers left the back of my balls and tickled the rim of my anus, there was no turning back. Reaching down, I parted Roxanne's wet and naked legs at the soft place where they met, placed a fingertip on her pulsing pearl and pressed.

Roxanne gasped, "Gabe, I love how you touch me." Collecting herself, she added breathlessly, "And don't worry about Sylvester. You aren't starting anything; I am."

We kissed and touched and moaned and I said, "Do you know what you're doing, Roxanne? What about our walk on the beach?"

Arching her back as I slid three fingers into her sopping wet pussy, her love nest quivered like a tiny bird and she cried, "We may not have a future, Gabe, but at least we've got tonight. Let's make it something to remember."

Hallelujah, Mothafucka!!!! Hallelujah!!!!

29

I woke up alone, and after checking my watch on the nightstand, discovered the time was nine-thirty. The last time I'd looked, it was a little after six and I had just dropped my fourth load. Not having achieved orgasm that many times in one night since I'd separated from Teresa, I felt a foolish sense of pride in knowing I could still perform at that rarified level, but along with that exhilaration came an unexpected sense of loneliness. As great as the evening with Roxanne had been, I was waking up in bed alone and wanted someone I really loved by my side.

In my drained state, sex was probably the last thing that should have been on my mind, but as I rose from bed I caught my reflection in the large mirror hanging over the dresser and saw the fresh scratches that ran across my chest where Roxanne had broken my skin. I recalled how I'd lifted her legs back and over her head, and in that position, with her sex completely exposed and totally vulnerable, I'd penetrated her deeply. She screamed my name with my first thrust and raked her nails across my chest. A gush of warm fluid poured from her almost immediately, lubricating my cock to its root, saturating my balls and puddling the bed between her legs. I'd never been with a squirter before, it drove me into an even greater sexual frenzy, and I pounded her like a great chef pressing pailliard.

OOOOOWEEEEE!!! Uh,oh!

Worn out, but feeling pretty studly, I showered and threw on some of the gym clothes I'd packed in my overnight bag. Opening the suite's door, I found a sterling silver tray waiting for me. I brought it in, uncovered the large cloth-covered plate and found three fried eggs, six strips of bacon, four slices of rye toast, a glass of orange juice and a small carafe of coffee. Nothing was very hot, but I'd discovered a microwave in a cabinet under the plasma television on the wall opposed to the bed, so hot was not a problem. Lifting the cup from the tray, I found a small, secreted note. Opening it, I read, "Thanks for a wonderful evening. I may never walk again. Enjoy. R."

I could have eaten ten trays of food but Roxanne's little note and one tray proved enough to get my day fitfully started. Throwing a towel over my shoulder, I left the suite and again found Conway in the hall waiting for me.

Leaning against the wall and displaying his usual bored attitude, he mumbled something that sounded like, "Morning, man."

"Good morning, Conway," I cheerfully replied.

"I saw the tray, man, so it looks like you already had your breakfast."

I responded, "Thanks for looking out for me, Conway. Say, I haven't had any exercise in a few days and I'm out of routine. Does Hightower have a gym in this place?"

A wiseass grin came over the punk's face and he said, "No exercise? Man, what do you call that shit you were doing with Ro last night, *memitation?*"

I put my chest into his face, looked down at him and snarled, "That's meditation, you stupid fuck, and if you don't wipe that grin off your face and answer my question I may have to teach you what the word exercise means … on your thick but empty head. Now, where's the fucking gym?"

Conway must have thought I was ultra cranky from lack of sleep because his grin disappeared and was rapidly replaced by the dull expression I'd gotten used to. Moving his neck in broad circles as if he'd developed a sudden crick in it, he said, "Shit man, I'm just playing wit you. Don't have to get all fucked up, man." After a shrug and a pull at his too long shirt sleeves, he added, "Follow me, man," and follow him I did.

Playthang's gym was at least the equivalent of Sag Harbor's American Fitness Center. There were Nautilus and Cybex machines for every body part, double racks of dumbells weighted from ten to eighty pounds, exercise mats, treadmills, ellipticals, and recumbent bikes, long bars, free weights and clamps, and a forty foot wall of mirrored glass to check your progress. It was like being in Weightlifter Heaven.

I'd finished my abs, chest, back and shoulders with only one particular basic movement for each body part and was about to start working my arms when the door to the gym opened and Romey stepped in. He walked over to the flat bench, right next to the inclined bench where I was doing my second set of concentration curls with forty pound weights, and sat.

Dressed casually, he was wearing black slacks and a tight black nylon muscle shirt that made his chest look like it had four separate slabs of muscle tacked onto an unexpanded sixty inches, and without a jacket covering his assets, his waist appeared to taper to a very trim thirty-four inches. Each of his exposed biceps looked to be the size of large coconuts, and huge veins and arteries popped perfectly along the undersides of both forearms, proving his vascularity to be of magazine quality. He still wore a pad of gauze under his shirt, covering his shoulder wound, but the sling was gone. Checking out his round vacant eyes and squashed face, I hoped I'd never have to tangle with the guy because kicking his ass would probably take quite a lot of effort and I knew I would probably get hurt as well.

"Mo'fo'," he said in greeting.

"Romey," I answered in a grunt.

Romey watched silently as I completed my third set of bicep curls and then continued with triceps kickbacks, again with forty pounds, and the last part of my routine for the day. I wasn't going to ride a bike or hit the treadmill, because as Conway had rightfully thought, I'd already had enough aerobics working out with Roxanne during the night.

"Fifteen," I said and placed the weight gingerly at my feet. Looking at Romey checking me out, I asked, "What's up?"

He said, "Sylvester don't like you."

"That's okay. I don't like him."

"I like you, though."

I replied through a smile, "Thanks, Romey. That's nice to know."

He went on to say, "Roxanne trusts you and that's enough for me to trust you, too. I just want you to know, that whatever you need, you can count on me. Don't go to Sylvester. He's got an artistic temperament and can fly off the handle. See me, instead. Just one thing, though, when you finish your business with these guys, I want to be there. They put a hole in my shoulder and I want to give them something in return. You okay with that?"

Okay with that? I'm delighted.

I answered, "Sure, Romey. I can understand wanting to get even. You'll have to move fast, though. When things start happening, they're going to happen fast."

"I can move fast, Mo'fo'. Just because I'm big doesn't mean I'm slow, and just because I look the way I do doesn't mean I'm stupid."

I replied, "I never thought you were stupid, Romey, just misguided."

After a thoughtful moment, Romey groaned, "Roxanne's gone."

More quickly than I would have liked, I asked, "Gone? Where is she?"

He passively replied, "She's with Sylvester, getting some last minute things they need for tonight. He took some of the boys with him for backup. Said I needed to rest my shoulder. We been together a long time, Sylvester and me. Don't want anything bad to happen to him. Roxanne's like my little sister. Don't want nothing bad to happen to her, neither."

I said, "Nothing will happen to Hightower. As for Roxanne, we have an agreement and nothing bad will happen to her either. I promise."

Romey's face clouded with thought, trying to weigh my promise, to see if it was worth anything. He suddenly winced, put his hand to his shoulder and through tightly clenched teeth said, "I believe you, Fortuna. Now, what do you need?"

I answered, "First, I need to stop at someone's place of business. I can't get there with the Caddy. The authorities would pull me over within five minutes and I'd probably have to hurt an innocent cop. So, I need a car. I shouldn't be gone for too long, maybe an hour or two. After that, we should be set."

"Car, huh? You got it, Mo'fo'."

"Oh, and I'll also need the use of someone's cell phone. There are a few calls I need to make and I don't want to use the house phone. The calls might get traced back here, or worse, the phones here may already be tapped. I want to play it safe."

"You can use my cell," Romey replied. He took his small phone from his pocket and tossed it to me. "What else do you need?"

Juggling the toss, I answered, "That should be about it. Thanks a lot, Romey."

The bodyguard readjusted his gauze pad and replied, "Ain't no thing."

I got my things together, headed for the door and as I was about to leave the gym, my new friend called, "Hey, Mo'fo'."

"Yeah, Romey?"

"Be careful."

30

The ride to Stump's place was a surprisingly easy one. None of the Southampton Police were looking for a neon gold 2005 BMW 325i with its top up, so I was able to cruise along the back roads without a hitch until I reached Mariner Drive. Not wanting anyone working for Stump to see what I was driving, I went past the blacktopped driveway leading into McNamara Collision and parked further down on the for-industrial-use only street, leaving the car about a quarter of a mile away, in front of the warehouse for The Southampton Gallery of Stone and Tile.

It was a warm and sunny day, and as I entered the open courtyard of Stump's place I saw that most of the guys who worked for him were sitting around doing nothing except taking a long coffee break. I recognized four of the six Hispanic guys in the third bay as fellows that had jumped out of Enrique's van at The Bridgehampton Commons. They were dressed all in black and we stared at each other in silent recognition before one of them tipped the bill of his cap to me. The other four guys working at Stump's were in the first bay and were locals. Each was dressed in stained and ragged blue jeans, oily flannel shirts and greasy old sneakers. They completed their unsavory uniforms with sweaty red bandannas wrapped around their foreheads and were lazily passing around a bottle wrapped in a brown paper bag. We glared at each other in silent distrust and I threw a surly expression at them, hoping that would be warning enough to keep them the fuck away from me. Reaching Stump's trailer, I gave the door a light tapping with the rounded tip of my initial ring and waited.

"Who the fuck is knocking on my door like some candy-assed pansy?" came the familiar roar.

I heard a chair drag across the floor and a few awkward steps before the door flew open revealing a glassy-eyed Stump staring into bright sunlight. He shielded his eyes from the light of day with his beefy hand and his vision slowly cleared, but I could tell it still took a few seconds for him to believe his bloodshot eyes. He smelled like he'd downed a quart of rye and his clothes were patchy with dampness, looking like the alcohol was sweating clean through them. We did not shake hands.

Smiling sloppily, Stump said, "Oh, it's you, Gabe. Didn't expect to see you here."

I replied, "Why not, Stump? I owe you money for fixing the Caddy. Never knew you thought me to be a chiseler."

He began, "Nah, it's not that, Gabe," but then, his grizzled face abruptly froze. His eyes started to dance, his back straightened and he let out a short, gurgling laugh. Running the thick fingers of his hand through his rusty hair, he said, "Sure, Gabe, you're an honest man. I knew you'd come by to pay me. It's because I do trust you that I didn't expect to see you so soon. Hah, I would have given you 'til the end of the week before I came after you."

I replied easily, "It's nice to hear you think so highly of me, Stump."

He gargled a laugh and said, "We go back a long way, Gabe. You're almost a local."

"But not quite, right, Stump?"

His blue and reddened eyes burned into me as he answered, "That's right, Gabe. Not quite."

We stood looking at each other for a few seconds, like two gunfighters about to draw, but it wasn't getting me anywhere pretending to be Paladin, so I decided to end the silence and asked, "Did you hear about Teresa?"

"Your ex-wife?"

"That's right."

Stump scratched his head, looked into the sky and tried his best to look dumbfounded before he said, "No, can't say as I have. We travel in different circles, your ex and me. Why?" he asked through a broadening smile. "Who's the cunt screwing now?"

You son of a bitch! How'd you like me to punch your fucking face in?

I answered, "She's not screwing anyone, Stump. Somebody killed her yesterday, somebody who was very strong and very mean. The bastard knocked her out and raped her. Then, he slit her wrists to make it look like a suicide. No note was left, though, so it probably was a spur of the moment decision on his part, something he felt he had to do and do fast. He probably sat there while she bled out just to make sure she wouldn't come around and escape. What kind of son-of-a-bitch does that to a woman, Stump? What kind of sick fuck kills a woman for nothing?"

Stump seemed to have been enjoying my description of what I thought had happened to Teresa until I said, "sick fuck." Then, his expression tightened and he took a step back into the shade of his door. Grimacing, he tilted his large head to the right as some saliva spilled from the corner of his mouth, and he spat, "I don't know, Gabe. I don't know who would do something like that. She was your woman. Maybe you should know. They say murdered people are usually done in by someone they know and I never had the pleasure of meeting your ex. That's too bad for me because I heard she'd do almost anyone."

Fighting the urge to deck the bastard, I responded through thin lips, "That's odd, I thought you and Teresa knew each other. After all, I saw you sitting with her at Al Shareef's place." I let the fact that I knew he was lying sink in and added, "Gasper thinks I did it."

Stump's eyebrows receded into his hairline before he whistled and said, "Shit, that can't be good for you, Gabe. Gasper is a fine cop and he usually knows what he's talking about." Retreating another step into his trailer, he asked, "You didn't do it, did you, Gabe?"

I answered, "No, but I have a pretty good idea who did, and when the time is right I'm going to make him sorry he ever lived."

Laughing drunkenly, Stump responded, "That's a good one, Gabe. Sorry he ever lived. I'll bet you would do that, too. You always were a mean mother." Falling against the door jam, he reached out to place an arm around my shoulders and said, "Come on into the office, Gabe. We'll fill out some paperwork and you can give me a check. Twelve hundred, wasn't it?"

I pushed his arm away and answered, "I'm not paying you shit, Stump."

Stump took on a shocked expression and then growled, "What's that? We had a deal. You agreed to twelve hundred. Is something wrong with the job? Just tell me what and I'll kick those Spics' asses."

"There's nothing wrong with the job, Stump. Those boys do fine work. Pretty soon they'll leave you and start their own business. They'll probably charge reasonable rates and force you out of business, too, you fucking thief."

"Fucking shit, they will," Stump hissed, smashing his fist against the wall of his trailer. "That's what's wrong with this fucking town. The people here have forgotten who made it great. Nowadays, rich outsiders come in and take all the land and all the money away from those of us who helped build this place and the Spics and the Niggers come in and rob everything they can get their filthy hands on. My family goes back seven generations in Southampton. Seven fucking generations! Back to 1780, and what have I got to show for it? Three fucking bays and a trailer in an industrial park that isn't worth a goddamned fucking nickel."

I caually interjected, "Can't even get a decent tee time, can you, Stump?"

He roared back, "That's right, but it isn't going to stay that way." Screwing his face into a diseased red ball of pus, he pushed it towards me and bragged, "We're going to build a great course, strictly for the locals. You'll have to prove family domicile for fifty years before you'll be allowed to play and it'll be the best fucking course in the Hamptons. It'll belong to us and no amount of fucking money will allow outsiders entry. That ought to show 'em."

I'd heard about all I needed from this maniac, so I broke in and said, "And if you have to get rid of a few outsiders to get it, what the fuck? Right, Stump?"

Stump was breathing hard, clenching and unclenching his big right fist, and he bellowed, "That's fucking right. If a few outsiders have to get it, well fuck 'em! And you know what, Fortuna? Fuck you, too!"

I balled each of my fists in case he came at me in his drunken rage, but he knew I was ready for him and wasn't too drunk or stupid to want to get his ass kicked.

He chose to snarl, "You owe me twelve hundred and I want it."

I calmly replied, "Well, you're not going to fucking get it. I've got something else to offer as payment, something I think you'll find more valuable."

Through a hot liquored breath, Stump asked, "What the hell could you give me that's worth more than twelve hundred dollars?"

I answered easily, "How about a nine-iron?"

He choked, "A fucking nine-iron. What the fuck do I need with another nine-iron? I've got ten sets of golf clubs if I've got one. You can keep the fucking club; I want my money."

I replied, "This one's different, Stump. This one came from a set of Calloway's that Conforti was going to dump for you after he paid Teresa a visit. The problem is that I saw it first and took it out of the bag that was in the front seat of his car. I knew it had to be yours because no one ever wears down a grip the way you do. Conforti probably thought he'd gotten rid of it when he threw the bag and all its contents into the 'bulk items' bin at the transfer station."

Stump looked a litle worried and then snapped, "I don't know what you're talking about." His eyes flashed and he added, "I don't own any Calloways."

I said, "Sure you do, Stump, or did. In early April, I saw you playing with them during The Blue Collar Open at Indian Creek in Riverhead. You shot a par seventy and won the tournament. I shot an eighty-six, not bad for me, but then, I'm not in your league. I remember how you kissed the seven-iron that placed your last shot six feet from the final flag, virtually guaranteeing you the win. There's no doubt about it, Stump; that nine-iron is yours."

Stump was working hard to control his temper. Knowing he couldn't take me by himself, not with the aid of ten golf clubs, he looked to his bays to see if any of the local boys were going to help. They recognized the meaning of his hard gaze and took a couple of steps towards us, but only a few seconds passed before The Zombies left their bay and surrounded them. It occurred to me that I'd have to call Enrique and thank him for having such a fine and upstanding crew of Zombies working for him.

Stump saw he was trapped, shrugged and said, "Fuck you, Gabe. What if it was my club? Why the fuck would anyone care?"

There was a worried look on my opponent's face and I was glad to be the one putting it there. Stump had tried to rip me off on The Caddy and he'd tried to pin the Al Shareef murder on me. He'd pretended to be my friend and now we both knew he was a liar.

Fool me once, shame one you. Fool me twice, go fuck yourself. Fool me three times, I'm going to fuck you royally.

"You see, Stump, I took the club to the hospital's morgue and placed its shaft into the crease someone put in Al Shareef's forehead. You know what? It fit perfectly. I think whoever killed him did it with that club. And Stump, I think that someone was you."

He responded hoarsely, "You can't prove that."

"I think I can. And here's what I'm suggesting to make sure I don't. I'll be nice enough to return your lost club. You, on the other hand, will give me fifty thousand dollars and the title to the Z4. I got used to driving that baby while you were working on The Caddy, and I've got to admit, I liked it. Also, I don't owe you shit for the work your guys did on my car. That's going to be a freebie. Those are my terms, Stump. If that's not good enough for you, I can drop the club off with The Feds."

Stump was bristling but he said, "Alright, you've got a deal. When do we trade?"

Tomorrow night, at midnight, at the scene of the crime. You bring the money and the title for the Z4; I'll bring the club. Come alone and we'll trade at the poolhouse. The Castle will be vacated because the Al Shareef Family has flown back to The Middle East to prepare a fine funeral for Binyamin." I pointed my ring finger at Stump's face and added, "And Stump, I'm warning you. If you do anything to try and fuck this up, I will screw you but good."

I turned my back on the collision specialist just to show him what a punk I thought he was and began walking towards my car. On my way out, I caught the happy smiles of The Zombies. They hated Stump's guts, too, and their grins told me how much they appreciated the shit I'd given their boss. I got into the 325i and started back to *Playthang*, taking the long way home via the backroads and hoping that Stump was too drunk, dazed and confused to figure out just how royally he was getting it.

31

Large American flags, spaced ten feet apart on ten-foot flagpoles, greeted me the moment I made the right onto Dune Road. The Stars and Stripes continued their parade of color all the way down the road, giving the rich man's avenue the quality of a beachfront Champs Elysee on Bastille Day. Reaching *Playthang*, the rows of fluttering symbols curved left into the driveway and continued up to the front of the house and beyond, forming a wall of red, white and blue around the huge parking lot that had recently been created on the tennis courts at the eastern end of the estate.

I was shaking my head at the thought of all the work that was going into planning this patriotic party as four fellows in red, white and blue uniforms waved me in at the gate. I pulled up to the main house, stopped the car, and Conway, looking like a malnourished Ethiopian Uncle Sam, came out of the doorway. Without a word to me, he took the dangling keys and drove off with The Beamer, leaving me standing alone at the entrance of the house to admire the army of workers flying around the place like a battalion of bees.

"Where you been, Muthafucka?"

It was The Infamous S.H.I.T. He'd just come out the front door and was greeting my backside in his usual hospitable way.

I turned around to face him and calmly replied, "I've been busy."

"Yeah, you been busy alright: busy with my woman, busy with my car and busy with my time. Muthafucka, don't you know when you should leave?"

Unable to take any more of his bullshit, I said, "Listen, Asshole, you think I want to be around you? If everything goes right, I'll be out of here tomorrow and we'll never have to see each other again. Just give me some space and I'll get the guy who shot Romey and who happens to want you dead. Or, have you forgotten that?"

Screwing his face into an overripe ugly-fruit, Hightower shrieked, "I ain't forgotten, Muthafucka! You just be careful with Ro, is all. We may not be sharing a bed, but she's still my girl. I know what you been doing with her and I don't like it. I told you before and I means it; you better not hurt her." Crossing his spindly arms over his narrow chest, he concluded, "Muthafucka, that's all I gots to say."

I didn't have anything more to say to him either, so I blew past him without another word and climbed the staircase leading to my suite. My door was closed but I smelled Roxanne's scent in the hallway and a chill raced through me as I opened the door, wondering if my beautiful lover was going to be waiting for me in my bed. To my surprise, I saw she wsn't naked and under the covers, but was instead seated at the game table, playing gin rummy with Romey.

Laying her cards down and rising from the table when she saw me, a bright smile washed her face and she gaily called, "Gabe."

"Mo'fo'," was Romey's deep greeting.

I closed the door behind me and was only a few steps into the room when Roxanne entered my arms and kissed me warmly on my lips.

"That was for last night," she whispered into my ear.

I knew nothing was going to happen with Romey around, so I whispered, "Thanks. You weren't bad, yourself." Looking over at Romey, I asked, "What are you doing here?"

The big guy didn't answer. He just shrugged, picked a card from the deck and placed it into his hand. Tossing a discard, he said, "Your play, Ro."

Roxanne ignored Romey, gazed lovingly into my eyes and said, "Come to the closet, Gabe. I've got something fun I want to show you."

Pulling me across the room by my hand, she opened the door to the gigantic walk-in closet and switched on the light. Inside the cherry wood cavern were several rows of Hightower's suits. They were hanging on three tiers of closet rods, came in various shades of pink, purple, puce and periwinkle, and most of them had rhinestones and other peculiar glittery applications on them, assuring that when the spotlight hit, Hightower would look like a multicolored flame.

Roxanne went to the back row and pulled out a hanger that held what looked to be a late eighteenth century styled blue suit, red leggings, a white frilled shirt and blue brocaded shoes. On her tiptoes, she reached and grabbed a powder white wig from a shelf.

"Here," she said, holding her filled arms out to me. "Here's your costume. Tonight, you're going to be George Washington, The Father of Our Country."

I never wanted to be the father of anything, so I said, "You've got to be kidding me. I'm not wearing this. This is embarrassing."

Roxanne laughed and said, "You've got to wear a costume for tonight's party, Gabe. It'll be fun. You'll see." Tossing my costume over her shoulder in a carefree manner, she sidled up to me and said, "I'll be *coming* as Martha." Her eyes got hot and sparkly and she purred for our ears only, "At least I hope so."

At that moment, there were a lot of things crowding my mind and going to bed with Roxanne dressed as our first First lady was certainly the best of them, but getting dressed as George just wasn't high on my list of priorities and I complained, "Jesus, Roxanne, I don't know. I'll feel foolish in this getup, and anyway, you know I have to leave the party early. I can't have a ridiculous outfit like this slowing me down." The joy left her face when I said that and I could see worry taking its place. Almost sorrowfully, I added, "You know what I've got to do."

From the game table, Romey called, "You all set for tonight, Mo'fo'?"

I answered, "Yeah, Romey. I made my calls and paid my visit. I'm done except for the meet. Hopefully, all will go as planned."

It occurred to me that very little in life goes as planned. I was sure no one had planned on killing Reggie and Carla, and I was sure that Teresa hadn't planned on having her wrists slit. Something almost always happens in life to change things and adjustments have to be made on the spot. That was something I didn't want to tell Roxanne, not then, at least, but looking at Romey's sad, flat face, I knew I had a partner when it came to understanding the vagaries of life.

He said, "Glad you finished with your business, Mo'fo', cause now you can gives me back my phone."

I returned his cell and he left the room without saying so much as a good-bye to Roxanne or me. She walked over to the window in a funk, pulled aside the curtains and gazed out at the broad expanse of Atlantic Ocean.

After a few lonely seconds, she asked, "You will be careful tonight, won't you, Gabe?"

I walked over to her, wrapped my arms around her waist from behind and answered, "Roxanne, You know that tonight is going to be dangerous for me. I'll be as careful as I can, but anything can happen. That's life."

Spinning from the window, she gazed deeply into my eyes and said, "We're still a team and I'm going with you."

I admired her pugnacity, but took a step back and responded sternly, "No, you aren't. You saw Teresa, you know what happened to my friends and you saw Al Shareef in the morgue. I won't be responsible for anything happening to you. You're staying here."

Placing her arms around my neck and pulling me down to her lips, she responded sensuously, "You aren't responsible for anything concerning me. I'm a big girl, Gabe. I'm responsible for myself." Kissing me sweetly, she let just the tip of her tongue race over my lips. Slowly, pulling away, she cooed, "Let's make love again, Gabe. You were right; who knows what tomorrow may bring?"

I didn't know about tonight or tomorrow, but I did know about that afternoon and making love with Roxanne would be a perfect way to start the Red, White and Blue Ball. When midnight came around, that would be another matter; I was determined to leave *Playthang* by myself.

32

By eight o'clock, *Playthang* was filling with an older and sedate Hamptons crowd, dressed as the invitation demanded, in expensive and varying shades of red, white and blue clothing. Most of the early arrivals wanted nothing more than a couple of free red-apple martinis and a quick departure, but by the time nine o'clock rolled around, the place was getting jammed with a much wilder bunch, looking not only for free drinks, but also for sex, drugs, rock and roll, and rap. Every moment, more and more of that particular multicultural type was cruising through *Playthang's* gates, while the older crowd, those who had dropped off their charitable checks and could now say with true Hamptonian pride that they had attended The Red, White and Blue Ball at Sylvester Hightower's place, fought their way against the oncoming tide of energetic revelers.

Celebrities of every race and nationality were in attendance, dancing, singing and drinking, making the place feel like The Oscars, The Emmys, The Tonys and The Grammys were all about to be awarded on a special episode of Soul Train. There was the real estate developer with the bad hair, and there was J.Lo with her celebrated caboose. There was Matt and Ben and Jen and Paula and Justin and Britney and Celine. There was Leonardo and Steven and Tom and Paris and Claudia and Kate and Tim and Susan and Halle. There were three of the guys from The Four Tops and Stevie Wonder and Hammer and Ja and Jay and the four girls from Sex and the City. There was Barbara and Cofi and Ed Koch and Rudy and scores more people that I'd seen on the covers of People or Us or The Enquirer or The Sun or on Page Six of the Post, whose names I did not know but whose faces were as familiar as the guy on the box of Quaker Oats. There seemed to be no end to the lineup of famous dignitaries, entertainers and unaccomplished celebrities who had done very little for the world but had somehow managed to become important to it, and every one of them, when they met with Hightower on the stage or on the patio or while walking through the magnificent grounds, embraced the guy like he was the King of the World.

I was walking around in my George Washington outfit with the welcome addition of a tri-cornered hat pulled down over my eyes. Although I'd protested at first to wearing the costume, it was perfect camouflage and several times during the course of the evening I was more than glad to be wearing it. I saw Gasper walking around the crowd, too. Uninterested in partaking in the color scheme of the party, he was in his tan and gray uniform, patrolling the party like an eagle searching for prey, which meant he was looking for me. I figured that he'd gotten the report on The Hummer's plates and found they belonged to Roxanne Rosario. It would have taken only one young officer who had a radio or an ipod to tell him who that was, and if Gasper saw a picture of her, knowing me as well as he did, it would have been easy for him to figure that I would be accompanying her to the party.

I tried to keep my distance from him, but getting caught in the massive crowd was often like getting caught in a riptide and I never knew when he might suddenly pop up. Once, finding myself trapped between the managing director of The Ross School and The Chancellor of Southampton College as they argued the role of education among the upwardly mobile, Gasper suddenly appeared in front of me. He turned and I was sure he would spot me, but saving me was the uniquely large ass of the cocktail waitress serving the educators their third martinis. I squatted behind those glorious cheeks until I saw Gasper's back moving away into the crowd and didn't stand until I felt safe.

Conforti was there, too, wearing a red cowboy suit and a white ten-gallon hat. A blue belt ran around his wide waist and a holster dropped from it. There was a gun in that holster, and I noticed that it didn't have the white plastic handle so many toy guns have. This one had a rectangular black handle, and when the helicopter zooming over our heads dropped a white strobe onto it, I could see it was made from dimpled metal. The fat bastard was standing behind his wife, suspiciously checking out all the black guys who walked past him as if they were suspected muggers about to kick his big white ass, and then, when finished with him, take their massive black dongs to rampage his helpless wife. He was sweating bullets, and considering how cool a night it was, I knew he wasn't sweating because of the temperature. My call to him that afternoon had put a different kind of weight on his soft, fat shoulders and pressure was written all over his face. As nervous as he was, I knew that even though he hated Hightower, Conforti still couldn't help himself from attending a popular Hampton's party that would get his name and face in the towns' papers. Well, Mr. Supervisor, your name is going to be in the papers, alright.

Read it and weep.

At around ten-thirty, I began to get nervous. Time was crawling, but it was still moving, and in less than an hour I would have to be at The Castle. I was just about to leave when multi-colored lights hidden throughout the estate began to flash on and off, bringing a kind of primal hush over the crowd for the first time that evening. Suddenly, the great stage that had been erected on the beach was showered in an eerie pulsating white light and a hard-driving bass beat began to breathe from a thousand hidden speakers, reverberating throughout the audience and setting everyone's ass to twitching. The bass grew louder until it overwhelmed everything in the crowd and suddenly there were a thousand white doves flying across the stage, blocking everything from sight. In seconds, they flew off in a stream of white chaos and a slow wave of screaming began, beginning in the rows in front of the stage and moving to the rear like a gigantic wave until the entire audience was raging.

The reason for all the craziness came into view in the flash of a brilliant strobe. Roxanne was standing in the middle of the stage with her head down and her arms crossed over her chest. No longer was she in her Martha Washington costume, but in its place was a blue thong, two red glittering pasties and a thick layer of baby oil. Her body was gleaming and glistening under the frantically moving white spotlights and the maddened crowd went into a greater frenzy waiting for her first move. The music was rhythmic and primitive and increasing in volume. Then, there was Roxanne, face up and arms outstretched to her audience, screaming like a banshee, "FUUUUCK!!! THIS AIN"T

NO DREAM!! THIS IS LIFE!!" and it occurred to me she might very well be rapping about us.

The place erupted into a total frenzy as she bolted around the stage and several young people attempted to jump up and join her. Phalanxes of large black men, none smaller that Romey, swatted them away like so many flies, and then, just as suddenly as it began, the music came to an impossible and sudden stop. The festive crowd was stunned into silence and then buzzed with life as a thick cloud of red smoke *whooshed* onto the stage. The roar of twenty cannons exploding their charges simultaneously electrified the crowd, and then suddenly, sliding through the smoke on his knees was The Infamous S.H.I.T. He slowly rose and approached Roxanne in deliberate fashion. Wearing a scarlet fur cape over a glittering sapphire blue jumpsuit decorated with thousands of light-reflecting sequins, he was as blinding as a flashbulb and had the magnetic power of a Black Hole. Even I couldn't take my eyes from him.

The music shifted from RoRo's rap to a fluttering low base, sounding what ten million butterflies on acid must sound like. Hightower opened his cape to the crowd and its underside of red, white and blue stripes were displayed, once again allowing the great star to show his patriotic tendencies. He went into a fast, hard rap that I couldn't make out, except for the chorus, which sounded something like, "USA is Fucking Okay, Kill, Muthafucka, Kill," and finally fell to his knees, cape and all, ala James Brown. And then, there was The Godfather of Soul, himself, arriving from out of nowhere to help the exhausted Hightower to his feet. It was all absolutely amazing.

Checking my watch, I saw it was eleven o'clock. I figured that by the time I reached my car and got to The Castle it would be eleven-thirty and I knew I needed to be early to set things up the way I wanted. I looked back to the stage one last time and saw Hightower, Brown, Roxanne and a world of unknown celebrities prancing about onstage, throwing miniature American flags out to the reaching audience. The Star Spangled Banner suddenly boomed through a pair of mammoth, stage-bound speakers, the recording coordinated to begin simultaneously with the million-dollar fireworks display that was that moment starting to fill the sky. Our anthem ended and Ray Charles' voice rang out, singing, *America,* and the cacophony of explosions and cheers increased until I just couldn't stand being around it any longer.

Glen Berkowitz

With all the tumult on the stage, I couldn't see Roxanne, but I said, "So long," to her anyway and started out for The Castle.

33

I pulled The Caddy into the waiting area to the right of The Castle's driveway, parked, and after a quick look around the place, got out of the car. Removing the nine-iron from the trunk, I held it tightly by its grip and felt a fool's confidence that if anyone had arrived early and was hiding in the surrounding woods with wise ideas about surprising me and maybe finishing me off, he would first be eating a lofted wedge for his late night snack.

The Castle's drawbridge was down, the portcullis was raised and the front door was unlocked. Inside, the furniture, the armor, the plants, the rugs and the sweet smell of money had been removed. All that remained were the hollow echoes of my footsteps, a heavy residue of sadness and the faux gaiety of kiwi and magenta walls. Walking out the French doors onto the bluestone terrace, I approached the railing and looked down upon the pool and the patio. The round stone table and six wrought iron chairs were still situated in front of the poolhouse, just as they were the other day when Teresa was alive, sitting there with her scared eyes begging me for help. I pushed that memory away as best I could and started down the stone steps. The unfamiliar tap of a pair of brocaded shoes reminded me that I'd left *Playthang* dressed in the George Washington outfit Roxanne had given me that afternoon. Removing the tri-cornered hat and the white wig, I tossed them onto a sprouting bush of hydrangea at the foot of the stairs, and remembering how Roxanne had helped me get dressed for the party, I recalled that the only thing under my costume was my birthday suit and I knew I would just have to remain the Father of our Country for a little while longer. Crossing the patio, I took a seat at the stone table and drummed my fingernails on its top. Time crawled again, but again it kept moving, and then, I heard a new and different tapping on the stone terrace. Checking my watch, I smiled and thought that at the least Stump was punctual.

"Good evening, Stump," I called, when I saw his face leaning over the marble balustrade. "I've got a nine-iron for you. Have you got the title and the money?"

Stump stared down at me. His little red eyes surveyed the patio area, probably to make sure we were alone, and when he must have felt satisfied that we were, he called through a drunken laugh, "What the fuck are you dressed up for, Gabe? Halloween's over." Not waiting for my answer, he cleared his throat, spat into the bushes below him and added, "Anybody with you?"

I answered, "You'd think I would be the one concerned about company, Stump. After all, I'm not the one going around murdering people. So, I'll rephrase the question and return it; did you come alone?"

Stump scoped out the downstairs area more closely for a while and then thought for a few more long seconds. Looking at me through bloodshot eyes, he answered, "Yeah, I'm alone," and then draping a rumpled carpetbag over the terrace, he spat, "The money is in here. I've got the Z4's title in my pocket."

Smiling, I responded heartily, "Well then, come on down, Stump, and let's make our trade."

He took a step back and said, "No thanks, Gabe. If you don't mind, I'll stay where I am, at least for the time being. You can leave the golf club at the head of the stairs and then go back to the table. I'll come down to check the club, and if it's what you say it is, I'll leave the bag up here and be on my way."

I replied, "That doesn't sound like a very good idea to me, Stump. If I do as you say, what's to stop you from just taking the club and leaving? And what if there's nothing in your bag but old newspaper clippings. No, Stump. I think I want to check things out before I return your club. After all, we both know it's a murder weapon and I wouldn't want to see it misplaced."

Stump busily jerked his head from one side of the yard to the other, using the time to think about what he should do and to see if I'd set any kind of surprise for him. Holding him up for fifty thousand and the title to a hot sports car in exchange for a hundred-dollar nine-iron wasn't helping him to relax, either. For Stump, I knew that trusting me was out of the question, but that club was his future. He thought for a few more gauzy seconds, and deciding that he didn't have much of a choice, tossed the bag over the wall where it landed beside my discarded wig and hat, snapping a hydrangea branch and crushing a set of new buds at the same time.

"There," he called. "There's your fucking money. You'll get the title when I have the fucking nine-iron."

I left the table and calmly walked to where the bag of money lay on its side. Opening it, I found several bundles of twenties and fifties rolled up tightly inside thick rubber bands. Closing the bag and smiling up at the repairman, I said, "Just like in the movies. I don't have to count this, do I, Stump?"

He answered succinctly, "Fuck you, Gabe. Just give me the club. You can toss it up here. I know how you feel about me and I don't feel like getting too close to you, neither."

I pretended to be as cool as a Bridgehampton cucumber, and with my back to Stump, I leisurely returned to the table. Placing the bag of money on its top, I sat and said, "I'm just a little curious about a few things, Stump. I checked with the Zoning Commission and found out that the Town Trustees, which everyone knows you head, had already given permission to Conforti and The Town Board to turn the five hundred acre reserve behind The Castle into a golf course. According to The Dongan Patent, you had the power to do whatever you wanted with that land. I figured that building the golf course was your idea and that Conforti couldn't resist building his prestige, the prestige of the town and getting tee times whenever he wanted. The sale of The Castle property to the town had already been arranged, or why else would Teresa have been involved? What I want to know is what happened with Al Shareef? He'd already agreed to sell the property. Why did you have to kill him?"

Stump wobbled back and forth on his short thick legs like a kid's play toy and then he leaned over the terrace railing and ranted, "The fucking towelhead was holding us up. We'd agreed on a price. We were going to give the son-of-a-bitch thirty million for the place. That was ten million more than the true valuation and he knew it. He also knew we needed his property for a scenic entry onto the course from Deerfield Road and that we intended to transform his fucking precious castle into the clubhouse and restaurant. The bastard must have figured he'd banged Teresa a couple of hundred times already, so that was old news, and that he really didn't need the money. The only fun left to him was to watch our faces when he fucked us over. During his party, we met privately at his indoor pool and he told me that nothing had been signed, he'd changed his mind and that we should forget about everything unless we came up with forty million. That fucking sandhog, if we gave him the forty he probably would have demanded fifty. He laughed in my face and told me that if I wanted to play golf so badly, a guy of my means should be able to afford practicing my game at Lynch's Miniature Golf behind The Omni. Then, he told me to get off his property before he had me thrown off."

Stump's confession blew me away. I couldn't hold myself back and screamed, "You sick, stupid fuck!! You mean you killed Al Shareef just because he was giving you a hard time building a new golf course in The Hamptons!! What the fuck is wrong with you??!!"

Stump's usually red face flashed bright crimson and he bellowed, "Not just a fucking golf course! It was going to be the best fucking golf course in The Hamptons … maybe in the whole fucking country. And, it was going to belong to me, me and the people who made this town great!"

I took a deep breath, and trying to clarify things just a bit more, said, "Let me get this straight, Stump; you brained a man with a nine-iron because he wouldn't sell you his land so that you could build a golf course. Are you fucking kidding me? We live in a place where there are already a hundred golf courses." Shaking my head, I laughed and added, "You need a lot of help, Stump. Turn yourself into the authorities, now. They'll probably put you in a looney bin and you won't have to do any hard time."

Stump's eyes went into a roll and he leaned further over the balustrade, to the point of his feet leaving the ground, forcing him to balance himself on the thin railing under his wide waist. I could see that this was not an easy thing for a one-armed guy to do, as Stump began pitching back and forth on that rail like a small ship caught in a fierce storm while traversing the Plum Gut.

Finally righting himself and returning to his feet, Stump hollered down at me, "I would have brained him with anything I had, that fucking turban. That evening, I just happened to be carrying that club. What's the fucking difference? The son of a bitch got what he deserved. Who needs any of his kind out here, anyway?" Breathing hard, Stump gulped some air and croaked hoarsely, "Now, give me my fucking nine-iron."

I wasn't about to give Stump anything, but at that moment, the club became the last thing on his mind because another voice suddenly joined ours, calling to him from the open French doors.

"McNamara, what are you doing here?"

It was Armand Conforti, still dressed in his red cowboy suit, white ten-gallon hat, blue cowboy boots and holster. Holding a brown leather briefcase, he looked like an extremely fat and uncomfortable Gene Autry going to work in a downtown Phoenix office building.

This new situation confused Stump and he looked down at me and then back at Conforti several times through wild, startled eyes. They finally settled on the supervisor and he shouted, "What am I doing here? What the fuck are you doing here?"

Conforti walked over to Stump at the railing, pointed down to me and said, "Fortuna called me this afternoon and told me that he knew I had his pistol. He said that if I didn't show up at the Castle with it at twelve-fifteen tonight he was going to tell my wife about my affair with Teresa. My wife is not a very understanding woman, Stump. She would have demanded an immediate divorce if news of my affair ever reached her. Fortuna went on to add that I would never be elected to office in Southampton again, that I'd be a political outcast and that I would probably become the lead suspect in Teresa's murder. He demanded that I return his gun and wanted an additional fifty thousand dollars. If I followed his instructions, he said he would forget about everything."

"And you believed him?" Stump asked.

"What choice did I have," was Conforti's answer.

I decided it was a good time to intervene and called to the beleaguered supervisor, "I don't get it, Conforti. You could get invited to play at any golf course you want. You're the town supervisor, a head honcho out here. You didn't have to kill Al Shareef just to get a chance to play."

Being called a head honcho seemed to settle Conforti, and with some of his fear gone, he answered haughtily, "My desires were not nearly so base as Stump's. I have more lofty goals than merely hitting a three-wood into an environmentally safe green. I was thinking of the townspeople whose children often had to move back-island because they could no longer afford to buy a home in The Hamptons. Families that have existed out here for more than a hundred years are being destroyed, Mr. Fortuna. My plan was to build affordable housing for our local children and continue the Southampton living experience for at least the foreseeable future. I estimated that at least two hundred middle and lower income housing units could have been built on that course, giving our less affluent townspeople pride of ownership. It was a wonderful plan. The only thing standing in its way was Mr. Al Shareef."

Stump's eyes nearly burst from his head and he spat, "You never said anything about low-income housing, you fat fuck. Who gives a rat's ass about housing? Building that stuff could have ruined the contours of the fairways."

Ignoring his one-armed partner's stormy disposition, Conforti tossed his soft leather briefcase from the terrace, where it fell beside the spot where the carpetbag had fallen, breaking yet another hydrangea branch.

He called, "There's the money, Fortuna. I don't want to throw the gun; it might accidentally go off. Why don't you come up here and take it and then we can all leave peacefully?"

From the comfortable distance of the poolhouse, I called, "Sure thing, Mr. Supervisor. I'll just walk up those stairs and let you shoot me the way you tried to shoot Hightower."

Conforti had been reminded of his precarious position and whined, "I didn't want to shoot anyone. I was forced into it. Murders had been committed and even though I hadn't performed any, it could be argued that I was at least partially culpable. Everyone on the board wanted Hightower out of our town and killing him would have been the easiest way to do it. It was supposed to look like you'd shot him because it would have been your gun used in his murder and everyone knew you were carrying on with his woman. At first, I was afraid to do it, but it sounded more and more like the only thing to do, especially after I was told what would happen if I didn't. They said things could be set up to make it look like I'd committed the other murders as well. I couldn't have that, Mr. Fortuna. Think of my reputation. Think of the upcoming election."

Stump's eyes bugged even further and he screamed, "You stupid, fat bastard, shut the fuck up! Don't say another word to this guy. Can't you see he's setting us up? Now, he knows everything."

I called, "Not everything, Stump. You said *they* could make it look like you committed the murders. Who's *they*, Conforti?"

Stump looked down at me and then threw an evil stare at Conforti. He held out his empty hand to his partner and said, "Give me that gun, Conforti. I'll end this now, the only way it can end."

From the patio, I replied, "That doesn't sound too friendly, Stump. It goes against our agreement."

"Fuck you and fuck our agreement, Fortuna. I used to like you when you were a kid, but that was a long time ago. I hope you've got a family plot back in Queens, maybe one next to your brother, because I'm going to see to it you're not buried out here."

With the mention of my brother, I wanted to run up those stone cold steps and choke the life out of both the bastards looking down at me, but I knew I needed to keep my cool only a little while longer. It turned out that I didn't have to wait too long because Stump suddenly appeared flustered and Conforti looked just plain helpless. Both of them backed against the marble railing with their hands raised above their head, and a few seconds later, Gasper's cruel face peered over the its edge. He threw me a wolfish grin and waved his service pistol at the duo, encouraging them to move away from him and towards the head of the stairs.

I called, "Hello, Gasper. Nice of you to join us. You're right on time, too. Twelve-twenty, just like I told you."

Keeping an eye on Stump and Conforti, Gasper responded, "Nice of you to invite me, Gabe. My guess is you already know who Supervisor Conforti is talking about. I think you've known for quite a while. What surprises me is that you were holding these two up for a hundred thousand. That isn't like you and makes me wonder. Well, I shouldn't look a gift horse in the mouth, so thanks a lot for the dough, too. It's too bad you're wising up so late in life."

I smiled and replied, "Just acting like a felon to catch a felon. I didn't think that either Stump or Conforti would show if I was going to act like their friend and just tell them what I knew without asking for anything in return. I was offering them a fair trade, my silence for some cash. What I can't figure out is why you would be a part of this. You never cared about golf. What was your end?"

Gasper must have been glad to finally get things off his chest because he openly answered, "I was going to be one of those fortunate recipients of fairway housing that Supervisor Conforti was alluding to in his pre-election speech. You know, Gabe, living in my parents' old place out on Sagg Main Turnpike, right between the daycare center and an auto salvage yard, is not a very prestigious spot for a police captain to live, and the way prices for land keep rising out here, I knew I'd never be able to afford better. Conforti called and promised me a prize lot on the golf course with a four-thousand square foot home and a wrap-around terrace. The town would have paid for most of it; all I'd need to put up was the money I'd get for selling my piece of shit. I was ready for a change of life, Gabe. I guess I just wanted a sweet slice of the Hamptons' pie, too."

As Gasper unloaded, I scanned the terrace and saw that there weren't any officers with him, as I expected there wouldn't be, and his gun remained pointed at his conspirators, as I knew it would be. It occurred to me that maybe this might have been the first time in history that things actually turned out as planned, and then I thought, not a chance, and got ready.

Gasper had a smirk on his face when he said, "Armand, I want you to take the Smith and Wesson slowly out of your holster and lay it on the ground beside you. If you don't do exactly as I say, if you make any sudden moves at all, I will shoot you in your fat, fucking head."

With this new and sudden threat, Conforti wheeled at his police captain and shrieked, "What!? You're going to shoot me? Why? We're in this together. Just get rid of Fortuna and our problems will be solved."

I called up to the trembling fat man, "You're such a putz, Conforti. Gasper's problems won't be over until he gets rid of you, Stump, me and anybody else I might have told about your little plan. Isn't that right, Gasper?"

My old friend responded calmly, "That's right, Gabe, and that includes that foxy little piece of dark meat you've been giving it to. I've got two lumps in the back of my head I owe her for, and after I screw her I'm going to make sure she pays for them." Laughing, he added what he thought must have been very clever, "In spades."

I was angry and shot back, "So, what are you going to do, Gasper? Rape Roxanne and then kill her the way you did Teresa?"

Conforti yelped with that bit of news, "You killed Teresa?" Taking a courageous step towards Gasper, he cried, "I loved her."

Gasper lifted the open-ended barrel of his gun at Conforti's face, sending the supervisor into a forced retreat. Smiling at his boss, he said, "That's better, Armand. Now, just stay there next to Stump and don't move until I tell you."

Conforti's shoulders slumped and he wept words, saying, "You said it was Fortuna who killed her. You said it was him. Why did you have to kill Teresa?"

I answered from the relative safety of the patio, "For the same reason he has to get rid of us all, Mr. Supervisor; we know too much. The good captain wants to remain the good captain. There are way too many people in the Suffolk County Jail who would like to meet him in private or behind bars and he doesn't want that to happen. He's still pretty sure he can blame all of this on me. Getting rid of us is his insurance policy."

Ignoring my response, Gasper murmured to his quivering boss, "Armand, place the gun on the ground and step away from it. Nobody has to get hurt except Fortuna. I'm just trying to make sure there aren't any problems."

Conforti was too weak not to do what he was told, laid the gun down and stepped away from it. Gasper picked up the S&W with his left hand and through a wicked smile, said, "Thanks, Armand." Waving his automatic at his partners, he added, "Now, both of you, get down the stairs."

Conforti started crying harder and took his first step down, but Stump still had balls. He gave Gasper a hard stare and hissed, "I ain't moving anywhere." Rearing his big red head, he cleared his throat and spat a wad of phlegm onto Gasper's chest, right next to where the captain's badge was pinned.

Gasper looked down upon the thick mucous and then jauntily replied, "Then, I'll shoot you where you stand, Stump. It will be only a minor inconvenience. I'll say you got caught in a crossfire between Fortuna and me. No big deal."

And so much for balls.

I watched the three men slowly descend the stairs, Gasper keeping his pistol trained on their backs, while my Smith and Wesson dangled from his other hand. They were halfway down when I called to my old friend, "Why did you have to kill Reggie and Carla? They were nothing to you. They didn't know about anything."

Gasper must have been feeling mighty confident because he quickly answered, "That was just a bit of bad luck on their parts, Gabe. That day, Stump and I drove over to your place in your Caddy, just to give your home a good tumble. We figured we could blame the trashing on Al Shareef's bodyguards and make it look like they were getting even with you for what you did to their boss, further figuring that would make you look even guiltier for the Muslim's murder. Unfortunately, your neighbors spotted your car parked out front, and thinking you were home, walked in the door to find out what all the noise was about. That's when I got the idea of getting rid of them, and you, for good. I gave Stump my service piece and had him hold it on the ladies while I went back into your locker and got your S&W. The ladies behaved like little lambs and did everything I said. We took them back to their place and I had them get into their bed and hold hands. After that, I made it fast and clean, figuring that after killing Al Shareef, the story would go you completely lost it and killed your neighbors." Smiling sickly, Gasper laughed and added, "You're going to become the first serial killer in Hamptons' history, Gabe. They'll probably make a television movie about you, maybe even a major motion picture. Hell, Gabe, I'm going to make you famous."

Stump coarsely broke in, "I told you not to shoot those girls."

Giving his partner a light tap across the back of his skull with the barrel of his piece, Gasper said, "Shut the fuck up, Stump, and just keep walking."

I called out, "You piece of shit, Gasper. You're nothing but a cold-blooded killer."

Gasper replied cold-bloodedly, "I thought you might think that, and you know what, Gabe, who gives a fuck?"

I gave a fuck and wanted to have everything out on the table, so I quickly asked, "And what about Teresa? She was helping you guys with the deal. Conforti was screwing her. She wouldn't have harmed you; all she ever wanted was the money."

Gasper calmly answered, "You're to blame for that one, too, Gabe. You scared the hell out of her with that jail-time bullshit. She called Conforti and told him she was going to tell you everything that had happened, and Conforti, being the helpless weasel he is, called me. I guess I'd never really forgiven Teresa for throwing me over all those years ago, and after killing your neighbors, I found it wasn't so hard to finally finish things with her for good. I dropped a *roofie* into one of her drinks and had sex with her for old time's sake, but it wasn't the same. You'd ruined her for me, Gabe, and even if she wasn't petrified that she was going to go to jail, she still would have been a lousy lay."

Staring at my old friend with nothing but hatred in my heart, I said, "Gasper, you are one sick bastard."

Reaching the foot of the stairs, he pushed his accomplishes towards me with the butt end of his pistol and replied, "Maybe so, Gabe, but what does that matter now? We've finally reached the end of the line, you and me. So long, old friend. It hasn't been fun."

The doors to the poolhouse suddenly flew open and the two Feds, Stern and Ledbetter, jumped out with their guns drawn. Each had a bead on Gasper's chest and Stern ordered, "Hold it right there, Captain Dupree. Drop your guns and raise your hands slowly over your head. You're under arrest for the murder of Binyamin Al Shareef."

"Among others," I added.

"Among others," Ledbetter agreed.

Gasper didn't look surprised as much as he looked angry and he wasn't lowering his weapon fast enough for my liking, but I smiled at my old friend and asked, "Did you hear all that, Inspectors?"

Stern answered, "We heard it and we have it on tape."

Ledbetter repeated the order, "Drop your guns, Officer Dupree. You're a murderer and you're under arrest."

I didn't know what planet those two dumb Feds came from, but in my world, someone who is guilty of murdering three people, assisted in the coverup of another, plans to commit at least four more murders and is holding two loaded guns and knows how to use them does not say, "Thank you so much, officers. Please, take me to jail."

I was already diving towards the stone table and overturning it as Gasper raised his revolver and fired. Stern took one in the shoulder and went down fast. Ledbetter fell to a knee and returned fire, but it's tough to hit anything when you're being fired at and your target is bounding quickly up a flight of stone steps. Gasper, taking three steps at a time and firing from both pistols, proved to be more accurate than either of the Feds. A thud came from Ledbetter's body and I saw him fall back.

Gasper disappeared, the firing stopped and I got out from behind the table. Ledbetter and Stern were lying on the ground, each bleeding pretty badly, but of the two, Stern appeared to have gotten it the worst. Picking Ledbetter's service revolver from the floor, I said, "Take care of your buddy, Bedwetter. I'm going after Gasper."

The Fed knew that there was nothing he could have done to dissuade me, and Stern was lying in an ever expanding puddle of blood in no condition to do or say anything. Fumbling in his pocket for his cell phone, Ledbetter grimaced and said, "Good luck."

I picked up the carpetbag from the ground, retrieved the briefcase from the hydrangeas and headed for the stairs. Stump was trying to fight his way through a thick garden of rhododendrons and azaleas at the rear of the yard, beneath the golden niobe, but he wasn't getting very far. Mustafa was behind him, grabbing his shirt collar and pulling him down the slope to where Mrs. Al Shareef and her son were waiting with long splintered bamboo canes. They were going to use those to beat the man who had killed their husband and father, but within reason, of course. When I'd told them my plan over the phone they had agreed not to kill Stump, but merely to beat him senseless so that he could not escape until the proper authorities arrived. To get that opportunity, they had faked closing The Castle and returning to The Middle East, a fair compromise for everyone.

Cornered at the top of the stairs by Romey, Conforti was wailing in front of the huge bodyguard, begging for mercy and understanding. The black giant's eyes should have been menacing enough to give the office holder a life-threatening coronary, and even though a hand had not yet been laid upon him, as Romey advanced, Conforti slid to the ground and wailed, "Please, don't hurt me. I never meant harm to anyone. All I wanted was a decent golf course, affordable housing and to get reelected."

I raced past as Romey tilted his head toward the open French doors and mumbled, "I've got this one. You get that other mo'fo'."

That was the general idea, and as I sped through the great room, moving quickly towards the front door of The Castle, I heard two shots ring out in rapid succession. Those shots were quickly followed by two distinct and nearly simultaneous wails that sounded something like, "Aiyeeeee!!" or "OoooWeeee!" It was difficult to make out which as they overlapped each other.

Passing the portcullis and the drawbridge, I saw Gasper's Trailblazer speeding down the driveway towards Deerfield Road. I flew to the parking area and found next to my Caddy, beside a late model BMW635csi and a banged up white Chevy cargo van, Hightower and Enrique laying wounded on the ground. Each was bleeding profusely, Enrique from a bullet in the arm and Hightower from one in his ass.

Stooping to the fallen Hispanic and cradling his head in my arms, I asked, "Are you alright?"

Enrique wailed, "MUTHAFUCK!! RoRo never said nothings 'bouts no fuckeeng guns. She saids ju needs my helps at The Castle and here I ams. Muthafuck, she never saids nothings 'bout no fuckeeng guns."

I rushed my words and said, "You'll be alright. An ambulance will be here, soon. I've got to stop that guy before he kills anyone else." Dropping Enrique's head onto the graveled ground, he shrieked, "Muthafuck!" but I wasn't listening to his bellyaching; I had a murderer to catch.

Hightower suddenly let out a fresh wail, "OOOOWEEEE!! What about me, muthafucka? You just gonna leave me here to bleed to death? My ass is on fucking fire, man. Muthafucka, I knew you were no good. I just knew it."

I answered the pain in the ass, quickly responding, "All you've got is a flesh wound, Hightower. You'll be fine."

"Easy for you to say, Muthafucka; I's the one with the bullet in his ass."

An ambulance was only minutes away and I didn't have time to waste. I tried my best to ignore the rapper's shrill complaints and was jumping into The Caddy when Hightower changed his complaining tone and called, "Hey, Muthafucka! That SOB's got Ro. He said you'd know where to find him. You better move fast, though. That is one mean, muthafucka cop."

Gasper's taillights had already turned off the driveway and were headed down Deerfield Road towards town. If what he'd told Hightower were true, I would know where to find him. It was the beginning of the summer season and he was probably going back to Saint Andrews Church of the Dunes, just like we had on Saturdays when we were kids, only this time was different. This time he was a murderer and I was determined to either bring him in or kill him. He had Roxanne, he'd promised to do some very bad things to her and it suddenly occurred to me, as I threw The Caddy into Drive, that I had no intention of bringing him in; I was going to Saint Andrews Church to kill Gasper.

34

He'd only gotten a minute's headstart on me, but with his police light whirling red on his rooftop Gasper was able to make far better time than me along the crowded Hampton roads. It was the Saturday night of Memorial Day Weekend and long rows of parked cars lined every lane and street I traveled, causing the usual two lane blacktops to narrow into one long and dangerous ribbon of road. Drunk drivers veered out of driveways or blinded me with their brights as they came at me, forcing me to jerk my steering wheel to the right or left, sending my Caddy scraping against one parked car after another, tearing off pieces of bumpers or fenders of too many rented or leased high-end vehicles for me to count.

I finally made it to Southampton Village, raced through the streets and around Agawam Lake, and reached Saint Andrews. Gasper's Trailblazer was parked in front, in the parking zone reserved for clergy, while the rest of the parking area was filled with vehicles belonging to the Memorial Day Weekend party goers at The Southampton Beach and Tennis Club, situated right next door to the church. I rammed The Caddy into the rear of Gasper's truck, sending the nose of my red beauty to kiss the sky in a shower of antifreeze and smoke, but I'd also slammed the rear of Gasper's truck into its cab and I knew that neither of us would be driving anywhere when this night was over.

Saint Andrews was one of the oldest churches in town, open only fifteen weeks a year during the height of the summer season, and then only for Sunday Mass. Tomorrow was supposed to be opening day, with church bells peeling brightly to welcome back the summer parishioners, but even in the darkness of night I could see that Gasper wasn't going to wait for the reverend to open the glass-paneled doors. He'd already smashed them open and one lay sadly dangling on its side, supported only by one hinge.

The interior of the church was dark. Gasper hadn't lighted any candles or overhead electric lights to make things easier for me, but the moon was shining its light through the lantern at the top of the church, sending a few bright beams of light into the holy place. Crawling on my hands and knees, I passed below the front windows and reached the church doors. Broken glass crunched under me, and in the silence and the darkness of night, I knew I must have sounded like an approaching army.

"Don't come in, Gabe," Roxanne screamed. "He's got his gun aimed at the entrance."

I heard a loud slap and then the dull sound metal makes when it cracks a skull.

I hollered into the darkness, "You sonofabitch, Gasper. If you've hurt Roxanne, I'm going to kill you."

He laughed like a madman and answered, "Then you're going to have to kill me, Gabe, because I think I've hurt her pretty badly already. I've got her tied up back here and her clothes are off, and man, I don't blame you for wanting to keep this one for yourself. She's feisty and beautiful and hot ... just the way Teresa was when you stole her from me. Well, payback is certainly a bitch, isn't it, Gabe? I'm just not sure if I'll rape her before or after I kill you. I guess that's up to you. Why don't you come and try and stop me, Gabe? I'm waiting for you."

The moon was at my back, making me a pretty good target if I decided to come in the front entrance, but I knew from years of coming here with my girlfriends that every other door in the place was kept locked, so there wasn't much of a choice. If I chose the center aisle, my one hope was that Gasper might be too busy and excited putting his grimy, murdering hands on Roxanne to enable him to shoot straight. I took a deep breath and a wild chance. Gripping a chunk of wood from the shattered door, I threw it high into the church, smashing it into one of Louis Comfort Tiffany's delicate stained glass windows, causing that piece of Southampton history to shatter into a thousand leaden shards.

I dove into the church and three shots rang out, two bullets splintering the wooden pews on my left and one tearing up the oaken-planked floor to my right. I kneeled behind a pew and went to the belt at my pants to get Ledbetter's gun, but it wasn't there and I realized that it must have dropped out of my pants when I'd smashed into Gasper's truck or when I dove for cover. I recalled that when I agreed to taking the job at The Castle I'd told Gasper, "If I can't handle things with my hands, then I can't handle things." It was hubris for me to say that then and I knew I would never say it again, but at that moment, in that church with Roxanne's life at stake, my hands were all I had.

I called into the darkness, "Gasper, let's end this. Leave Roxanne alone. It's all over for you, anyway. It's me you want. Leave her alone and I'll meet you on the beach. You can do whatever you like to me. Just let her go."

Gasper answered, "Screw you, Gabe. I can have both of you. I'll kill you and then finish with her. I haven't yet decided whether or not I'll kill her. You see, I'm not the ruthless murderer you think I am." Laughing villainously, he amended his statement, adding, "Wait a second, yes, I am. I've got nothing to lose. When I'm finished with her, I'll kill her, too. Then' I'll go to the yacht club and take a boat back island. They'll never find me, and if they do, you won't know it because you'll be dead." Laughing again, he called. "Your girl's got great tits, Gabe. Hey, look, she's coming around. That's good. I want her to know what I'm doing. I want her to feel it, too."

Gasper had been careless. All his talking had helped me to zero in on his position. His voice was coming from the first row of pews on the left, just in front of the speaker's lectern. Breathing hard, I weighed my chances and decided to go on the count of ten.

Roxanne moaned loudly a few times and then suddenly shrieked, "Let go of me!! You're hurting me! Get away from me, you fucking-son-of-a-bitch-bastard-motherfucker."

That was my cue. Jumping out from behind my pew, I raced down the center aisle towards the lectern. Shots rang out the moment I hit the planks, but I kept my head down and kept running as bullets whistled past, one blowing away an epaulet from general Washington's coat and another taking a finger from my right hand, the middle one, the really important one. The shooting stopped and I raised my head to see Gasper's twisted face captured by the moonlight. He was training his eye down the barrel of his gun, pointing it straight at my heart. I watched him slowly pressing his finger down on the trigger and I expected to hear an explosion followed by the white light that means the end has come, but instead, I saw a gorgeously curved ankle attached to a marvelously naked brown leg spring through the moonlight to deliver a kick to the side of Gasper's head. The cop went over sideways, the shot whistled past my ear, and in another second I was on him, raining blows on his face and head in an never-ending avalanche of pain.

People from the parking lot and beach club streamed into the church and Roxanne screamed at them to pull me off Gasper. I was told it took eight lifeguards serving as waiters to tear me away, and by the time I was peeled off him, Gasper was a bloody pulp.

I was streaming blood, too. Aside from the epaulet and my finger, he'd also hit me in the right hip, left shoulder and left side and probably couldn't believe I was still coming at him when he was aiming down the barrel of his gun to finish me.

With a large American flag wrapped around her body to cover her nakedness, Roxanne rode with me to Southampton Hospital in a town ambulance. I kept going in and out of consciousness, but I remember hearing Roxanne whispering into my ear, "Hold on, Gabe. You can make it. We're almost at the hospital. Hold on, Baby. Just hold on."

I opened my eyes to smile at my lover and saw a small corner of our banner fall from Roxanne's chest, revealing a generous portion of her magnificent breast. There came a sudden and vigorous movement under my pants, and as I closed my eyes to welcome oblivion, I was not afraid. Everything was going to be alright.

THE END